THE COLOUR OF WINTER

THE SEASONS OF BELLE SERIES: BOOK 3

MICHELLE MONTEBELLO

Michelle Montebello is an Australian author and British English spelling is used in this novel.

Editing by Lynne Stringer and Marcia Batton.
Cover by Kris Dallas Designs.

ISBN: 978-0-6452296-7-7

To my dad,
for showing me the magic of books.

BLURB

After enduring a long-distance relationship for three years, Belle and Andre are finally reunited.

Now, blissfully married and living in Andre's Tuscan family home, they have their whole lives ahead of them. They're desperate to start a family and Belle is working to put the trauma of Paris behind her.

But when Christmas brings unexpected guests, Belle is caught off-guard. Andre's ex-fiancée, Mary, along with her newborn baby and parents, are staying at the Tuscan house for the holidays.

Determined to make the best of a bad situation, Belle opens her home to them but is quickly undermined by Mary and her meddling mother. The baby is a delight but is a constant reminder to everyone that Belle is yet to fall pregnant. And is it her imagination or are Andre and Mary spending too much time together?

Struggling with distrust, her inability to conceive and the ghosts of the past, Belle wonders if she'll make it through the holidays and if the life she's always wanted with Andre will still be waiting for her on the other side.

'I wonder if the snow loves the trees and the fields,
That it kisses them so gently?
And then it covers them up snug, you know,
With a white quilt; and perhaps it says,
"Go to sleep, darlings, till the summer comes again."'

~ Lewis Carroll

ONE

It wasn't how she'd imagined her wedding day. A rush to Rome's Town Hall to satisfy visa requirements, the simple white dress and heels she wore, the small gathering of people bearing witness to it—her parents, Riley and Uncle Benito. Once upon a time she'd imagined extravagance—walking down a church aisle, a trail of bridesmaids in procession, a ballgown dress, and her beloved waiting by the altar for her.

But as she stared up at Andre and he read his vows aloud, she realised how perfect this was, their rushed little ceremony, striking in its simplicity. No overpriced, over-sized day with strict ceremony and hundreds of guests she hardly knew, no anxiety and sleepless nights and the constant looming thought that something would go wrong. He was all she needed. *This* was all she needed.

'Because without you, I am nothing,' Andre was saying. 'From the moment I met you, I knew my life wouldn't be the same again. For better or for worse, you are the only person I want by my side.' He folded the sheet of paper containing his vows and tucked it into his trouser pocket.

His dark eyes welled, and he wiped them with the back of his hand, grinning sheepishly. 'Sorry.'

She reached for his hands and squeezed them gently. 'Don't be sorry,' she whispered. 'It was beautiful.'

'You're beautiful,' he mouthed.

She beamed. Yes, the day was perfect. They had waited years for this moment, a wedding that had always seemed unattainable given their long-distance relationship, living on separate continents, thousands of miles apart. For years they'd persevered with phone calls and video chats in the hope that one day, they could be together.

Her mind drifted back to a morning only months earlier. She'd been drinking coffee in her Camden house in Sydney with her laptop perched on her lap and her email had tinged. She'd flicked absentmindedly to her inbox and there it had been—the approval for her temporary Italian working visa newly arrived. She'd blinked once, then had almost flung her coffee cup into the air with shock.

Italy was allowing her back. All the questions and interviews and endless amounts of paperwork proving that what she and Andre had was genuine, coupled with the interminable waiting, never knowing if she'd be successful, had paid off. The temporary working visa would still need to become a spousal one if she wanted permanent residency—marrying had always been the plan—but at least the first hurdle was over. She could return to Andre.

After reading and rereading the email, just to be certain she hadn't dreamed it, she'd woken him in the middle of his night to tell him the news. There'd been tears, lots of them. And elation, disbelief, laughter, more tears. He'd told her to book the first flight she could, that he'd be waiting for her on the other side. So she'd informed her mother and Riley, packed up the Camden house, quit her job at The Olive Grove and moved to Italy.

That was three months ago—how quickly things could change—and now here they were, standing in a quaint room in Rome's Town Hall, in the city where they'd fallen in love all those years ago, surrounded by the people who mattered most to them, and it couldn't have been more perfect.

The celebrant cleared his throat, and Belle realised she'd fallen silent. 'Is it my turn for vows? Sorry.' She giggled, Andre laughing nervously too. She pulled a piece of paper containing her handwritten vows from the sleeve of her dress and unfolded it.

'Andre,' she began, her voice quivering. 'We haven't had the easiest journey so far. We've loved and lost, endured time apart, and lived on different continents, but through it all, we've always found our way back to each other.' He squeezed her free hand, and her heart was beating so loudly, she wondered if he could hear it. 'You are my soulmate, my voice of reason, my patience and calm. You're the mornings and the evenings, and all the hours in between. My love starts and ends with you.'

She heard a sob in the front row and glanced at her mother. Grace was wiping tears from her cheeks, Callum gently patting her arm. Andre's father, who she still affectionately thought of as 'Uncle Benito', because that's what his niece Avery had called him, sat beside them, blowing his nose noisily into a tissue. Riley was next to him, shaking her head, a wide grin on her face.

Belle smiled fondly at them, turning back to Andre to exchange rings. They slipped them on to each other's fingers, then Andre's lips were on hers before the celebrant had a chance to declare them husband and wife.

AFTER THE CEREMONY concluded they left Town Hall, stepping down the Capitolina's picturesque stairway to the Piazza d'Aracoeli. Belle and Andre had chosen a restaurant for lunch a short walk away, to celebrate before they left for their honeymoon in Sorrento.

It was a warm day, puddles of sunshine dappling the cobblestones, statues and spires washed in light. Belle's hand was tucked in Andre's, and he slowed their pace a little, letting her parents, Uncle Benito and Riley walk ahead.

'Are you happy, Mrs De Luca?' he asked. His eyes were full of pride as he gazed down at her.

Mrs De Luca. She smiled, moving closer to him. 'The happiest I've ever been, my love.'

He grinned widely. 'Me too. I feel like the luckiest man alive.'

'Well, you are,' she teased.

He laughed. 'I know it was only a small wedding. I promise you a bigger one soon, with a church and celebration.'

'You know none of that matters to me. Today was perfect. Everyone we love was there.' Everyone except her father Edward and her dear friend Avery, even Ben, but she pushed that thought away. *Not today*, she told herself. *They wouldn't want me to be sad today.*

They crossed the piazza and turned down a narrow lane delineated with pots of tumbling geraniums and determined ivy climbing up amber stone walls. The restaurant was unassuming, nestled among apartment doors. No one commented on how tiny it was as they stepped over the threshold, the dining room large enough to hold a handful of white-clothed tables and a bar. But it was elegant and away from the busy piazzas, which made Belle's heart hammer less in her chest. She still struggled with crowds. Or crowds in restaurants.

'It's a little small...' she began apologising, as they waited for the maître d to come for them.

There was a pause, then everyone rushed to reassure her.

'Nonsense.'

'It's perfect.'

'One of the best in Rome.'

Andre gripped her hand, squeezing it encouragingly, but she was still embarrassed. She'd carried Paris around with her since that fateful night and, while she tried not to let others see how it still haunted her, she was humiliated that they couldn't celebrate somewhere livelier on her wedding day for fear of how it would affect her.

The maître d came to seat them at their table, a waiter appearing instantly with bottles of wine and baskets of bread. Their orders were taken promptly, glasses filled with Barolo and the owner arrived to congratulate them, discussing the menu at length with Uncle Benito and Callum.

'Will you be tossing your bouquet?' Riley asked Belle, indicating the posy on the table.

'Why? Are you planning on catching it?' she quipped.

'God no.' Riley looked horrified. 'Throw it to your mother.'

Callum must have heard for he stopped discussing the menu with the owner and gave the posy an intrigued glance.

Their orders arrived, dishes of *tagliolini* with cuttlefish ink ragu, ravioli with ricotta and coffee caviar, and seafood risotto on stark white plates. More bread came out, then more wine, followed by dessert and a round of espressos.

'And in the next few months, we'll have the big wedding,' Uncle Benito was telling Grace. 'All the family will come.'

'Oh that sounds lovely,' Grace said, sipping her coffee.

'Because this eloping thing, it's strange for me,' he said, hands gesticulating. 'Italian weddings need to be in the church, no? And with the celebration, with the family, with all the food and wine.'

'Yes, of course,' she agreed, catching Belle's eye and winking.

Although Andre's father had initially been opposed to their Town Hall wedding, he'd eventually relented with the realisation that it would secure Belle's residency in the country and that they could have the 'real' wedding—the Italian wedding—a few months later, when they'd had a chance to plan it. And he liked to remind everyone that it was coming indeed.

Belle felt Andre lean in close to her and she was brought back to the table by his voice in her ear. 'Want to leave for our honeymoon?'

She pulled back, surprised. 'You mean now? We're about to order more espresso.'

'I don't care about espresso. I want to make love to my wife.'

Heat spread through her body at the thought, and she grinned. 'What about our family?'

'They'll understand.' He stood, tossing his napkin on the table.

He was serious.

'We're going to leave before the traffic builds up,' he explained to the group, reaching for Belle's hand as she climbed to her feet and collected her clutch. 'Thank you for coming. We'll see you in two weeks when we're back from Sorrento.'

The table chatter stilled, someone cleared their throat, then everyone understood and quickly rose to their feet. Uncle Benito cried noisily again, and Belle hugged Riley, then her mother.

'You should have this.' Belle handed Grace her bouquet. 'Riley wants no part in it.'

Grace gave an unnaturally high laugh, her cheeks colouring as she grasped it. 'Well only because it's yours and it will look lovely in my hotel room. No other reason, right?' Her eyes darted to Callum.

'No other reason,' Belle said.

Grace stepped to the side, a bemused smile on her lips as she stared at the bouquet.

Callum hugged her next, fatherly and protectively and full of emotion. 'Congratulations, lassie.' His voice wobbled in his thick Scottish brogue. 'Every day you make me proud as punch to be ye da.'

Uncle Benito held her last, cheeks wet with tears, telling her in Italian that she was the daughter he'd never had. 'Valentina would have loved you.'

Everyone followed Belle and Andre out to the laneway, waving tearfully, as they watched them walk towards the main street where Andre had parked their rented Maserati sports car.

'I thought they'd never let us go,' he said, one hand on the wheel, the other on Belle's knee, as he guided the car away from the restaurant and through Rome's streets towards the motorway.

'I feel bad,' she said. 'We should have stayed with them a little longer.'

'I want to spend the rest of the day in bed with you, not sitting around the table with our parents.'

'We could have had one more espresso with them.'

He tsked and she laughed. One more espresso would have been agonising for her too. She was desperate to get to Sorrento and start their honeymoon. Lazy days lying in bed or by the pool, hot nights spent eating and dancing. And maybe, just maybe, they'd fall pregnant quickly, something they both desperately wanted and were now at liberty to do. The long-distance and uncertainty was over. They were married, living together in Italy and eager to start a family, to fill their Tuscan house with children.

Belle had a good feeling about Sorrento.

TWO

EIGHT MONTHS LATER

Belle traced her finger through the condensation on the windowpane, slivers of the white world outside becoming visible. Winter in Tuscany—it never failed to enchant. Crystallised pencil pines and snow drifting like confetti, polar-white hillsides rolling to the whitewashed sky; the wind, sometimes gentle, sometimes howling, bending stark trees and turning lips blue.

The thought made her pull her robe tighter around her, grateful for the fire crackling in the hearth, woodsmoke mingled with fresh pine from the Christmas tree and a *pane di casa* baking in the oven.

A drove of hares stole across the back yard, down near the fence, kicking up snow as they burrowed under it. She saw them often at this time—early morning, the sun barely risen. She normally crossed paths with them during her hike, but the weather was poor that morning, cold and snowy, so she'd decided to stay curled up beside Andre instead, promising herself she would walk later.

'I want you to exercise,' her psychologist, Emilio Bianchi, had instructed her during their first session together. 'For thirty minutes a day. More if you want. Walk, swim, run, cycle. Whatever you prefer. Just focus on your body and how it feels to move it.'

She'd never been overly athletic. Aside from walking to and from Valentina's when she was in Rome, she preferred to cook rather than pound pavements. Besides, she wasn't sure she needed a psychologist to tell her to go for a walk. But Andre had insisted that she start therapy—she hadn't been able to control her PTSD on her own—so she'd given in. And there she was, in her first, extremely expensive consultation, being told to exercise.

'And how will it help?' she'd asked, sceptical.

'Aside from the endorphin rush, exercise can reduce hyperarousal and ground the state of mind,' Emilio had explained. 'It won't be the only technique we work on, but it's something you can start immediately.'

She'd sighed a little at the thought. 'All right, I'll give it a try.'

That had been seven months ago, and she wasn't too proud to admit that Emilio was good at his job. She knew at times she could be treatment-avoidant, and probably not one of his most agreeable clients, but even she had noticed progress since she'd begun working with him. The exercise had particularly helped. Her head felt lighter, her body stronger, and her legs craved the hills. And while standing in a packed restaurant still made her heart hammer wildly in her chest and her thoughts trip and scatter, most times she could breathe through it, grounding her mind, applying everything he'd taught her.

It was these small steps that had given her the courage to work again at Valentina's, four days a week with Andre, braving the tourist-packed streets and piazzas as they walked from Uncle Benito's apartment in Rome to the trattoria each day. She hadn't worked up the courage to walk through Piazza Navona though, or down the Corsia Agonale to Avery's old apartment, where they'd spent that year together with Andre and Riley. To sit on her front steps and remember. But she supposed Rome wasn't built in a day.

Belle felt someone slip behind her, then strong arms circled her waist, pulling her close. She turned her head slightly to nuzzle against Andre's cheek.

'What are you looking at?' he asked in her ear.

She pulled his arms tighter around her, leaning in, inhaling clean cotton and aftershave. 'The snow falling. It's lovely.'

'They said it's going to last beyond Christmas.'

Snowfall was common in some parts of Tuscany. But while it was unusual to experience significant falls in December, their town's proximity to the Apuan Alps meant it sometimes started early and lasted until January.

Belle turned to face her husband, cupping her hands around his jaw, worrying thoughts filling her mind automatically. 'You'll be safe on the roads, won't you?'

He smiled. 'Of course.'

'Because they can get icy.'

'I know,' he said, nudging the tip of her nose with his. 'I'll be safe.'

'Call me as soon as you get to Rome.'

'I will.' He bent to kiss her lips.

A passion rose in her that she was forced to quell, given her mother and Callum were due down at any moment.

'What time are your parents leaving today?' Andre asked, his hands finding their way beneath her robe and under her pyjama top.

'Mum's flight is this afternoon.' One hand discovered

the swell of her breast and stroked it. She moved closer to him, their hips touching. 'Callum's is this evening.'

'I'm sorry we can't take them to the airport,' he murmured, his lips close to hers. 'If I didn't have to work, I'd drive them there.'

'They understand,' she replied breathlessly. 'Besides they have a rental car here.'

'You could go with them, and I could slip away later and pick you up from the airport, take you back to Rome with me,' he said.

'I have a session with Emilio tomorrow.'

He shrugged. 'It was worth a try.'

She laughed as he leaned against her, pressing his lips to hers with a fierce intensity. She threw her arms around his neck and they fell back against the windowsill, his hands roaming her abdomen, sliding lower, making her stomach erupt with butterflies. Then he pulled away with a groan. 'Ugh, torture.' His fingers squeezed her hips, then he adjusted the crotch of his jeans. 'I should go now before I can't.'

'Yes,' she said reluctantly. 'I don't want you to hurry on the roads.'

'I'll see you in four days, my love.' He dropped one last kiss on her lips before scooping his duffel bag up from the floor. He walked to the door, opened it, and with a last smile and a blast of glacial air that made the fire sputter, he left, the purr of his car retreating down the driveway a few minutes later.

Normally she would be with him, driving to Rome together for their four-day working week at Valentina's, where he tended the bar, and she was a sous chef in the kitchen with his father. But her parents had come to visit, and she'd taken two weeks off to spend with them.

Her heart palpitated at the thought of Andre making the journey without her, of them being apart if something happened, just like they had been in Paris when she'd waited for four agonising hours to learn if he'd survived the bomb blast outside the theatre. Therapy helped with thoughts like those, but it didn't completely prevent her mind from jumping to the worst conclusions. What if he was in a car accident? What if there was a terrorist attack in Rome? What if Valentina's was held up?

There were footfalls on the stairs, and she glanced up to find Grace stepping down into the lounge room. She was dressed in cream trousers and a blue cable knit jumper, her short ash-blonde hair wet from the shower. She rubbed her hands together in the warmth. 'Not going for a walk this morning?'

'The weather's not great,' Belle replied. 'I might go later if it clears up. Hungry?'

'Starving.' Grace frowned. 'I'd offer to make breakfast although judging by the smell of baking bread I'd say you've beat me to it.'

Belle tilted her head with a smile. '*Pane di casa*. But we can have bacon and eggs with it.'

'Then that's what I'll make. It's my turn to cook.'

They left the window and Belle led the way through the dining room to the kitchen, her mother behind her.

'Have I missed Andre already?' Grace asked.

'Yes, he just left,' Belle said. 'He had to get on the road so he wouldn't be late for his shift. But he said to say goodbye.'

With an ease she'd acquired during her visit to the house, Grace collected eggs and bacon from the fridge and checked the *pane di casa* in the oven. 'Is this ready to come out?'

'Should be. Let me check it though.' Belle had made the dough the night before, allowing it to rise overnight so that when she'd woken that morning, it was ready to be kneaded. Then she'd shaped it into a batard, placed it in the banneton to proof, then put it in the oven. It was a tried-and-true method Uncle Benito had taught her, to prepare bread dough the night before, especially for breads like focaccia or Italian sourdough, which benefited from long fermenting times.

Belle pulled the loaf out of the oven. She could tell it was ready—a golden crunchy crust and soft, dense crumb, the aroma of hot bread filling the kitchen. 'Is Callum awake?' she asked, placing it on a wire rack to cool.

Grace laid strips of bacon in a frypan. 'He was just coming out of his room as I was heading down.'

Belle heard the old pipes in the bathroom above grumble to life. 'I wish you could stay for Christmas,' she said, turning the coffee machine on.

'We've been here for two weeks,' her mother said. 'We don't want to be a nuisance for Benito.'

'You're not a nuisance. It's his house, but Andre and I live here. I can invite people to come for the holidays. He wouldn't mind.'

'Next year sweetheart, I promise. The girls are waiting for me in New York.' Grace's social life was far more impressive than Belle's these days, with quilting club and book club, tennis club, all sorts of clubs. She was flying to New York to spend Christmas with her friends from her gardening club. 'Anyway, by next year, I'll have a little grandchild to visit, then you'll never get rid of me.'

Belle pretended she hadn't caught the hopeful look Grace flicked over her shoulder as she cracked eggs into the frypan. She busied herself instead, centring a coffee mug under the machine's dispenser.

'And hopefully, you'll come visit me in Sydney too,' Grace persisted. 'I can set up a nursery next to your old room, the one overlooking the garden. I certainly have the space in that big house.'

Belle forced an uneasy smile. 'We're not even pregnant yet.'

'Maybe not,' her mother replied. 'But you've only been back in Italy a year. Some couples try for a lot longer than that.'

'Or they don't have to try at all,' Belle mumbled, thinking of Andre's ex-fiancée, Mary, who'd had a one-night stand with an Italian naval officer ten months ago and had fallen pregnant, to her parents' horror.

Belle and Andre had attended her shotgun wedding in Rome, the evidence of her premarital sin protruding through her wedding dress, as the priest cringed, and her mother sobbed in the front row. Her groom, Dante, a handsome but solemn man, had stood at the altar looking shell-shocked, as Mary had walked down the aisle towards him.

Belle's hand flew unthinkingly to her stomach. Even Mary, who hadn't meant to, had fallen pregnant. She'd given birth to a healthy baby boy last month called Sebastian. Everywhere Belle looked, women were having babies. *Don't think about it, then it will happen*, people told her. But no amount of 'not thinking about it' worked when it was all she could think about. When every month her period frustratingly returned to taunt her.

She sighed, preparing a cappuccino, then reaching for another mug to start the next one. Emilio said her body was still finding its rhythm after Paris. *It'll take time.* But at forty years of age, time wasn't on her side. Maybe that ship had sailed, something she didn't want to contemplate, given Andre was as desperate as she was to start a family.

'Why don't you get the wedding celebration out of the way first, then focus on falling pregnant,' Grace suggested, transferring eggs and bacon to three plates. 'You did promise Benito he'd have his big wedding within three months. It's been eight.'

'I'm kind of happy to remain eloped.'

'But it means a lot to him sweetheart,' Grace said. 'It *is* the Italian way.'

'What's the Italian way?' Callum entered the kitchen, clapping his hands together, smelling of cologne and soap. His brown hair, salted with grey, was wet, brushing the collar of a cream sweater, paired with dark jeans and canvas trainers.

'Nothing,' Belle said, eager to change the subject. 'How did you sleep?'

'Great. Something smells good.'

'Bacon, eggs, *pane di casa* and coffee.' Grace handed him a plate.

'Sorry,' he said. 'I should have come down sooner and started all this.'

'Nonsense,' Grace said firmly. 'With two chefs in the house, I've hardly been allowed to lift a finger in the kitchen. On my last day, the least I can do is make my family breakfast.'

At the mention of the word *family*, Belle caught a surprisingly tender look pass between them, before Callum took the plate and her mother blushed and turned away.

'Coffee?' she asked her father.

'Please.' He sat down at the island bench with his plate. 'Did I hear talk of a wedding?'

Belle groaned inwardly. 'It's something I haven't quite got to yet.'

'Ah, the big celebration,' Callum said. 'Benito still seems keen. He couldn't stop talking about it when we visited Valentina's last week.'

'You could probably tell he wasn't thrilled we eloped,' Belle said. 'He had his heart set on a traditional church service and a party afterwards.'

'Sometimes that thing called a spousal visa won't allow for it,' Callum said. 'Ye had to move quickly.'

Now that the spousal visa had been granted, Belle couldn't help feeling guilty that she hadn't yet honoured her side of the bargain—planning the wedding. It was on her and Andre's list of things to do, but she was the first to admit that she kept moving it to the bottom.

'If they get the wedding out of the way, then they can concentrate on having a baby,' Grace insisted.

Belle frowned and Callum's cheeks grew pink. He cleared his throat, mercifully changing the topic. 'Have you thought about your Christmas menu yet?'

Belle sipped her coffee. 'No. I'll work on it tonight. I have no idea who's coming. Uncle Benito likes to invite people at the last minute.'

'And Riley's coming too?' Grace asked.

'She'll be here in three weeks. I need to call her and confirm which day.' She gave her parents a chastising look. 'I wish you were staying for the holidays.'

'Ah, ye couldn't possibly want us around anymore. And ye'll have enough to do anyway,' Callum said. 'A house full of guests.'

It was true, Christmas was a busy time at the house with locals visiting, but there were enough bedrooms upstairs for her parents to stay, and she'd missed so many Christmases with Callum that there was a need to catch up.

'Next year, lassie. I promise,' he said.

They ate their breakfast, snow falling again outside the kitchen windows, as they talked about Christmas menu ideas. The topic moved to Grace's visit to New York and Belle fell silent, her mother and Callum becoming lost in a conversation for two.

After she'd finished eating, she quietly stepped away from the bench, placed her plate and mug in the dishwasher, and slipped out of the room, leaving them to talk.

THREE

Although Grace's flight departed four hours before Callum's, he offered to drive her to the airport in his rental car well before he needed to be there. They'd finished breakfast, then Belle showered, coming down the stairs later to find her parents scampering about, gathering bags and passports and coats with a familiarity that reminded her of an old married couple.

She still remembered that night, three years ago, when they'd reunited for the first time after almost forty years. It was during a visit Callum had paid to Sydney shortly after Belle had returned from finding him in Scotland. Andre had still been there, on his three-month hiatus from Valentina's, and the three of them had invited Grace to dinner in Camden, to a teppanyaki restaurant.

Grace had sat perched on the edge of her chair, wild-eyed, like she might flee at any moment, while Callum stole dubious glances at her. Afterwards, outside on the street, Grace had broken down in a flood of tears.

'I'm so sorry,' she'd sobbed, looking utterly bereft and

apologetic. Belle had been about to step forward when Callum beat her to it.

'There, there,' he'd said soothingly, one hand on her arm. 'No need fur tears.'

'But I did the most dreadful thing to you. I kept you from your daughter,' she'd cried. 'And we just spent a whole meal pretending like it never happened.'

His arm had gone around her shoulders, pulling her close to him. 'And we will talk about it,' he'd said gently but firmly. 'I dinnae plan on leaving Sydney without an explanation. But please dinnae cry. It's nothing we can't fix.'

Her parents had met again for lunch the next day and Callum told Belle later that they'd talked extensively about the past, and what had driven her to keep Belle a secret from him.

'We can't change what she did. But she's remorseful, a hundred times over,' he'd said. 'What is there to do but move forward? I can't stay angry at her forever.'

At that moment, she'd realised her father was a deeply kind man—forgiving and empathic and perhaps still a little in love with her mother.

Luggage wheels clattered over the stone floor and Belle blinked, brought back to the present. Callum dragged both suitcases towards the door as Grace's arms were suddenly around her. 'I'll call you as soon as I reach my hotel in New York,' she said. 'And on Christmas morning, of course.'

'Aye. Ye'll be hearing from me too,' Callum added, looping his scarf around his neck. He threw his arms open, and Belle stepped into them, hugging him. 'I'm going to miss ye, lassie.'

'I'll miss you both.'

'Take photos of all the dishes ye make for Christmas.' He stepped back to look at her.

'I will.'

'Have you got your coat?' Grace asked him.

'It's over there on the sofa. Did ye get your hairdryer? I saw it on the vanity when I was packing.'

She nodded. 'I've got it.'

Belle watched them gather up their things and check, then recheck for wallets and purses and passports. They rarely saw each other outside of visits with Belle, yet when they came together, they seemed to click like jigsaw pieces. She saw that now, a sense of ease with each other, and she wasn't sure yet if it consoled or unsettled her. The father she'd known all her life—Edward—had only been gone three years, and while she was growing to love Callum dearly, seeing him with her mother felt a bit like a betrayal.

'We'd better go then,' Callum said, glancing at his watch. 'The roads will be slow.'

He opened the door and dragged both suitcases out onto the porch, then lifted them one by one, carrying them over the sludgy snow, to deposit them into the rental car's boot.

Grace and Belle watched him from the doorway.

'You two are getting along,' Belle said.

Grace still watched him as he packed the car. 'He's been a good sport about everything, even though it hurts him. All those years not knowing you have been lost forever.' She winced like her remorse was physically painful. 'I see it in his expression when the two of you are together. I can never give that time back to him.'

'But he's forgiven you. He's moving on. You need to as well.'

Grace pulled on her leather gloves. 'I'm trying. Regret can be burdensome, though.' She turned to Belle, placing her hands on her arms. 'I'm more concerned about you than us.'

'Why?'

'I know falling pregnant hasn't been easy. And I can get a little over-excited about being a grandmother, which doesn't help. But I do know what you're going through.'

Belle couldn't see how she could. Her mother had fallen pregnant after a brief affair with Callum. Belle and Andre had been trying for eight months. They'd expected to fall pregnant during their honeymoon in Sorrento. When they'd arrived home and Belle's period had been a few days late, they'd even rushed out, deliriously excited, to buy a pregnancy test. But their elation had been short-lived. Her period had arrived before they could take the test and the disappointment of it had been breathtaking.

She remembered how foolish they'd both felt, thinking they could have been that lucky on the first go. 'Don't worry, my love,' Andre had said. 'Next month.'

But next month came and the one after that, a soaring spiral of hope always followed by the plummeting let-down that felt, at times, like grief. Soon after they'd married, Belle started her therapy with Emilio and picked up shifts again in Valentina's kitchen, but always in the background was the constant monitoring of her ovulation cycle and the timing of sex until it had almost become clinical. She wasn't sure how her mother could possibly know what that felt like.

'I wanted more children with your father. Edward, I mean,' Grace said, as though sensing her scepticism. 'I wanted four or five. I wanted our house to burst at the seams with children.' She gave a sad laugh. 'But he couldn't have them and it wasn't meant to be. So I *do* know how you feel, that ache in your stomach to carry a child. The disappointment when you realise another month's gone by and it hasn't happened.'

'And what if it never happens?' Belle whispered, too afraid to ask out loud in case the universe heard. In case she jinxed herself and sealed her fate.

'I know this is terribly cliché but try not to worry so much about it. Enjoy married life. You've only been back for a year. For just a few months, forget about biological clocks and ovulating and all that calculating and date-watching I know you do. When your mind and body aren't so fixated on making it happen, it will do what it's meant to do.'

Belle, unconvinced, sighed deeply. 'I'm not sure I trust leaving it to chance anymore.'

Grace smiled softly, sweeping aside a brown curl from Belle's eye. 'Just be kind to yourself.'

Belle stared out at the front garden, wishing she *could* relax about it, but logic and emotion rarely spoke the same language in her mind. 'I just never thought I'd be at this stage of my life and childless. When I was with Ben, I thought I had it all figured out. If I'd known it would have been this difficult, I would have tried for a baby years ago.'

'We can never know what the future holds. There's no point torturing yourself over it now. And, honestly, I'm not sure having a child with Ben would have been a good idea. He was unfaithful after all.'

The boot closed and Callum returned to the doorway. 'Ready?'

Grace nodded. 'Yes. We'd better go.' She embraced Belle fiercely this time, her arms strong around her daughter, before kissing the top of her head. 'I love you so much, sweetheart.'

'Love you, Mum. Bye, Callum. Have a safe flight.'

Callum hugged her again, before taking Grace's hand

and helping her step through the snow to the passenger side of the car.

The sun emerged bravely through thinning clouds as they climbed in. A minute later, the rental vehicle drove down the driveway, past the row of snow-capped pencil pines, her parents waving goodbye from the front seats. Belle waited until their car disappeared around the bend before she stepped back into the warm living room and closed the door behind her.

The house was silent, almost sullen, without Callum's Scottish cheer and her mother's laugh. With Andre away until the end of the week, she was almost tempted to catch the train to Rome to see him, but she had her appointment with Emilio the following day, one that she'd rescheduled several times around her parents' visit and she didn't want to reschedule it again.

Her phone trilled upstairs, and she climbed the stairs two at a time, finding it on the nightstand in their bedroom. It was Andre.

'I made it,' he said.

Relief washed over her as she heard the boot of his car close. She could almost see him swinging his duffel bag over his shoulder and beginning the five-minute walk to his father's apartment on the east side of the city, where he'll drop his bag and head straight back out again to Valentina's. She wished she was with him.

'Did I miss your parents?' he asked.

'They just left.'

'What are you going to do after your session with Emilio tomorrow? Want to catch the train to Rome? I could get the dinner shift off and we could drive to Naples, visit that little winery you like.'

She smiled, dropping down on the edge of the bed. 'I had considered it. But can you get away?'

'I can try.'

'While I'm there, we could talk about Christmas. Do you know who's coming yet?'

'About that.' Andre cleared his throat. 'My father called while I was on my way in. He's, uh, invited some people.'

'Great. Who?'

There was a pause. 'Mary's parents, Giovanni and Teresa.'

Belle sat up a little straighter. 'Mary's parents?'

'Yes.'

'Oh.' She bit back the desire to protest. 'Okay. Anyone else coming?'

'Mary as well. And the baby.'

This time, Belle couldn't hide her feelings. 'Mary and her baby? Why is *she* coming? Is her husband coming too?'

'No,' Andre said carefully. 'Dante is on a mission in the Gulf of Guinea. Mary's coming with her parents and baby Sebastian.'

Belle pursed her lips. She shouldn't feel insecure when it came to Mary—the girl had moved on, was married now, had a baby and yet, at her wedding, from her spot on the bridal table, her gaze had still followed Andre's every move. Belle had brushed it off at the time, putting it down to nostalgia on Mary's part, particularly since her life had been thrown into upheaval—a one-night stand and an unexpected pregnancy resulting in a snap wedding—but occasionally, Belle thought about it, and it still bothered her.

She shook her head at herself. *Stop.* Mary was in the past—they hardly saw her anymore. And she'd clearly moved on. New husband. New baby. Surely one Christmas with her couldn't hurt.

'Belle, are you there?' Andre asked, interrupting her thoughts.

'I'm here,' she said. 'It's fine. They can come. It's just for one night, right?'

'Well, that's the other thing,' Andre said slowly. 'Papà invited them to stay until Epiphany.'

'Epiphany!' She hadn't meant to yell. 'They're going to stay with us until January the sixth? The four of them? Here?'

'Yes.'

'But why?'

'Because my father wants to spend the holidays with his friends. It was only meant to be Giovanni and Teresa. Mary would have been with her husband and his family. But he's away on duty, so she's coming with them.'

Of course she is, Belle wanted to say. She exhaled slowly, trying to be reasonable.

'It's not ideal,' he said, his voice full of apology.

'No, it isn't. I was willing to compromise for a night or two. But the four of them, for Christmas, New Year *and* Epiphany? What about Riley? She's meant to be staying with us on Christmas Eve. Where will she sleep?'

'We have the daybed downstairs. I'm sure Mary wouldn't mind sleeping on it. We can put the baby next to her.'

'We can't put a mother and her newborn baby on a fold-out bed in the lounge room.' She sighed, irritated, wishing more than ever that her parents had stayed for the holidays. *Sorry, all the guest bedrooms are taken.* The perfect solution. 'Riley can sleep on the daybed.'

'I know this is inconvenient,' he said. 'I'm not keen on them coming either, but I'm not sure we can say no.'

That was the crux of the problem. She loved the house

in Tuscany and living there with Andre, but it wasn't *her* house. She had no right to tell Uncle Benito who could and couldn't visit his family home for Christmas.

She ran a hand through her chestnut-brown hair, fingers tangling in soft curls, watching the late afternoon gather outside. Really, what was the worst that could happen? That she might grow to like Mary? That the new mother might have some useful advice about pregnancy and babies? They could find common ground and maybe, just maybe, become friends. She sighed. 'No, it's fine. Of course they can come. I'm making a big deal out of nothing.'

'It's not nothing,' he said kindly. 'I know they're not who you'd prefer to spend Christmas with—my ex-fiancée and her parents.'

'Maybe it will be good for us all. A new start.'

'And the baby?' he asked. 'Will you be all right with him in the house?'

Her back stiffened. 'Why wouldn't I be?'

He hesitated. 'It's just that we haven't... you know. I'm worried it will make you sad.'

Tears pushed at the corners of her eyes, and she blinked them back, resenting the pity in his voice. 'I'll be fine. It will be lovely to have a baby in the house.'

'Are you sure?'

'Yes,' she said brusquely, then hurried to change the subject. 'I might give Rome a miss. I'll need to get the guest rooms ready again, clear some space for Sebastian's things.'

'Oh.' He sounded disappointed. 'Sure. Well, Mary will appreciate that.'

Belle fell silent. She picked instead at a loose thread on the quilt cover.

'Anyway, I better go,' he eventually said. 'I have to get to work.'

'Okay. I might go for a walk. The snow's stopped here.'

'Be careful. It's getting late.'

'I will,' she said. 'I love you.' She emphasised the words, because their conversation had felt uneasy, and she didn't want to leave it that way.

'*Ti amo tanto*,' he said, with equal feeling.

They hung up and Belle dropped her phone beside her, flopping back onto the covers. She stared up at the dark oak timber beams above. Mary was coming for Christmas. *Mary*. The woman Belle had no reason to resent other than that she was Andre's former fiancée. Yet, as much as she told herself that Mary had moved on, the memory of her watching Andre at her wedding, her large, brown eyes following him as he moved around the room, ate his dinner, danced with Belle...

Her stomach churned at the thought. She was staring down the barrel of an awkward Christmas and Epiphany with people she didn't like and who didn't like her. But she was a De Luca now—Andre's wife, Benito's daughter-in-law, and part of the family—and this was expected of her.

Somehow, she would have to make it work.

FOUR

The next morning Belle showered and dressed warmly for her commute to Emilio Bianchi's office in Pistoia. Usually, she drove herself there in Andre's car, but since Andre was in Rome, she caught the train instead.

She walked briskly to the station, the cold air clearing her lungs and making her eyes water. Trains ran regularly from Barga to Lucca and she caught one easily, reaching Lucca fifty minutes later and changing over to the Pistoia line. The time passed quickly, with headphones and a book and a Christmas menu to plan.

She reached Pistoia two hours and ten minutes later—a northern Tuscany town that sat snugly at the base of the Apennines. From the station, she set off on foot, retreating into her coat as she turned down damp laneways and into breezy piazzas. Dr Bianchi was on the top floor of an apartment block turned office complex, in a part of town that had outgrown its medieval ramparts. It was slightly more modern there, with upmarket bars and restaurants, and chic clothing boutiques, with the historic centre in the opposite direction.

Belle arrived at the building and climbed the three flights of stairs to Emilio's office. The elevator had long given up the ghost—one of those rickety cage door contraptions that were beautifully ornate but slightly toe-curling to ride. Belle preferred the stairs anyway. It was an easy, endorphin-charged climb that she could master without breaking a sweat now that regular exercise had become a part of her routine.

At Emilio's suite, she opened the glass door quietly and let herself in. The waiting room was empty except for Greta, his secretary, who glanced up from her typing, giving Belle a wide smile.

'*Buongiorno, come sta?*' she said, her slick, grey bob gently stirring.

'*Salve. Bene grazie, lei?*' Belle asked, unravelling her scarf.

'I am well,' Greta replied. She indulged Belle often by slipping into English for her. The older woman said it gave her practice too. 'Are you ready for Christmas?'

'I should be, but I'm not.'

'Is the celebration at your house this year?'

'Yes. We're having guests stay until Epiphany.'

Greta screwed up her nose. 'That's a long visit. I hope they're people you like.' She chuckled at her joke. 'Emilio won't be much longer. He's just on the phone.'

'That's okay. I can wait.' Belle settled on the sofa, placing her bag and scarf down next to her.

She noticed the latest issue of *Vogue Italia* on the coffee table in front of her and reached for it, flicking through its glossy pages. She'd been practising her Italian reading over the past months in that little room, studying the articles. It passed the time, and the room was pleasant to wait in—calm blue walls and dark grey patterned carpet, a comfortable two-seater sofa and two plush armchairs, a coffee table with a pile of magazines, the gentle tap-tapping of Greta's fingers on her keyboard.

Belle was reading an article on Donatella Versace when the door to Emilio's office opened, and her psychologist stepped out. He smiled warmly at her, said something softly to Greta in Italian, then indicated with his hand that he was ready for her.

'Belle, *buongiorno. Come sta?*'

Belle closed the magazine and placed it back on the table, rising to her feet. She collected her bag and scarf and walked to Emilio. '*Salve. Bene grazie.*'

She followed him into his office, and he closed the door behind them. 'Take a seat,' he said. 'Usual spot or wherever you like.'

Just like the waiting room outside, the walls were the same gentle blue. Emilio's desk was by the window, the pale colours of a winter afternoon casting patterns across his laptop and paperwork. She found that view of Pistoia particularly soothing, with its rolling hillsides dipped in syrupy sunlight, tinting the rooftops and church spires, the snow-capped Apennines in the distance.

She chose the sofa, where she often sat, and Emilio sat in his regular spot, in the armchair opposite her. He looked relaxed today—a white collared shirt with no tie, dark blue trousers and brown leather shoes. His glasses were black-rimmed, hair boyishly brown and always flopping over his eyes. He had a nice smile and was smart and kind, sometimes even funny.

Sitting in that chair opposite him, Belle often wondered about his life. He was around her age, she thought, hands absent of a wedding ring. So was he married? Divorced? Did he have children? He never shared personal details with her, obviously, but it didn't stop her from wondering who Emilio Bianchi was and what he did when he wasn't being her psychologist. She wondered, not because she was attracted to him, although Emilio *was* attractive, but because she'd spent the last seven months pouring her heart out to this man, sharing her deepest, darkest fears with him and it had made her curious. Not in a friendship kind of way—that wasn't allowed—but just... curious.

'Is all well?' he asked, crossing his legs and pushing his glasses up his nose.

'Yes,' she said, settling back into the sofa.

'And last time we spoke, your parents were coming to visit? Your mother and biological father.'

'That's right. They went home yesterday.'

'And how were your two weeks with them?' Her file was open on Emilio's lap and although he appeared relaxed, he was poised to take notes as soon as she spoke.

'It went well. I didn't realise how much I'd missed them until they arrived. Now they're gone and I wish they'd stayed longer, even over Christmas.'

'Do you feel lonely here?'

'Not lonely,' she clarified, 'just homesick sometimes.'

'It's perfectly natural to miss your family and feel homesick,' he said, smiling and making a note. 'Did you take them out anywhere?'

'Mainly restaurants and cafés,' she replied. 'A few wineries. Andre and I drove them to Rome too. We stayed there for a few days so they could see Andre's father, Benito.'

'How did you go with visiting all those places?' he asked, his pen scratching against the paper again. 'Any dissociation, physical reactions to crowds or noises, flashbacks, nightmares when you tried to sleep?'

She'd be lying if she told him that she'd moved through those two weeks and the endless places they'd visited with ease. He would see straight through it anyway. 'Rome is becoming easier. I have a routine there and there's rarely time to deviate from it. But other places, *new* places, still affect me.'

'Because you lack a sense of control in those places?' Emilio asked.

'I guess.'

Emilio made more notes. 'Describe some of the symptoms you faced when visiting a restaurant you'd never been to before. What went through your mind?'

Belle wiped her hands down the legs of her jeans. They felt clammy suddenly. 'My heart sped up when I walked in, and my thoughts were a bit scattered. I was looking for places to hide.'

Emilio nodded. 'Were you able to apply your grounding techniques?'

'Yes. I'm getting better at controlling the symptoms when they come on.'

'What about before that? When you first made the plans? What went through your mind?'

'I googled whether it was a busy place, out in the open or down a laneway where we might get trapped.'

'If you were attacked?' Emilio prompted. 'You don't want to get trapped if the establishment is attacked?'

'Yes. I always like to study the layout of the restaurant before we go, whether it's big or small or narrow or open, just to be safe.'

'You would like to know if there's something like a closed-in alfresco where you might get trapped by hedges?'

She cast her eyes down. *Like the Papilles.* 'Yes.'

Emilio smiled encouragingly. 'Anxiety and PTSD

sufferers tend to maintain highly controlled lives. When they have a plan, even a plan for the plan, it helps give them a sense of control and quietens the anxiety. When things are left to chance, that's when the sufferer feels out of control.'

'But I feel like I'm doing it all the time. Trying to account for every possible scenario. It's exhausting.'

'What does Andre say about the motions you go through?'

'I don't... I mean... I don't really tell him.' Her voice became small.

'Why don't you tell him?' Emilio, ever persistent, watched her intently.

'Because studying the layout of a restaurant to make sure you have an escape plan in case terrorists attack sounds a little crazy.'

'I don't like the word "crazy".'

'You know what I mean.'

'Would he be upset, confused? Would he think you're crazy?'

She sighed. 'No, he wouldn't. He would worry himself sick over it. We haven't fallen pregnant yet and we have the wedding to plan, and I don't want to add to that with all my psychobabble. I don't want to be a burden.'

'Do you think he would be supportive?'

'Yes, he would be.' There was no doubt in her mind how much Andre loved her and worried about her. 'But that's precisely the reason why I don't want to bother him with this.'

'Talking to your loved ones about your hypervigilance or any of your PTSD symptoms is not a bother. Have you ever thought that maybe Andre would like to know? Would like to help? Bottling everything up and trying to cope on your own exacerbates the issue.' Emilio gave her a pointed look. They were covering old ground. Every session, Emilio drummed it into her to communicate more with Andre and every session she promised to until she got home and the gruelling shifts at the trattoria and falling pregnant and planning a very expensive, very big wedding wore them both down and she decided he didn't need to deal with her issues too, not when, for the most part, she *was* making progress.

It was just occasionally, when a deviation from routine happened, like two weeks spent visiting a string of new restaurants and cafés with her parents, that all her coping techniques were put to the test. Emilio had warned her that she might occasionally relapse, but she didn't want Andre or anyone else to know about it.

The session continued and they covered the usual grounding techniques—anchoring phrases, memory games, breathing and the five senses—then they spoke about Valentina's and Rome, the wedding, Edward and Callum, and how much she wanted to have a baby.

And as always, they discussed that night in Paris in depth, about what happened to Ben and Avery, her survivor's guilt, and processing the events in a constructive, healthy way, something she hadn't been able to do in the aftermath of the attack. Emilio called it Prolonged Exposure therapy. By regularly addressing her memories in a safe and controlled environment, over time, they would become less painful to deal with.

They'd almost come to the end of the hour when Emilio gave her a long look and tapped his pen contemplatively against his lips. 'Something's on your mind.'

She blinked at him, then laughed. 'Isn't that why I'm in therapy?'

He chuckled. 'No, I mean you seem distracted today. Not your usual self. Did something happen before coming here?'

She frowned as she thought of Mary and Christmas. 'Well, sort of. But it's nothing, really.'

Emilio glanced at his watch. 'We have ten minutes left.'

Belle gave him an embarrassed smile. 'My father-in-law invited some people to the house for Christmas.' When Emilio's eyebrows drew together with puzzlement, she elaborated. 'It's Andre's ex-fiancée and her parents, who don't like me very much. Well, the mother doesn't like me. She thinks I stole Andre away from her daughter. Maybe I did. I don't know.'

'And they're coming for Christmas, the ex-fiancée and her parents?'

'Not just Christmas. They're staying until Epiphany. In our house.'

Emilio nodded. 'And that obviously bothers you?'

'It should be water under the bridge, I guess. He ended his relationship with Mary over five years ago. She's married to someone else now; they have a baby. And Andre and I are married. But I think she still carries a torch for him.'

'But her husband and baby will be with her?'

'The baby only. The husband is away on a naval mission.'

'I see.' To her relief, Emilio didn't make notes. He'd closed her file and had set it aside and she hoped that meant there was nothing wrong with how she was feeling. That this was a perfectly natural response to having her husband's ex invade her home for Christmas.

'Does your father-in-law normally invite people to your house for celebrations?' Emilio asked.

'It's his house,' Belle explained.

'But it's your house too. You live there with your husband.'

She tilted her head to the side, conceding. 'Yes, I live there, but it's Uncle Benito's family home, one that he owned with his late wife, Valentina.'

'So you live there and it's your home, but you don't feel like you have a say in who visits and who doesn't?' His tone wasn't accusatory. He was simply asking a question.

Belle shrugged. 'I guess.' Up until this Christmas, it had never been an issue. There had been the occasional request to entertain his friends or have a party at the house, nothing unreasonable, and his friends were always lovely. But this time was different. This time it was Mary, and Belle wondered briefly what would have happened if she'd just said no. *No, they can't come. No, I don't feel comfortable. No, I don't want them staying until Epiphany!*

What would Uncle Benito think? What position would that put Andre in? The truth was, she wouldn't have dared because even though she lived there, it wasn't *her* home.

The last ten minutes flew by, and she was silently relieved as she said goodbye to Emilio and scheduled her last session for the year with Greta. She'd felt guilty talking about Uncle Benito behind his back, as though she was betraying his goodwill. But as usual, Emilio got her thinking too, got her unpacking the complex layers of emotions that she was used to burying deep down. And as she left his office later, walking back to the train station, his questions continued to niggle.

Yes, Mary's visit bothered her more than she'd realised.

FIVE

Belle rinsed toothpaste from her mouth and turned the tap off. She flicked off the bathroom light and walked across the hall into the bedroom. Andre was sitting up in bed shirtless, wearing only pyjama bottoms, an assortment of coloured brochures on his lap.

She smiled. It was something she would never grow tired of—the freedom to share the same bed with him, to lie beside him and to wake up together. He'd arrived back that afternoon from Rome, throwing open the front door, tossing his bag on the floor and carrying her straight up to bed.

Longing stirred in her stomach as she stared at him, his gaze locked on one of the brochures, lips slightly turned up, activating those impossibly deep dimples. Even after all these years, he still evoked something primal in her, a need to have him and to be consumed.

'What are you looking at?' she asked, climbing in beside him, draped in one of his sweaters, which was enormous on her.

He leaned across and kissed the top of her head as she curled into him, entwining her bare legs around his. 'Wedding venues. We need to agree on something soon so we can set a date. These places book out months in advance.'

'So I guess having a baby first is out of the question,' she said, picking up one of the brochures and glancing at it.

'Not out of the question. But if we wait for that to happen, we might never get this wedding done.'

She bit her lip and nodded, his words making her eyes sting with tears.

'Oh, my love, I didn't mean it like that,' he said, wrapping his arm around her and pulling her close to him. 'I just meant that it hasn't happened yet, so maybe we should get this wedding out of the way first. Then the stress will be over, and we can concentrate on falling pregnant.'

She played with her engagement ring, a white gold band with a square cut diamond, that he'd presented her with the day she'd arrived back in Italy. It had been New Year's Eve. He'd brought her straight to the Tuscan house, lit the fire, and had bent down on one knee in front of it to propose. That night and all the nights since had been filled with their hopes and dreams of a blissful life together and a house full of *bambini*.

She swallowed back the disappointment that always sat heavy in her soul when she thought of babies. 'I guess I just never expected it to be so difficult. And it hurts knowing that the problem is me.'

Andre's hand went instinctively, protectively, to hers. 'It's not you.'

'Well, we know it's not you,' she said. 'That's been proven.'

Several months ago, they'd tested Andre's fertility and it was confirmed he was carrying healthy, robust, superstar sperm. When it became clear that the problem wasn't with him, the reality that it was her had been like a punch to the stomach—her and her useless uterus or underachieving eggs, or whatever the problem was. She'd made an appointment immediately with a local GP to get evaluated too.

'Come back and see me when you've tried for at least twelve months,' the elderly doctor had said, as though she hadn't given conception a good enough go yet.

'But surely we can run some tests now,' she'd said.

He didn't seem to agree and was already at his door, ushering her out. 'See you again next year.'

So that was that.

'It's no one's fault,' Andre said. 'It's just not our time yet, that's all.'

'Then when will our time be? Because I'm running out of it.' She hated being obsessed with the idea of pregnancy, with a biological clock that she was certain everyone could hear ticking, but the more months that slipped by and the more her period doggedly pursued them, the more she was aware of it.

He turned and cupped his hand under her chin, forcing her blue eyes to meet his dark gaze. '*We* are not running out of time. And *we will* fall pregnant,' he said.

She appreciated how he used the term 'we' and not 'you' like she was less to blame for their barrenness, even though it was *her* stubborn reproductive system that refused to cooperate.

'Maybe this is the small break we need,' he said. 'We can plan this wedding, enjoy ourselves a little. It will give your body time to figure out what it's doing, and when we're less fixated on it, it will happen.'

'What if it never happens?' she persisted.

'It will.'

'But what if it doesn't and it's just you and me? The two of us, every day, forever. Could you be happy with that? Am

I enough for the rest of your life?' It was a question that plagued her repeatedly because of the answer that he might give.

He kissed her gently on her forehead, her cheeks, then her lips. '*Mia cara*, we have waited so long to be together. Do you honestly think the two of us wouldn't be enough?'

She shrugged. 'I know you want children. I don't want to be the one to take that away from you.'

He frowned. 'Belle, you're not taking anything away from me. If it doesn't happen naturally, then we have options, like IVF or surrogacy, even adoption.'

She knew it was reasonable to expect those next steps, but it didn't prevent her feeling like a failure for what should come naturally for her body.

'And besides, you're the love of my life. I'd be happy if it were just the two of us for the rest of our days.'

She closed her eyes, resting her head on his bare chest, his chin perched on her head. She wasn't sure she believed him entirely, but she let his words soothe her all the same. There was nothing else she could do.

'So,' he said, 'where would you like to get married... again?'

She reached for one of the brochures, a lavish reception hall set on a sprawling estate in Chianti.

'You like that one?' His question sounded hopeful.

'It's nice,' she said. 'A bit big, though. It caters for over four hundred guests. Do we need all that room?'

'I have a big family.'

'How about something a little smaller and less expensive?'

'Like this?' He reached for a glossy booklet displaying a majestic villa in Lucca on its front cover, with accommodation and several rooms to choose from for the reception, as well as a Catholic chapel on the grounds. He flicked through the pages, pointing at different options.

'Yes, better,' she said. The smallest reception room was still grander than she'd hope for, with a vast coffered Renaissance ceiling and rich, ornate cornices, a Venetian glass chandelier, and stiff tablecloths, but at least it wasn't enormous.

'Let's call them in the morning. It's by appointment only, so we can arrange to see them before Christmas.' He kept flicking through the pages. 'My dad will probably prefer Chianti, but this one is nice as well.'

'Chianti is a bit much, don't you think?' Belle asked carefully.

Andre compared the two brochures side by side. 'Not really.'

'I mean, it would be nice if I could have a say too.'

He glanced down at her, his brow furrowed. 'Of course you have a say. Where did that come from?'

Belle shrugged, chewing on her bottom lip. 'I don't know. Just this whole thing with Mary and her parents coming to stay.'

Andre put down the brochures. 'What do you mean?'

'Well, I just thought Christmas could be spent with people we want to spend it with. Two weeks with your ex-fiancée and her parents wasn't what I had in mind.'

Andre untangled himself from her arms to look at her better. 'Okay,' he said slowly. 'I didn't realise you were upset about this.'

'I'm not upset,' she said, although the more she thought about it, she realised she was. 'I just don't want to spend my first Christmas back in Italy with *them*.'

'Neither do I,' he said. 'But we talked about this a few

days ago and you said you were okay with it. So I told my father it was fine. Now, it seems it's *not* fine?'

'All I'm saying is that it would have been nice to have been consulted before they were invited, especially for two weeks.'

'You *were* consulted.'

'No, I was *told* they were coming. I wasn't given a choice.'

Andre's jaw ticked.

'I know this isn't my house,' she said, softening her tone, for she could feel the tension stretching like a tightly wound coil, 'but I live here too. And Mary isn't just some family friend. There's history between the two of you. Of course it's going to be awkward for me. It would have been nice to have had a say. Anyway, Emilio and I were chatting about it—'

'You spoke to your psychologist about this before me?' A flash of annoyance crossed his face.

'He noticed I was distracted, and he asked me what was wrong. I mentioned that Mary was coming for Christmas.'

'So he knows about Mary? I thought you were discussing your PTSD, not my ex-girlfriends.'

'We talk about lots of things,' she said, feeling equally annoyed that he would turn this back on her. He was missing the point.

'He must know you very well if he can see when you're "distracted". Better than I can, apparently.' Andre turned his head away from her and she flinched.

They sat in stony silence for a few minutes, surrounded by glossy brochures of wedding venues and the very touchy topic of Mary.

'Hey,' she said, reaching out and placing her fingertips on his arm.

He faced her, hurt and confusion in his eyes. 'I didn't realise your psychologist knew things that I didn't. What does that say about me as your husband?'

'He's just a therapist. A professional. Someone whose job it is to make me talk.' She studied his face, but he still looked insulted. 'Okay, no, you're right. I should have told you how I felt about Mary coming. But it only happened a few days ago, then Emilio brought it up at the end of our session and we spent a couple of minutes discussing it. That's all. I wasn't hiding it from you. I was just getting my head around it.'

Andre's jaw softened and his shoulders relaxed. He shook his head, sighing deeply. 'No, I'm the one who should be sorry. I know this is an awful situation for you. And you're right—we live here, but it's not our house. I mean, it's my house, the house I grew up in, but it's not *ours*. It's my father's. It's hard to tell him he can't invite people for Christmas.'

'And I would never want you to,' she hurried to say, for he needed to know that. She'd never claimed the house to be hers. It was Valentina's and Benito's house, and she was grateful to live there. But it was becoming apparent that she had little say about certain matters and, maybe, if she were to live permanently in Italy, she would like to have a say every now and again. Especially about who stayed at the house and who didn't, who she'd have to entertain or live with for two weeks.

'Once we've finished paying for the wedding and we have more money to spare, we'll look for our own place,' he said.

She shook her head, feeling ashamed. 'No, I don't want you to leave your home. That's not what this is about.'

He placed his hand on hers and stroked it gently. 'I

know that, but you're right. The lines are blurred. It's our house, but it's not, and I understand that.'

'I want to stay,' she assured him. 'I love it here. Maybe we just need to have a conversation with your father.'

Andre laughed. 'He will be highly offended.'

She grinned. 'Of course he will be.'

Andre snorted this time, then rolled over and pinned her beneath him. 'I missed you while I was in Rome.'

She clucked happily, then kissed him intensely on the mouth.

'You're not allowed to stay here anymore while I'm gone,' he said, his voice thick with desire as he kissed her back. 'It makes me too lonely.'

'I was lonely too.'

His hand found its way under her oversized sweater, long fingers caressing her bare stomach. She pressed her lips to his throat, sucking his skin, drawing it in with her teeth and gently bruising him. His breath hitched and a moan escaped. She repeated it, enjoying his reaction.

He discarded his pyjama pants and pulled her into a sitting position, raising her arms above her head so he could slide his sweater off her. Then he pulled her onto his lap with quiet, yet wilful fervour, strong arms looped around her back, holding her steady.

He smelled of fresh soap and shampoo. And he smelled of her, of her perfume and her skin, and she liked the way they'd marked each other, like a fingerprint.

Heat spiralled in her belly, warming her thighs, and Andre's chest was smooth and taut beneath her hands, his heart quickening in time with hers. For a moment, they kissed deeply, lips languorous and tongues seeking, a rhythm they knew by heart, as they knew each other. Then his hands found her hips, gripping them gently, lifting her up off his lap then back down again, so that he was inside her.

He let out a sigh of ecstasy, and she wrapped her arms around him, pressing her body to his so they were one. Their mouths met again, Andre murmuring her name against her lips, as though desperate to cling to every part of her. They rose and fell together, their lovemaking bathed in hope, pouring everything out and leaving nothing behind. And because she wasn't ovulating and there was no pressure, the spontaneity of it left her even more breathless. She realised, not for the first time, how much she'd missed the simple act of *just* making love.

Afterwards, he held her close and kissed the tip of her nose, then her lips, until he drifted off to sleep and she watched him with silent reverence. They were lucky to be together—it was more than some couples in their predicament managed, when time and distance conspired, and years were spent satisfying visa requirements, sometimes without success. Belle would never take their life for granted, would always protect it fiercely, for all the months and years it had taken them to find each other again.

She traced a fingertip along the scar that Paris had left on his temple, smoothing away a lock of brown hair from his forehead, and he stirred, smiling softly in his sleep. She didn't withdraw, instead bent to kiss him, to touch the tip of his straight nose, his full lips, the strong jaw she loved, revelling in that moment when the world grew soundless, and their worries were hushed.

SIX

Belle barely had time to catch her breath as Christmas approached. The week before the holidays, she visited Pistoia for one last session with Emilio, to resume again after Epiphany, then she and Andre travelled to Rome for their final four days at Valentina's for the year. They also called the villa in Lucca to enquire about an appointment to tour the wedding rooms, but the venue was booked solid for the next two years.

'I was afraid of this,' he said, shaking his head. 'Everything is booking out.' He picked up the brochure for Chianti, with its huge reception rooms, the kind that sent anxiety crackling up her spine. Big rooms meant lots of people. 'I know you think this one is too extravagant, but we should give them a call. You might like it.' And because waiting two years for Lucca was probably out of the question, she agreed.

Amidst the long hours of working, frequenting the market to purchase food for Christmas, and preparing the house for their guests, Belle almost forgot that Riley was coming.

It was the day before Christmas Eve and she and Andre had been in their local town of Barga doing last-minute shopping. When they returned home, a dark sedan followed them into the driveway, parking alongside them.

Riley climbed out of the back, wearing a dramatic brown faux fur Cossack hat, a coat and leather gloves. '*Buongiorno!*' she cried.

Belle gasped and glanced at Andre.

'You forgot she was coming, didn't you?' he asked, shutting the engine off.

'I was meant to call her and confirm which day she was arriving.' She grimaced.

'Well, she's here now,' he said with a laugh.

They climbed out of the car and trudged through the snow to Riley's Uber.

After a flurry of hugs and '*ciaos*', Andre scooped up Riley's luggage and clomped to the house, Belle and Riley following, arms linked. The Uber backed out of the driveway and drove away.

Belle squeezed her friend's arm. 'I'm so glad you're here. I meant to call and find out what time your flight was coming in, but it slipped my mind.' They reached the front door and kicked the snow from their boots. 'We could have picked you up from the airport.'

Riley waved her hand. 'The train and Uber were fine. You have enough to do getting ready for Christmas.'

'It *has* been crazy,' Belle admitted.

Inside, she closed the door and removed her boots, Riley doing the same, as Andre stacked kindling in the fireplace and lit it.

'How was your flight?' Belle asked, unlooping her scarf.

'From Vienna, fine,' Riley said. 'I was in Dublin before that, did I tell you?'

'I knew you were in Stockholm for a few weeks.'

'Stockholm was before Dublin.' Over the past year, Riley had become what she liked to refer to as 'a citizen of the world'. She'd visited nine countries in twelve months, sometimes staying a month or a few, finding work, a place to stay, and a lover each time. 'I'm not married, and I have no plans to be,' she'd said the last time they'd spoken on the phone. 'There's no reason for me to be stationary.'

It felt reminiscent of the conversation they'd had five years ago when Riley had been unsettled in Sydney, a one-way ticket to London on her kitchen bench and her best friend next to her, nursing a broken heart over Ben. Belle had joined her on that trip to London, where they'd landed in Rome with Andre and Avery. It seemed that not much had changed. Little could tether Riley's free spirit.

'Are you still staying for Christmas?' Belle asked, shrugging off her coat and draping it over the back of the sofa.

'Yes but remember I'm leaving on Christmas Day for Florence. I have a date and tickets to the *Nutcracker* the following day.'

'A date?' Belle asked, raising her eyebrows. 'How did you get a date so fast? You've only been back in the country a few hours.'

'I have men in many cities,' she declared theatrically. 'Besides, he's following me here from Vienna.'

'I'm going to unpack the shopping from the car,' Andre said, catching the tail end of the conversation and chuckling as he opened the door, a blast of frigid air making the fire crackle and spit.

Riley removed her Cossack hat and slipped out of her coat.

'Let's put your luggage upstairs,' Belle said. 'Then I'll make us lunch.'

She took hold of Riley's hat and coat and led the way, as Riley tugged her suitcase across the stone floor and up the stairs.

Belle laid the hat and coat on the bed in the room Riley occupied whenever she came to stay. Then she sat down, watching as Riley set her bag on the ground.

'So we have a small situation,' she said.

'What situation?' Riley asked, unzipping her luggage and pulling out a blouse and jacket, ready to hang in the closet.

'Some guests are coming for Christmas, and we might need to move you to the daybed downstairs. Just for Christmas Eve.'

Riley turned to face her. 'Oh. Okay.'

'It's Mary and her parents. That's who's coming for Christmas.'

Riley blinked several times. 'Mary? As in Mary Mary? Andre's Mary?'

'She's not Andre's Mary,' Belle replied tersely. 'She's just Mary. And yes, she and her parents and her newborn are coming for Christmas.' She sighed. 'And they're staying until Epiphany.'

Riley's face screwed up as though she'd smelled something rotten. 'Whose idea was *that*?'

'Not ours,' Belle said. 'Uncle Benito invited them. And we couldn't say no. They're his oldest and dearest friends.'

'And you're his daughter-in-law. Does he understand how awkward this will be for you?'

Belle shrugged. 'I'm not sure he does.'

'Why does Mary have to come? Isn't she married?' Riley looked as affronted as Belle felt, and she was suddenly glad that her friend was there. Only Riley could understand why this Christmas was going to be so uncomfortable.

'She is, but Dante's away with the navy, so she's coming with her parents.'

'And the baby?'

'And the baby,' Belle confirmed.

'Jesus Christ.' Riley looked bewildered.

'I'm sorry that we're relegating you to the daybed.'

'Don't worry about me,' she said, lifting her chin defiantly. 'That daybed is comfortable.'

'You can stay up here until Christmas Eve.'

'Just don't unpack, right?'

Belle winced apologetically. 'We'll need the space for the baby's things.'

Riley raised her perfectly arched eyebrows, then placed her clothes back in her suitcase. 'Okay, then.'

THE MORNING of Christmas Eve arrived under a fresh blanket of snow, the world outside cold and grey. Although she had plenty to do, Belle was reluctant to leave Andre's arms or their warm bed.

'*Buona Vigilia di Natale, amore mio,*' he murmured in her ear. *Merry Christmas Eve, my love.*

'*Buona Vigilia di Natale,*' she whispered back and sank deeper into his arms.

She could have stayed there all day, except the simultaneous squeak of the shower taps across the hall and the front door opening downstairs meant that Riley was awake, and Uncle Benito had arrived.

Andre groaned. 'Why is everyone up so early on Christmas?'

'Because we have a lot to do.'

'Ten more minutes,' he said, wrapping his arms tighter

around her, his lips finding her neck. They traced a path to her earlobe, then down to her shoulder, his hand stroking her breast. 'We can do a lot in ten minutes.'

'Andre!' Uncle Benito shouted up the stairs. '*Sei sveglio?*'

Andre sighed loudly and rolled onto his back, running a hand through his hair. 'How can I *not* be awake?' he shouted back.

'Come on,' Belle said, pushing the covers away. 'We'd better get up.'

After showering and dressing, they found Uncle Benito and Riley in the kitchen. The kitchen benchtops were covered with ingredients, pots and pans. Uncle Benito whipped around the room like a hurricane.

Riley stood by the fridge, horror stamped on her face. 'He's asking me to start the tagliatelle,' she cried. 'I don't know what that is. Do something.'

Belle grinned as Riley snatched up a pastry from a box that Uncle Benito had brought with him and scampered out of the kitchen.

'*Buona Vigilia di Natale,*' Uncle Benito said, setting down the tray he was holding to embrace Belle.

'*Buona Vigilia di Natale,* Papà,' she replied. He smelled like a comforting blend of Old Spice and coffee.

'Let me look at you,' he said, pulling back, assessing her with his dark eyes. '*Come sei bella!* Are you well? You look well.'

'I'm well,' she said, as he pinched her cheeks hard between his fingers.

Then he turned and wrapped his arms around Andre. '*Buona Vigilia di Natale,* son.'

Andre hugged him back. 'Same to you, Papà.'

'Okay, we have lots to do,' Uncle Benito declared, clapping his hands together. Although Belle and Andre had constructed the menu already and had made some dishes the day before, like the panettone and the lasagne, they still had fresh seafood to prepare, the tagliatelle to roll and cut, the cannoli to pipe, and the ossobuco to slow cook. And she wanted to try her hand at a struffoli wreath if she had time.

Belle launched herself into prep, stopping briefly for a coffee and a pastry, eager to distract herself from the clock on the wall and its steadfast approach towards the arrival of Mary and her parents.

By three o'clock, Belle, Andre and Uncle Benito had finished most of the preparation. The hot dishes were in the oven or on the stove simmering, and the pasta was drying. The cannoli shells were piped and dusted with icing sugar, the limoncello was chilling, and Riley was setting the table for dinner.

Belle and Andre dashed upstairs to change out of their food-splattered clothes. As they made their way back down to the lounge room, car tyres crunched up the driveway.

'They're here!' Uncle Benito said, hurrying out of the kitchen. He sunk his socked feet into his boots, flung open the front door, and trudged out into the snow to help Giovanni with the luggage. Andre cast Belle a look that said, 'here we go', and went out to help his father.

Riley stood beside Belle, shaking her head. 'Remind me again what Uncle Benito was thinking.'

Belle shrugged. 'Maybe it won't be that bad.'

Riley responded with a frown.

Andre arrived in the open doorway balancing a suitcase, four packets of nappies and a portable cot. 'There's a lot of stuff,' he said breathlessly, setting it down in the lounge room and heading back out for more.

Soon the room was crammed with suitcases and baby

equipment—the portable cot, a rocker, a rainforest-inspired jungle gym, packets of nappies and wipes, a change mat and baby carrier, a baby bath—and still the men were transporting items in. Then Mary walked through the door, her sleeping infant swaddled in her arms. She looked around the room, casting Belle and Riley a guarded smile.

'Welcome,' Belle said. '*Buona Vigilia di Natale.*'

'*Grazie.* And to you too,' she replied, turning away from them and walking to the window, offering nothing further.

She positioned herself by the glass to watch the activity outside. Her brown hair was pulled back into a ponytail and her usually petite frame was curvier since she'd had the baby. She wore a knee-length black skirt, a red cable knit jumper, and black knee-high boots. Belle recalled that Mary was a year younger than her, almost four years younger than Andre. There was a sense of contained stillness about her, aloofness almost, and she seemed as wary of them as they were of her.

Several minutes later, the door burst open again, everyone from outside tumbling in, discarding coats, dislodging snow from the bottoms of boots, and carrying in more bags, all in a flurry of jubilant Italian.

Teresa, Mary's mother, wearing a maroon dress and high leather boots, brushed past Belle like a frigid gale, throwing her a haughty '*Buona Vigilia di Natale*' as she passed, before taking up residence by her daughter's side.

Giovanni was less frosty. He grabbed both of Belle's shoulders and pulled her to him like they were old friends, kissing her cheeks several times and wishing her a merry Christmas. He did the same to Riley before Uncle Benito slapped him good-naturedly on the back and they joined Mary and Teresa, to dote over the sleeping child.

Andre came to stand by Belle's side and draped his arm around her shoulders. 'Are you okay?'

'Of course,' she said, determined not to let Teresa's indifference bother her.

'Are they staying for two weeks or two months?' Riley mumbled, eyeing the pile of luggage in the middle of the room.

'Babies need lots of things,' Belle said, staring at the bottle steriliser and breast pump, the portable cot and the endless supply of nappies. Her lower abdomen tugged at the sight of it all, and she looked away. It was all the things she'd eyed repeatedly at the stores but had not had a reason yet to purchase.

The others had moved away from the window and were standing by the Christmas tree, passing the baby around, the adults cooing and purring, leaning in close to rub his head and kiss his fingers.

'Andre!' Teresa boomed self-importantly. 'Come have a hold of baby Sebastian.'

Belle waited, wondering if the invitation might extend to her too, for she would have loved to hold the baby. But no offer came.

'That's okay, Teresa,' Andre called back. 'I'll hold him later.'

'Come now, while he's sleeping,' she insisted. 'Mary will show you how. She's an excellent mother.'

Andre glanced at Belle with defiance in his eyes.

'It's okay, go,' she said. 'It will be good practise.'

He leaned in and kissed her forehead. 'We'll have our own to practise with soon enough.' He turned back to Teresa. 'Later, Teresa. Let him sleep.'

Teresa's face dropped and she scowled at Belle before returning to the circle to coo again at Sebastian.

A few minutes later, Sebastian woke and began to grizzle from being passed around too many times. Giovanni and Uncle Benito sprang into action, carrying the cot and other baby items upstairs so that Mary could settle him and put him back to sleep.

While she waited, Mary began a gentle bounce, trying to calm him, Teresa alternating between spurts of advice and irritating high-pitched baby talk. Eventually, Mary took the baby upstairs, Teresa selecting two small suitcases from the pile and scrambling up after her. Once they'd left, the energy in the room deflated and it became quiet again.

Riley let out a breath. 'Jesus Christ. Mary's mother is intense.'

Andre chuckled. 'Teresa can be... well, Teresa. She's a lot to digest sometimes, but her heart is in the right place.'

'Is it?' Riley muttered. 'She didn't ask if Belle wanted to hold the baby.'

Andre glanced at Belle. 'Did you want to hold the baby?'

Belle shrugged. 'It would have been nice.'

'She was rude,' Riley said pointedly.

'I don't think she intentionally meant to leave you out,' Andre said to Belle, then he looked unsure. 'Did she?'

'Whatever. I'm not worried.' Her mind had already moved from Teresa to the millions of things she still had to do in the kitchen before dinner.

Andre smiled. 'She'll calm down, I promise. Give her a day and a few limoncellos and she'll be a completely different person.'

SEVEN

After Mary had put the baby to sleep upstairs, everyone gathered in the living room around platters of antipasto and trays of *aperitivi*—a pre-dinner drink to whet the appetite. Belle remained in the kitchen with Riley, with still so much to do before dinner.

After twenty minutes of being sociable, Andre joined them. Shouts of *'cin cin'* and laughter followed him as he pushed up his sleeves and finished cleaning the seafood. Riley made espressos and helped deep-fry arancini balls, and Belle took the ossobuco off the stove and boiled the tagliatelle for the seafood pasta.

At eight pm, with snow falling again outside and *Venite Fedeli*—the Italian version of *O Come All Ye Faithful*—playing in the dining room, they sat down to eat. Andre was right. Teresa had thawed a little with a few limoncellos before dinner, but her good nature didn't extend to Belle. Somehow, she grew louder and more obnoxious towards her. After the meal, she thanked Uncle Benito and Andre for the food, raising her glass of wine to them.

'The tagliatelle is the best I've ever tasted,' she crooned, kissing her fingertips in that *'belissimo'* kind of way. 'And these clams. *Squisito!*'

'Belle did most of the cooking,' Andre said. Seated beside her, he draped his arm proudly around her shoulders, giving her a tender smile. 'She's been in the kitchen for days.'

'It was nothing,' Belle said, feeling her cheeks flush at the attention.

'It wasn't nothing,' Andre said. 'You worked hard and you're an incredible cook.'

Uncle Benito and Giovanni raised their glasses enthusiastically in a toast. Teresa sipped her wine, her mouth puckering sourly, as though the meal wasn't nearly as *squisito* as she'd first thought.

Belle ignored her, her eyes falling instead on Mary. She was sipping her juice, her gaze trained on Andre from over the rim of her glass. There was a longing in her stare, as she watched him talk and laugh, his arm still draped fondly around Belle's shoulders. It made Belle's skin prickle, that stare, just like at the wedding when that same adoring gaze had followed him all night.

When Mary realised she'd been caught, Belle boldly held her eye, until the girl, red-faced and embarrassed, looked away.

They finished dinner and Sebastian woke again. Mary and Teresa dashed upstairs to change and feed him while Andre and Uncle Benito cleaned up and Belle, Riley and Giovanni drank mulled wine by the Christmas tree.

Giovanni was drunk and ruddy-cheeked, but delightfully funny. His rambunctious laugh boomed around the room, his large belly wobbling in time with it. He was less intense than his wife and warmer than Mary, speaking to them in capable English, unlike Teresa, who was intent on break-neck speed Italian.

At eleven-thirty, they pulled on their coats, beanies and scarves, waved goodbye to Mary, who was staying in with Sebastian, and trudged out into the cold night for the drive to the Collegiate Church of San Cristoforo in Barga to attend Midnight Mass.

Andre, Belle and Riley climbed into Andre's Alfa Romeo, and Giovanni and Teresa climbed into Uncle Benito's little red Fiat. It was a ten-minute drive to the church high on the hill, made slower by dark, winding roads covered in snow.

They arrived at an already-packed church, the cold doing little to keep the faithful away. The town of Barga sprawled below the hilltop, snow-drenched terracotta-tiled rooftops and distant hillsides glowing white under a frosty moon. They found seats near the back, the doors closing shortly after their arrival, the medieval church slowly warming.

Belle had been in this church before, discussing their wedding with the priest, and she'd always thought it primitive and imposing, with its formidable white marble exterior, overlaid with stone, and a high-vaulted ceiling. The structure was as old as the eleventh century, assembled with a blend of Romanesque and gothic architecture.

Inside smelt heavy with age, wax and burning wicker thickly perfuming the air. Belle was still unsure if it was the kind of church she wanted to marry Andre in. It was beautiful, yes, but vast and dim. Uncle Benito wanted them to marry there, and Andre said Belle could choose, as long as they made a decision soon.

Mass was predictably long and ceremonious and at one am, the congregation stood and heaved towards the doors and out into the frigid night.

'No need to remind me why I'm an atheist,' Riley said as she, Belle and Andre clambered back into the Alpha Romeo and followed Uncle Benito's Fiat through the winding streets of Barga, to the house. 'Can't Catholics do Christmas mass when the sun is up and it's a bit warmer?'

'Jesus was born at midnight,' Andre explained. 'So we celebrate by having mass at midnight too.'

'You must relish in torture then because I lost all feeling in my fingers and toes about two minutes into the service.'

'You weren't singing loud enough,' Belle said. 'It's the singing that keeps you warm.'

Riley yawned and shivered simultaneously.

Back at the house, they tumbled out of the cars and into the warm living room, Mary greeting them at the door, a sleepy look on her face betraying the nap she'd had while they'd been out.

'I'll get the cornetti and hot chocolate ready,' she said.

'I'll show you where everything is,' Belle said, unlooping her scarf.

'We know where everything is,' Teresa snapped, shoving past her. 'We've been visiting this house longer than you've lived in it.'

Teresa's aggression rendered Belle so speechless that all she could do was gape as the two women retreated to the kitchen. She tugged off her coat and hung it with her scarf on the coat rack, wondering if somehow she'd misheard or misunderstood. Teresa always spoke in rapid Italian, but Belle was certain she'd interpreted the insult correctly.

She walked to Andre's side, stunned into silence. He

smiled down at her, placing his hand on her back, seeming not to have noticed Teresa's hostility or how much Belle was attempting outward calm despite stewing on the inside.

Ten minutes later, the women reappeared with trays of hot chocolate and Nutella cornetti. Everyone reached for a cup and a pastry and took a seat as Uncle Benito began handing Christmas presents out.

Belle gave Andre several crime-fiction books that he'd been eyeing at the bookstore and a new A.S Roma football jersey. He gave her a long velvet jewellery box containing a white gold necklace with a diamond pendant. When Belle turned so that Andre could clasp the necklace around her neck, Uncle Benito clapped, and Teresa and Mary exchanged a look.

More gifts were passed around, wrapping paper torn away and discarded. Belle had bought baby Sebastian a musical carousel in pewter, along with clothes and a Sophie teething giraffe. Mary seemed surprised by the gifts at first, then thankful, while Teresa assessed them with cool eyes and a downturned mouth.

'I have a gift for you, Andre,' Mary said, passing him a square, wrapped box.

Andre looked confused as he accepted it. 'For *me*?'

'Well, it's to say thank you for having us in your home.'

Andre pulled Belle a little closer. 'Belle and I are happy to have you here. You didn't have to buy me anything.'

Mary blushed, then glanced at her mother. 'It's um... just something small.'

Andre tore at the paper, revealing a black box underneath. He met Belle's eyes. It was from a reputable jeweller in Rome.

Andre sat forward and opened the lid. Inside was an

enormous heavy gold watch with a large gold clockface. Andre gasped and looked up at Mary. 'You bought me a watch?'

'Do you like it?' she asked breathlessly.

'It's uh...' he stammered. 'It's huge. And it's too much. I can't accept this.' He stole another look at Belle, who was equally stunned beside him. It *was* too much. Easily over three hundred euros and not a simple gift of gratitude by any means. A bottle of wine or some homemade biscotti would have been appropriate, but this, this was a statement.

'Mary knows your style perfectly,' Teresa said. 'The minute she saw it she knew you had to have it. As a thank you, of course, for having us.'

Mary blushed profusely again, her smile wide, hopeful.

Belle stared at the watch. Andre was forever misplacing the one he wore. A loose link in the band caused it to slip off sometimes and despite getting it fixed twice, the same link kept failing. He liked his watch, but it gave him equal parts joy and frustration, and he regularly complained that he needed a new one.

She'd had her eye on another watch for his birthday next year—sleek and black, with a partial cut-out on the face that revealed beautiful silver clockwork beneath. It was smaller in size and more elegant than the gaudy chunk of gold sitting on his lap, which hardly seemed his style at all. And, if she was completely honest, she resented being beaten to the chase.

Andre replaced the lid on the box and cleared his throat. '*Grazie*, Mary. It's a very generous gift.'

'Very,' Belle said, her syllables tight.

'I'm glad you like it,' Mary said with giddiness.

Andre swallowed thickly, his Adam's apple bobbing as

he placed the box on the sofa beside him. He looked as uncomfortable as Belle felt. Riley's eyes were on them both and when Belle met them, Riley mouthed, 'What was that all about?'

Belle frowned. It was called flirting.

christmas.

EIGHT

It was after four am when everyone trudged off to bed. Belle stayed behind to help Riley make up the daybed, then she dragged herself upstairs too.

Mary's lamp was on in the guest room and Belle could hear her moving about, preparing to feed the baby. She was tempted to knock on the door and ask her about the watch, but she was reluctant to bother her if she was settling Sebastian, especially with something as trivial as a Christmas gift. Besides, it was almost dawn, and she was too tired to have that conversation, also second-guessing whether she'd interpreted Mary's intention correctly. Maybe it was customary in Italy to give expensive gifts of hospitality to old friends. She tried to tell herself that that was all it was, but something inside her simmered with suspicion. Why was the gift only for Andre?

She walked into her bedroom and closed the door behind her. Andre was already under the covers, eyes half-closed as he watched her. The box with the watch was on the tall boy with the other gifts he'd received. She undressed and climbed into her pyjamas as he flicked the covers back for her and she slid in beside him. His side of the bed was warmer, so she wriggled close to him, his arms folding around her to draw her in.

'Big day,' he said sleepily.

'Yeah,' she replied. She was utterly spent, every muscle crying out with relief to be lying down finally. But her mind wouldn't calm. 'That watch.'

He shifted beside her. 'What about it?'

'It was a bit extravagant.'

He yawned. 'It was a bit. I suppose Mary's just grateful to be included and she wanted to show her appreciation. Otherwise, she'd be at home on her own.'

'But an expensive watch? It felt more like a play than gratitude.'

Andre fell silent and she wondered if he'd gone to sleep, until he sighed. 'It wasn't a play. Teresa plays games, but not Mary. Besides, she knew I needed a new watch.'

Belle craned her neck to look at him. 'How did she know that?'

'Because she and Teresa came to Valentina's a few weeks ago.'

'They did?' It was news to her; he'd never mentioned it before. 'I didn't know that.'

'You were here with your parents,' he said.

'Still, you never said anything.'

'It wasn't a big deal. They were out shopping, then they dropped in to say hello. I was looking for my watch at the time and Mary helped me. She probably realised then that I needed a new one.'

Knowing that Mary had visited Andre while Belle hadn't been there irked her more. She knew he wanted to go to sleep, but she couldn't let it drop. 'Are you going to wear it?'

'I don't know.'

'It's not really something you'd wear,' she persisted.

He yawned again. 'No, it's not.'

A few minutes later, she heard his breathing slow and felt his arms grow heavy, and she realised he'd fallen asleep. But it wasn't until the sky lightened outside and Sebastian stirred once more for a feed, that she finally fell asleep too.

BELLE WOKE SOMETIME LATER, the bedroom awash with late morning sun. She stretched and rolled over, touching the spot beside her. The sheets were cold, and she saw that Andre was up. She glanced at the clock on her phone on the nightstand and groaned when she saw it was midday.

She threw back the covers, pulled on jeans and an over-sized sweater, and hurried down the stairs. Mary was sprawled out on the rug beside Sebastian. He lay swaddled in his rocker, awake, struggling against a muslin wrap. The fire was crackling, and the room was warm. The daybed Riley had slept on was packed away, blankets, sheets and the pillow piled neatly on top of it.

'*Buongiorno*, Mary,' Belle said, as she stepped down into the living room.

Mary glanced up and flicked her a small smile. '*Buongiorno*.'

Belle walked over to them and crouched beside the rocker, as Mary sat up on her knees.

'He's very cute,' Belle said. At eight weeks old, Sebastian was a bundle of perfect softness, with dark eyes and a shock of dark hair to match his parents.

'Yes,' Mary said, 'although not so much at four in the morning.'

One of Sebastian's tiny hands finally freed itself from the wrap, and Belle reached out and touched it. His fingers grasped hers, holding on tight. Her heart tugged at the sheer littleness of him, her soul aching for the place in her uterus that remained empty. She would give anything to be woken at four am by hungry cries, to have a baby fill her arms as she fed it, to witness Andre be a dad. It was yet to happen, if it would ever happen, and that's what frightened her the most. That she may never fall pregnant. That she may never know the wonderous joy of being a mother, of nurturing that warm, milky weight in her arms. And that she may be denying Andre the opportunity too.

She cleared her throat, still watching Sebastian as he held tight to her fingers.

Then Mary leaned over suddenly, unfurling his grip from Belle's and quickly tucking his hands away. 'Sorry, if I don't keep him wrapped properly, he'll scratch his face with his nails,' she said.

'Oh, right, of course.' Belle stood up and backed away. 'Sorry.'

Mary gave her a tight smile, then finished wrapping the baby. 'That's better.' She gently patted his tummy. 'No more escaping.'

'Dante must miss him when he's away,' Belle said.

Mary gave her a sideways look. 'I suppose.'

'Especially at Christmastime. But you're a great mother. You handle it well.'

Mary frowned. 'I don't have a choice when I'm the only parent around.' She turned away, looking affronted. Belle cringed, wondering what part of her compliment had been insulting.

Her eyes scanned the living room, desperate to get away now. 'Is everyone else up?'

'They're in the kitchen,' Mary mumbled. 'Eating leftovers.'

Belle quickly muttered goodbye and hurried out of the room. She found the others awake and dressed in the kitchen, the air rich with the aroma of coffee beans and warmed lasagne. Teresa was at the stove, stirring minestrone, her voice discernible over everyone else's. Andre and Giovanni were at the island bench drinking coffee, and Uncle Benito was kneading dough.

'*Buongiorno amore mio.*' Andre held his arm out to Belle, and she went to him, letting him pull her close for a kiss. 'Did you sleep well? I tried not to wake you when I got up.'

'I didn't hear you go. I must have been tired,' she said.

'It's no surprise,' Giovanni said. 'You made a wonderful dinner for us.' He rewarded her by smacking a loud kiss on each of her cheeks.

'*Grazie*, Giovanni. I'm glad you enjoyed the food.'

'We did. Look, we're still eating it.' He slapped the benchtop and laughed at his own joke.

Riley strolled into the kitchen, dressed in jeans, boots and a coat. Her hair was in a stylish high ponytail, and she had a face of dewy makeup. '*Buon Natale* everyone,' she announced.

A chorus of merry Christmases were returned. Giovanni gave her svelte figure a cheeky wink.

'Would you like a coffee?' Belle asked, leaving Andre's arms.

'I've already had one. My Uber's out the front. I'll be off now.'

'You're leaving?' Belle asked. Then she remembered

that Riley was heading to Florence that day. 'I forgot you had tickets to *The Nutcracker*.'

The car outside honked its horn.

'Come, I'll walk you out,' Belle said.

Riley waved goodbye to everyone, kissing Uncle Benito and Giovanni. Andre and Belle led her to the front door where Riley's luggage stood upright in the foyer. Mary and Sebastian were no longer in the living room, footsteps sounding on the boards above in Mary's room.

'I wish you could stay,' Belle said, opening the front door to a glacial morning. The air was like ice, but the sun was out, turning the snow a blinding white.

'I'll be back before Epiphany,' Riley said, tossing her scarf around her neck.

'Andre and I could come to Florence and visit you,' Belle suggested.

'We could bring Mary,' Andre said.

Belle shot him a sharp look.

'What?' He shrugged. 'She could leave the baby with her parents and have a day out.' He gave Riley a sheepish smile. 'Or not. Terrible idea. It'll just be us.'

He carried Riley's suitcase outside, meeting the driver halfway, who took it and placed it in the boot, then he walked back to the door, hugged Riley, and disappeared inside.

'I think I'll go crazy without you here,' Belle said, as they stepped out onto the porch.

Riley held her hand up to the driver to indicate she'd be a minute. 'Just think, twelve more days until Epiphany. Then you'll be rid of them.'

'I'd like to be rid of Teresa a lot sooner,' Belle muttered.

Riley squeezed her arm sympathetically. 'Hang in there, kid. She's just asserting herself as the alpha female.'

'But she forgets that I live here,' Belle said. 'She has no right to act like the woman of the house or to be disrespectful. And that watch Mary gave Andre...'

'Yes, what was that about?'

'I have no idea, but it wasn't right.'

The driver opened one of the passenger doors to get Riley's attention.

Riley ignored him. 'You should speak to Teresa. Ask her what her problem is.'

'I know what her problem is.'

'If it's about Andre, she's going to have to get over it. Mary's moved on, Andre's moved on. Everyone but Teresa has moved on.'

But had Mary moved on? After giving Andre that watch the night before, Belle wasn't so sure.

The driver clapped his hands together and bounced up and down on his toes, indicating that he was cold and wanted to get going.

'You better go or we'll have to invite him in for lasagne,' Belle said.

Riley gave her a reassuring smile. 'Call me if you need me. I'll come back in a heartbeat.'

They hugged, then Belle watched as Riley climbed into the backseat of the Uber and the driver started the engine, turning the vehicle around and heading back the way he came.

Belle returned to the warm house, closing the door behind her. The living room was deserted still, so she walked back to the kitchen, eager for a coffee and something to eat. As she approached the kitchen doorway, she saw Giovanni still at the island bench, holding the baby. She sensed Teresa and Mary just out of sight, by the stove, and Uncle Benito was setting his dough by the windowsill to rise.

No one had noticed her reappear, least of all Teresa, who was speaking slowly in Italian now, enough for Belle to fully comprehend what she was saying.

'So she's yet to fall pregnant?' she asked Uncle Benito.

He shrugged, placing a tea towel over the dough. 'They're trying. But it hasn't happened yet.'

'What if she can't?' Teresa asked, sounding outraged as though Belle had somehow offended her with her inability to conceive.

'She will soon enough,' Uncle Benito said calmly, with certainty.

'It's been a year already,' Teresa declared. 'Maybe there's something wrong with her. Maybe she's *infertile*.' She enunciated each syllable for effect.

'These things take time,' Uncle Benito said, sounding annoyed with the questioning. 'It will happen when it happens.'

'Poor Andre,' Teresa said, moving into Belle's line of sight, shaking her head melodramatically. 'Someone should tell him that if it hasn't happened by now, it probably never will. Not like my Mary who had Sebastian so easily.'

'Too easily!' Giovanni barked from the bench, before laughing.

Mary gasped and Teresa glared at him.

'Valentina would be turning in her grave if she knew what was happening,' Teresa added, a sign of the cross and a kiss to the heavens for effect.

'You are too dramatic,' Uncle Benito said, still sounding annoyed.

'Tell me that again in two years when she still can't give you grandchildren,' Teresa retorted.

Belle had heard enough. Humiliated, she turned and

left the doorway of the kitchen, colliding straight into Andre on her way out.

'There you are,' he said. 'Is Riley gone?'

'Yes,' she murmured and pushed past him.

'Hey.' He reached for her hand. 'What's wrong?'

'Nothing. Going for a shower.' She wriggled from his grip, tears stinging her eyes that she didn't want him to see. And although he looked confused and she probably should have explained, all she wanted to do was get as far away as possible from Teresa and her hurtful words.

NINE

They spent the rest of Christmas Day gorging on coffee and leftover food, which was promptly exchanged at three pm for antipasto and wine. Teresa asserted herself as the cook of the house and took up residence by the stove and oven, refusing to let Belle near it. When Belle offered to help or grabbed a knife to start chopping, she was urged out of the kitchen like an unwanted pest.

'I've been cooking in this house since before you were born!' Teresa declared, her voice becoming louder with every drink she had. 'Way back when my dear friend, Valentina, was alive. This is still her house. God rest her soul.' She mumbled a prayer, then returned to her cooking.

For dinner that night, Teresa served minestrone and chicken risotto, followed by veal scallopini. All throughout the meal, she spoke at lightning speed, her Italian too fast for Belle to follow properly, as though she were intentionally trying to exclude her.

'Teresa, can you speak in English please, so Belle can understand too?' Andre asked.

Teresa blinked several times at him, her mouth twitching. 'You mean she's been here for a year, and she doesn't know how to speak the language?' This time she spoke slowly enough so that Belle interpreted every word.

'I understand,' Belle replied in Italian. 'But I can't follow if it's spoken too quickly.'

'She's still learning,' Andre added.

'Well, it's not my fault if she hasn't learnt quickly enough,' Teresa said. She laughed coldly, looking at everyone in astonishment. 'Must we all speak a different language now because someone hasn't taken the time to learn? Ridiculous!'

'Teresa,' Giovanni said, his voice carrying a warning.

'Have another wine, Teresa,' Uncle Benito said, topping up her glass. 'You are too tense.'

'I'm not tense,' Teresa said, picking her wine glass up and waving it around. 'I just don't like being told I cannot speak in my native tongue. That's silly.'

'It's not silly,' Andre retorted. 'It's called respect.'

The table fell silent. Teresa's mouth pulled into a thin line, but she didn't return fire, just gulped from her wine glass and set it down on the table again.

Andre glanced at Belle, rolled his eyes and mouthed the words, *she's drunk*. Mary caught the exchange and when his gaze met hers, she gave him a hurt look. He flushed red and looked down at his plate, his expression full of guilt.

———

'HOW'S NEW YORK?' Belle adjusted the phone against her ear and pulled the quilt up to her chin. The next morning had dawned bright, early sunlight splaying patterns across her bed covers. From her spot by the window, she could see that fresh snow had fallen overnight, making the ground glisten.

'It's wonderful. So cold here,' Grace replied. 'And Christmas was a delight. The tree at the Rockefeller Centre is something else.'

'Is it snowing?'

'Yes. But we've still managed to get out. We're going to Chinatown tomorrow.'

'And Callum—I'm assuming he caught his flight okay?' She'd yet to ring him. The day before had been busy and this was her first chance to call her parents for Christmas.

'He did...' Grace said slowly.

'Why do I feel a "but" coming?' Belle asked. 'What happened? You didn't argue in the car, did you?'

'Not exactly,' Grace said.

'Well, what then?'

'He's here.'

'Where?'

'Here. With me. In New York.' Grace rushed the words out, hoping, perhaps, that Belle wouldn't hear them.

But she did. 'Oh!'

'Yes.'

'Right...'

'Well, you have a lovely Christmas and I'll call you in a few days.'

'Wait!' Belle wasn't about to let her drop the news and run. 'What do you mean Callum is in New York with you? He was supposed to get on a plane to Scotland.'

'Yes, well... we got talking in the car and...' Grace hesitated, 'we agreed it would be a nice thing to do.'

'For him to go to New York with you?' Belle wasn't displeased, just a little surprised and trying to fit the pieces together.

'Yes.'

'And what's happened in New York?'

'Nothing,' Grace said a little too quickly. 'Nothing like that. We're just friends. We're spending the holidays together.'

'Hmmm.' Belle pursed her lips. Suddenly, she felt like the parent, trying to rein in her wayward teenagers. 'And is Callum having a good time with all the ladies?'

'He's fitting in with my friends surprisingly well,' Grace said. 'You know what he's like. Charismatic; dazzling them all.'

'But is he dazzling *you*?' Belle asked. She winced at how sour her words sounded. Who was acting like the teenager now?

'It's just a holiday, sweetheart. We're friends, that's all.'

'Sorry,' she said sheepishly. 'I didn't mean it that way.'

'I'd understand if you did.'

'I just feel bad for Dad.'

Grace sighed. 'Oh, Belle...'

'I know, I get it. I'm too old for that.'

Her mother chuckled lightly. 'You're never too old to miss your father.'

'It *has* been a few years, though and you need to move on. It's not my place to say anything.'

'Yes, I do need to move on,' Grace said. 'But I'm not. So you don't need to worry.'

Grace's tone was kind, although it didn't stop a surge of guilt from rolling over Belle for how poorly she'd handled the conversation. She loved her mother and Callum. The question was, did she love them together? Edward's death had been such a shock and she was still reeling from it. But just because she was stuck in the past, did it mean everyone had to be?

Feeling a need to put their awkward phone call right, she changed the subject and told her mother about Teresa, Giovanni, Mary and the baby joining them for the holidays. She hadn't had a chance to mention it yet and she explained it all now, as Grace listened.

'I adore Benito, you know that,' Grace said, 'but what possessed him to invite *them*?'

'They're his friends. And this is his house,' Belle replied. 'I could hardly say no.'

'Yes, but you live there too, darling. Surely he understands how awkward it is having Mary and Teresa there.'

'I honestly don't think he does. Teresa and Giovanni are his best friends. They've known each other for decades. He seems oblivious to it.'

'And Mary, is she behaving?'

'I'm not sure what to make of her, to be honest. I know Teresa can't stand me.'

'She hardly knows you.'

'She's asserting herself as the woman of the house. She won't let me cook in the kitchen and she refuses to slow down her Italian so I can understand it. And she talks about me when she thinks I'm not around.'

'What does she say?'

'That I'm infertile.'

There was a sharp intake of breath. 'She said what?'

Belle fell quiet and stared out the window, uncomfortably close to crying.

'You know this isn't about you, right?' Grace said, gently. 'This is about Mary and Andre not working out, and Mary falling pregnant to someone else before marriage. This is about Teresa's humiliation and her need to blame someone for it.'

'Yes, but why me? Andre and I got together months

after he and Mary broke up.' It wasn't like she'd met him while he'd been in a relationship with Mary, the way Olivia had met Ben. Andre hadn't strayed or been unfaithful. Their relationship just hadn't worked out.

Belle sighed and pressed her fingers to her forehead. Talking about Teresa left her drained. It was only seven in the morning, and she was already exhausted by it. 'Is Callum around? I'd like to wish him a merry Christmas.'

'He's not here at the moment. I'm in my room.'

'So you have different rooms?' she asked tentatively.

'Yes, we have different rooms. I'm sharing with Deirdre from my gardening club.'

'Right. Not that it's any of my business,' she was quick to add.

'I think you have enough going on without worrying about me and Callum too.'

Belle accepted that as her mother's polite way of asking her to stop meddling. 'I love you, Mum.'

Grace's voice was full of her smile. 'I love you too, honey. And don't worry about Teresa. I'm sure she'll calm down.'

They ended the call as Andre opened the bedroom door and walked in. He'd just showered, his hair still damp. He sat beside her, and she inhaled his aftershave and the sharpness of clean cotton, scents that were always comforting and provocative to her.

'Did you call your mother?' he asked.

She flicked back the covers and he climbed in, letting her wriggle into the spot between his legs so that her back was to his chest. His hands found her shoulders and he began to massage the knots.

'Yes,' she said, letting her head drop as he kneaded her muscles. 'She's having a wonderful time. Callum's with her.'

Andre stopped massaging and she glanced back to find him shaking his head with a smile. 'I wondered if that would happen.'

She scrunched her nose up. 'You did?'

'Of course. They're crazy about each other. You couldn't see it?'

'While they were here? No. I mean, I knew they were friends but...'

'I think they're more than friends.' He resumed massaging as she leant back into him. 'Would you be okay with that?'

She was unsure how to answer. 'They're my parents and I'm happy for them, but it feels strange. I've only ever known Mum to be with Dad. Now she's with my *other* dad.' She shook her head. 'It's just thrown me a bit.'

'I get it. It's confusing.'

'Yes. And if Mum and Callum were always meant to be, then what does that say about Edward?'

She felt Andre nod. 'Do you think they're betraying him?'

'Maybe he's just been forgotten.'

Andre stopped massaging and rested his chin on top of her head. 'Families can be tricky, no?'

A gross understatement.

His hands returned to her shoulders, fingers gently pressing into her muscles. 'You're so tense.'

'I can feel it.'

'When was the last time we walked? It's been days.'

'Before Christmas, I think.'

He climbed off the bed, helping her up. 'Then let's get you dressed, my love. We're going for a walk.'

WHILE EVERYONE WAS in the living room drinking coffee, they snuck out the back door and trudged through the yard down to the fence line, where the back of the property met the woods. Snow was thick underfoot, their boots crunching through it, breath frosty on exhale.

They reached the fence and climbed over it, dropping down to the ground on the other side. It was routine to visit the stream first, where the shy roe deer gathered to graze and drink, and the buck shed its antlers in winter. Sometimes, if it was early morning or late afternoon, the crowing call of a red fox could be heard as it trotted tranquilly with its pack in search of food.

They always spent a few minutes skipping rocks along the stream's surface, then they headed in the opposite direction of the current, uphill, working their legs and lungs, following a forested valley of chestnut trees which eventually relented to beech trees, if they climbed high enough. They never took music or their phones. They were always happy to listen to what the forest had to tell them.

'Are you warm enough?' Andre asked, reaching for her gloved hand with his, helping her over the remnants of a fallen trunk.

'I'm okay,' she said. A weak sun was shining, but it hardly penetrated the canopy of trees to reach the forest floor. Still, there was a pureness the snow had lent the air, and the beauty of this far surpassed the discomfort of the cold.

'It's nice to get away from the house,' he said.

'And everyone in it,' she half-joked.

He smiled knowingly. 'Teresa has been difficult, I know. She and my mother were best friends when my mother was alive.'

'Has she always been so hard?'

'Not always,' Andre said. 'She was softer in her younger years. Just like my mother. They were beautiful friends.' He kicked at a mound of snow with his boot as they walked. 'Teresa and Giovanni have been coming to this house since before I was born. Sometimes she forgets it's our place now.'

'It's not just that,' Belle said. 'She thinks I'm the reason you and Mary aren't together. You see what she does—excluding me from conversations. And yesterday morning, I caught her talking about me.'

Andre glanced at her. 'What did she say?'

'That I'm infertile and someone should warn you. That if we haven't fallen pregnant by now, it'll never happen.' She fixed her gaze forward, tears stinging her eyes. She hadn't intended to tell him about it, had tried to put it out of her mind, but she was tired and emotional, worn down by Teresa's constant barbs, and it had tumbled out.

'She *said* that? *Che cazzo,*' he swore, his jaw clenched. 'Is that why you were upset when I ran into you near the kitchen?'

'She caught me by surprise.'

'Yes, because she has no right to say things like that about you.'

'But it's true, isn't it?'

'It's not true!' he exclaimed. 'We haven't fallen pregnant yet, so what? It takes some couples years to conceive.'

'Or one night, like in Mary's case.'

'That's different,' he said. 'Mary hasn't been through what you've been through. You're still dealing with a tragedy and your body is catching up. And although I'm stupidly jealous of your psychologist sometimes,' he grimaced contritely, 'I know he's helping. You can't compare your situation to anyone else's.'

They reached the stream, the current chattering

towards the river, dense woods surrounding them. Bare trees, gnarled and skeletal, lifted their arms upwards, forming a ceiling of crystalised branches. Belle adored the forest in the winter. Although it was cold and the silence unfathomable and deep, it was also beautiful—a true wonderland. In two months, the forest would transform again with spring, another season to adore. The snow would melt, hidden colours would emerge, and tree branches would reach exultantly towards a warmer sky.

'I'll speak to Teresa,' Andre said, as they held hands against the cold and stared out at the stream, the water gurgling over rocks. 'What we do is none of her business.'

'But then what? She'll complain to Giovanni and your dad. It will only make it awkward for everyone.'

'But she's a guest in *our* home. She can't treat you like that. I don't care who she is.'

Belle smiled and wrapped both her hands around him, cuddling him tightly. 'Thank you.'

He raised an eyebrow. 'For what?'

'For being on my side.'

'I'll always be on your side,' he said like it was incomprehensible to assume otherwise.

'I know, but this is a difficult situation. It's our home, yet in her mind, it's not. It will always be your parents' home. I'm just an outsider.'

'You're not an outsider,' he said firmly. 'You're my wife. And you belong here more than any of them.'

'I was thinking,' she said, 'maybe we could spend a couple of days in Florence with Riley, just to get away for a bit.'

She was certain he'd shut the idea down. It was hardly the Italian way, to skip out on guests, but he wrapped his arm around her and pulled her close, kissing the top of her beanie. 'I like that idea.'

'You do?'

'Yeah.'

'Your father won't mind?'

He chuckled. 'I don't think so. And if Teresa wants to run the house, she can. It's all hers. Because we won't be here.'

TEN

Later that night, after another dinner prepared by Teresa—Belle was promptly banished from the kitchen when she asked if she could help—they digested their meal with limoncello by the fire, the Christmas tree lights blinking across the branches. Baby Sebastian had been fed and was awake, gurgling as he was passed from adult to adult.

When it was Teresa's turn, she took him and adopted the bounce that all people holding a baby seem to adopt, cooing and shushing him, blitzing him with an array of crazy noises that made his eyes grow wide with fear and his bottom lip tremble. 'Andre, now you will have a hold of Sebastian,' she wheedled. 'You haven't held him yet.'

'That's okay, Teresa,' Andre said. He was beside Belle, one arm around her, the other holding a small glass of limoncello. His jaw was tight, and she could tell he was still smarting over what she'd told him earlier that morning on their walk. 'Maybe Belle can have a hold.'

Teresa harrumphed. 'Don't be silly, Andre. Here, take him.' She walked to the spot where Andre was sitting and held Sebastian out to him so that he was left with little choice but to accept.

'*Mio Dio*,' Andre protested, rushing to put his limon-cello on the coffee table and remove his arm from around Belle. He took Sebastian tentatively in his hands. 'I'm not sure I'm good at this.'

Once the baby was transferred safely to him, Teresa clapped her hands together and glanced at Mary. 'Look at Sebastian and Andre! Just beautiful.'

Mary smiled happily, as Andre held Sebastian like a fragile piece of glass. 'Am I doing it right? He looks uncomfortable.'

'You're doing great,' Belle said, leaning over and touching Sebastian's head. But then the smell of him hit her, all that softness and baby soap and sweet milky skin, and she couldn't ignore the way her heart ached because it wasn't *their* baby Andre was holding.

'He's tiny,' Andre said, gazing down at Sebastian. His arms relaxed around him, and Sebastian relaxed too.

'Babies look good on you, eh?' Uncle Benito said to them, his eyes growing shiny. 'One day it will be your turn. Very soon. I know it.'

Sebastian gurgled and yawned, growing sleepy in Andre's arms. 'He's so cute,' Andre whispered with awe. 'Look he's falling asleep.'

'He's divine,' Belle said. And he was—a bundle of utter perfectness—making the ache in her heart grow physical.

'Would you like to hold him before he falls asleep?' Andre asked, preparing to transfer Sebastian to her arms.

But Teresa swooped in quickly. 'Maybe tomorrow. He needs to go to bed now, otherwise, he will be unsettled and keep Mary up all night.' She took Sebastian from Andre's arms. Before Andre could protest, she flicked her head at Mary. 'Let's go.'

Mary stood, her face contorted in something Belle couldn't decipher—apology or maybe approval—then she said goodnight and scampered up the stairs after her mother.

'Cigar?' Uncle Benito said to Giovanni, and the two older men rose, then swayed unsteadily to the front door with the bottle of limoncello and a box of cigars.

The living room emptied, and the fire died quietly behind the grate. Andre glanced at Belle with a perplexed frown. 'Sorry about that.'

'What are you sorry for?' she asked.

He indicated upstairs with his head. 'Teresa. Sebastian. She wouldn't let you hold him.'

Belle leaned her head on his shoulder. 'You don't have to apologise for that.'

'But I see what she's doing. And it's not okay.'

'Maybe she's right. Too much passing around and he'll just keep Mary up all night.' She said this as much to assuage Andre's unease as to take the sting out of what Teresa had done. Teresa was happy to pass the baby around when it suited her. But when Andre suggested it was Belle's turn, suddenly it would unsettle the baby.

He reached for her hand. 'Come on, let's go to bed.'

He led her up the stairs and into the bathroom to brush their teeth, then they ducked across the hall to their room and closed the door. Andre switched the lamp on and, as they changed into their pyjamas, he gave a light chuckle. 'Sebastian's cute.'

Belle slipped her arms into her top. 'Yeah, he is.'

'And so tiny,' Andre said, indicating the size with his

hands. 'His fingers, his face, his little eyelashes.' He pulled a sweater over his head.

'He's adorable.'

'It's amazing how the female body works. How it can make something like that,' Andre mused.

Or in Belle's case, couldn't make. She turned away from him so he wouldn't notice how deeply his comment had cut. It wasn't his fault her body couldn't do what it was meant to do. And while it was endearing to watch Andre's excitement over Sebastian, to know that he would one day make the most incredible father, it was also wrapped in the knowledge that she may never be the one to give him that opportunity.

A few minutes of awkward silence and he was beside her, his hand on her arm and his expression full of apology. 'Hey, I didn't mean to...'

She swallowed and faced him, shaking her head. 'It's okay. I'm just a little sensitive tonight.'

'No, I shouldn't have said that. I wasn't thinking. And I shouldn't go on about Sebastian.'

'No, of course you should enjoy Sebastian. He's beautiful. I just wish...' she inhaled shakily, frustrated with how emotional she'd become lately, 'I just wish it was our baby you were holding.'

He pulled her into his arms and stroked her hair. 'It will happen soon.'

She nodded half-heartedly, not as certain anymore.

Andre cupped his fingers under her chin and tilted her head up to his. 'Do you know how babies are made?'

Despite her sadness, she broke into a reluctant grin. 'Yes.'

His hands found their way under her pyjama top to her

bare breasts. 'We haven't tried to make any babies since before Christmas.'

'No,' she said. 'Why is that?'

'Because we're too busy worrying about everyone else.' He slid her top over her head, her hair flicking out and tumbling down her back. The cold air hit her skin, goose-bumps erupting on her arms.

'Let's get you warm,' he said. In one swift motion, Andre scooped her up and carried her to the bed, lowering her onto the covers.

He discarded his sweater and their pants, then moved on top of her, kissing every inch of her body—her lips, her face, her collarbones, her breasts, the places that made her cry out with want.

He took his time with foreplay, as she liked him to do, fingertips tracing her skin, while her body became desperate for him. If there was one thing Andre knew how to do, it was to make love, slowly and sensually, sending her hurtling to the edge every time until he carefully pulled her back again.

'You are beautiful, my love,' he whispered, his deep gaze drinking her in. 'And one day, you *will* be a mother. An amazing mother.'

Her eyes filled with tears, and she pushed her lips to his, the words she needed to hear, as he gently nudged her legs apart and slid inside her.

He kissed and caressed her with his lips, the slight stubble on his face gently scraping her skin, hands explor-ing, tongue pleasing. She tried not to moan too loudly, conscious of others in the house, but it was difficult, as their rhythm quickened and they reached ecstasy together, teetering at the edge, neither wanting to tip over yet. Belle was the first to lose control, then Andre, and they rode the wave in sync, their breath finally slowing and their heart rates calming.

Andre rolled onto his back and took a deep, languorous breath. 'If that doesn't make a baby, I don't know what will.'

Belle laughed, lost in warm oblivion.

Andre shifted onto his side to face her, tiptoeing his fingers around her stomach, circling her belly button. 'Florence tomorrow?'

'Yes, please,' she said sleepily.

'We can leave in the morning. I'll call my friend who runs a boutique hotel there. He might have a room for us.'

'Are you sure your father won't mind?' she asked.

'Don't worry, I'll speak to him.'

She was pulled swiftly to sleep after that, wrapped in Andre's arms, spent and satiated, looking immensely forward to Florence in the morning.

ELEVEN

Belle opened her eyes to the pale morning sun streaming in through the curtains. She stretched and yawned, then tossed back the covers and quickly climbed out of bed, her feet hitting the cold floorboards. Andre was already up and had pulled two bags out for them, his one open, with a few sweaters tossed in.

She smiled. *Florence.* She would have coffee and a quick bite to eat, come back up to shower and pack, then call Riley to let her know they were coming. Now that Florence was in sight, she was desperate to get away from the house for a few days and be free of Teresa.

Belle opened the door and slipped out into the hallway, trotting down the staircase. Even before she reached the kitchen, she could hear a commotion, several frantic voices firing rapid Italian at each other. She was surprised to see three suitcases lined up by the door.

Belle walked quickly through the dining room and into the kitchen. Everyone was in there, speaking quickly, hands gesticulating. She sidestepped Giovanni and Mary, who was holding Sebastian, and went to stand beside

Andre and Teresa, while Uncle Benito spoke urgently into his phone.

'What's going on?' she asked them.

Andre turned to her and frowned. 'A water pipe burst at Valentina's. The bar next door called Papà this morning. Apparently, water is leaking out from under the back door of the kitchen.'

'Oh no!' Uncle Benito usually turned the water mains off during the Christmas holidays. He must have forgotten in the typical frenzy that succeeded the last shift. 'What will he do?'

'He's going back to Rome now. He's already packed his bag. Giovanni and Teresa are going with him to help check the damage and clean up.' He smoothed a hand over his stubbled jaw, then through his hair, leaving it ruffled.

'So everyone's leaving?' she asked.

'Not Mary,' Teresa interjected. 'She will stay here with you and Andre.'

Belle glanced at Andre who shrugged, as though this was news to him too. 'But—' she started.

'We will be busy with the trattoria,' Teresa said, waving Belle's protest away. 'Mary will stay here and enjoy the holidays. There's no reason why not. You can both help her with Sebastian.'

'But—' Belle said again. She looked imploringly at Andre. 'Florence,' she mouthed.

He shook his head, bewildered.

'Let's go!' Uncle Benito declared, ending the call. 'The plumber will meet us there.' He kissed Andre and Belle on both cheeks, then hurried out of the kitchen, Giovanni and Teresa hurrying after him.

Andre and Belle followed, along with Mary, who was still holding Sebastian, and they all gathered around the front door, as coats were tugged on and suitcases were dragged out to the cars, Italian on fast forward making the birds startle and flee from the trees.

'I will call you,' Uncle Benito cried out to Andre as he loaded his bag into his little Fiat. 'If the damage is not too bad, we will come back.'

After Teresa hugged Mary and kissed Sebastian, she went to Andre and put her hands on his shoulders. With a serious expression, she said, 'Look after my Mary and Sebastian.'

'Maybe they should go with you,' he said.

'Nonsense. There's no one her age to keep her company in Rome. She will be happier here.' Teresa shook his shoulders as though trying to drum the words into him. 'Promise me you'll take care of them.'

He sighed, looking annoyed. 'We'll take care of them.'

Standing beside him, Belle scowled as Florence began to slip through her fingers like grains of sand.

After the bags were loaded into each of the cars and Uncle Benito, Teresa and Giovanni had climbed in, they waved from the windows and navigated down the driveway, tyres crunching over gravel and snow.

And just like that, they were gone.

Mary glanced at Belle and Andre. 'I guess it's just the four of us.'

BELLE MARCHED upstairs and into their bedroom, Andre dashing up the stairs behind her.

'Did that just happen?' she cried.

'Keep your voice down,' he said, closing the door behind them. 'And yes, it happened.'

'What about Florence?' she asked, refusing to lower her voice. She didn't care if Mary heard her.

'We can't leave Mary and Sebastian behind,' he said.

'So just like that, our plans are ruined because we have to babysit her.'

'Okay, calm down,' he said, taking her hands in his. 'I don't like this anymore than you do.'

'Then why couldn't we just say no?' she said. 'Why does Teresa get to decide for us?'

'You're right. She shouldn't be allowed to do that.'

'And yet, here we are, being dictated to by that woman.'

Andre placed his hands on his hips and tipped his head back to stare at the ceiling.

Belle watched him, still seething inside. 'Why can't Mary go back to Rome too?'

Andre dragged his eyes away from the ceiling to meet hers. 'I guess she wants the company.'

'Mine or yours?'

Andre frowned.

'What?' Belle asked.

'Don't turn this into something it's not. The girl's lonely. She wants to spend time with people her age.'

'You sound like Teresa.'

Andre sighed with strained patience. 'Belle, we're married. Mary is married. Can't we just get along with her? She's a new mother and a nice person, not your enemy.'

Belle turned away from him and crossed her arms. Even if Andre was right, she was still disappointed over Florence, still annoyed that Teresa could wield such authority over them. She just wanted her and Mary gone. But while lashing out at Andre was the only way she could vent her frustration, it was also unfair. This wasn't his fault.

'Darling,' he said. 'I don't want to argue. What should I do? Tell me.'

She shook her head and turned back to face him. 'Nothing. You can't do anything. That's what upsets me the most. We have no say.' She glanced around the room for her parka and sweatpants, finding them draped over the blanket box at the end of their bed. 'I'm going for a walk.'

'I'll come with you.'

'No, it's okay.'

A flicker of hurt crossed his face. 'You don't want me to come? I always come with you.'

She reached for his hand and squeezed it. 'Not today. I'd like to be alone. Do you mind?'

He hesitated. 'No.' But his expression told her otherwise.

THE AIR WAS BITINGLY cold when she stepped outside, but she trudged with purpose anyway, up to the back fence, climbing over it and jumping down on the other side. Although she longed for time alone to gather her thoughts and make sense of the morning, it took only minutes for her to regret the decision to walk without Andre.

She rarely walked alone. Occasionally, Andre had an appointment or something that kept him busy at the house, and she would venture out by herself, but it wasn't often. He was her constant companion. Even in Rome, they walked to and from Valentina's together. He'd adopted her exercise regime as though he were the one in recovery. Her progress was his progress, every step of the way. So it felt odd that she was out there walking without him, especially given the way they'd just left things.

She crunched through melting snow, down to the stream, where she spent a few minutes watching icy water rush over the rocks. The hares were in their warrens, and it was too early for the roe deer to come out, their shy and crepuscular nature keeping them deep in the woods until sunset. Even the birdsong seemed to have dried up. The forest was empty and quiet, with a stillness that echoed.

She wrapped her arms around herself. The fight she'd had with Andre weighed heavily on her. She hadn't intended to take her frustration with Teresa out on him, but his defence of Mary had irked her. She couldn't understand why the girl was still with them or why Andre failed to find this odd. Her family had returned to Rome. She should have returned with them. Surely the girl couldn't be so devoid of friends that she felt the need to spend the holidays with her ex-fiancée and his new wife. Or was Belle somehow reading the situation wrong?

She sighed and picked up a rock, skimming it across the rushing water. It hopped once, then sank. She wanted to trust Mary, but it didn't come easily to her, not after Ben and Olivia's affair. The heart could take a long time to heal before it allowed itself to be vulnerable again.

It could also take a long time to get over someone. And she was afraid, even after all this time, that Mary wasn't over Andre yet.

BACK AT THE HOUSE, Belle kicked off her boots and opened the back door that led into the laundry. She could hear voices as she shrugged out of her coat and scarf and removed her beanie—conversation and a woman laughing, Sebastian gurgling, the coffee machine whirring.

She rounded the corner into the kitchen and found Andre making espressos and Mary sitting at the island bench, nursing Sebastian in her arms. Andre's attention was on the machine, and he was explaining to Mary in Italian the intricate reasons why his favourite football team, A.S. Roma, had lost their recent match against Napoli.

He glanced up, noticing Belle's arrival, and the conversation stopped. He reverted to English. 'Belle, you're back.'

Belle stepped into the kitchen, still clutching her beanie. 'Don't switch to English on my account. I was heading upstairs anyway.'

Andre glanced at Mary, then back at Belle with an uncertain expression. 'Would you like an espresso?'

'No, thank you.' She gave Mary a small smile, then continued through the kitchen to the dining room.

'Belle, wait,' Andre called. He caught up to her near the staircase and reached for her arm, turning her gently towards him. 'Can we talk?'

She nodded, for the walk had calmed her enough to know that she didn't want their argument to linger unresolved. 'Yes, we should.'

He followed her up the stairs and into their bedroom, closing the door behind them. She sat on the bed, and he lowered himself beside her. There was a gap between them, she noticed, that felt miles wide.

'About before—' he began.

'I want to apologise,' she said.

He looked surprised, then he smiled. 'No, I need to apologise. I should have been more understanding. Having Teresa, Mary and the baby here hasn't been easy for you. You've handled it better than most would.'

'Not really. I got angry earlier and took it out on you. I shouldn't have. None of this is your fault.'

He put his arm around her, and she leaned into him. 'I don't like fighting with you,' he murmured into her hair. 'It hurts me.'

'I don't like fighting with you either,' she said. 'I'm just disappointed about Florence. And Christmas. It wasn't enjoyable.'

'I know.' He pulled her a little closer to him. 'I spoke to Mary. It wasn't her idea to stay, but she would like to if we're okay with it. She doesn't want to impose. There's just not much for her to do in Rome without Dante. She doesn't want to spend every day with her parents.'

'So she's going to stay until Epiphany?' Belle asked.

'Yes. But if you would prefer that she went home, I'll drive her and Sebastian there today. This is your house too. You have a say.'

Belle hesitated. As much as she would have liked Mary gone that day, it was a slight overreaction to send her and her baby packing. And it would only make things difficult for Andre and Uncle Benito once Teresa found out. There was nothing left to do but be the bigger person and make the best of a bad situation. 'No, it's fine. They can stay with us.'

'Are you sure?' he asked, watching her closely. 'I don't want you to feel like you can't make decisions here.'

'I know,' she said. 'It's okay. What's another ten days?'

He nodded slowly. 'And Sebastian is nice to have around.'

'Sebastian is lovely to have around,' she agreed. The baby *was* a delight, and she was still hoping she might get to hold him.

Andre smiled and kissed the top of her head. 'There are so many reasons why I love you.'

'I bet jealousy isn't one of them.'

He laughed, pulling her backwards onto the bed with him. 'I like your jealous streak.' His hand traced a path under her sweater.

'Oh please.'

'No, it's kind of sexy.' His hand cupped her bra.

'Well don't get used to it.' She frowned at him. 'Unless I have a reason to be jealous.'

He smiled before kissing her in a way that obliterated their earlier argument into dust. 'No *signora*, you do not.'

TWELVE

The next morning, Belle was flipping pancakes in the frypan when Andre padded into the kitchen, tossing a pile of glossy brochures onto the benchtop.

'The wedding,' he announced.

She eyed the brochures warily. 'What about it?'

Andre slid into a seat at the bench and began flicking through them. 'We need to call some venues.'

'Will they be open over the holidays?' They should have called them weeks ago when they'd discovered Lucca had been booked out, but they'd never got around to it in the lead up to Christmas.

'Probably not, but we could leave a message, see if we can visit after Epiphany. I'm worried if we don't do something soon, we'll get back to work and forget about it.'

She nodded, reducing the heat on the stove. 'Okay.'

'So, I still *really* like Chianti,' he said, his large eyes hopeful. He held up the brochure he'd shown her before Christmas of the sprawling Chianti estate with its lavish reception rooms that catered for four hundred guests.

Belle stacked pancakes onto a plate and placed it on the

bench in front of Andre, glancing at the brochure. 'It's nice, but don't you think it's a little big?'

'Big?' He studied it again, turning the pages, reading the information. 'I don't think so. I have a big family, so it makes sense to have it there.'

'Just so we're clear, you want four hundred people at our wedding?' She poured more batter into the pan.

'Not four hundred,' he said. 'Maybe two or three hundred. It doesn't have to be as big as the venue can hold.' He covered his pancakes with berries and maple syrup, and he cut into them.

'I just figured, since we're already married,' she said, choosing her words carefully, 'that we could have a sort of intimate celebration.'

He glanced up at her, inclining his head. 'Intimate? You mean small?'

'Yeah,' she said.

He nodded slowly, as though needing to digest what she'd just said. 'But we already had the small one.'

'Well not that small. I was thinking fifty guests this time.'

'But I have a large family. Aunts, uncles, cousins, second cousins, third cousins and all their children. And what about our friends? Valentina's staff? The Barga locals? My father's known some of the people around here for more than thirty years.'

'I've been here a year and aside from your friends and Valentina's staff, I've never met any of those other people,' she said, one hand on her hip, the other waving the spatula at him.

He laughed, spearing a strawberry with his fork. 'Okay, you're right. But I still must invite them. There'll be arguments if I don't.'

She flipped the next batch of pancakes and returned to the bench where the brochures were. 'I like this one.' She pointed to a small venue near Cortona, Arezzo. There was an option to have the reception outside on the lawn, beside a small chapel and a cheerful garden. 'What do you think?'

He studied it, screwing his nose up slightly. 'I don't know. It's a bit... plain.'

'I'd be happy to have the wedding there,' she said, retrieving Andre's empty plate and stepping back to the frypan, sliding fresh pancakes onto it. 'We could have it outdoors.'

He studied the brochure, brow furrowed, and she could tell he wasn't convinced.

'How about a beach wedding?' she suggested. 'Some places do private beach ceremonies. Or maybe a clifftop overlooking the ocean. Or a castle.'

He nodded slowly, but his eyes, which she knew so well, never lied. He didn't like the idea. 'But it will be small, right? We can't fit all my family on a private beach.'

'We'd have to reduce the numbers, yes.'

He sighed, flicking through the brochures again.

'Anyway, we can work it out,' she said.

His phone beside him rang and he set the brochures to one side and answered it. She gathered immediately that it was his father calling. Through Andre's calm Italian, she discerned that the flooded kitchen at Valentina's wasn't as bad as first thought, but that some produce and skirting had been damaged. Mostly everything was just soggy.

He ended the call and placed the phone down as Mary walked into the kitchen. Her dark hair was pulled into a ponytail, and she wore an A.S. Roma football jacket with tight black leggings. She looked svelte, sporty and very pretty, the fitted clothing clinging her hips.

She plonked down onto a bench stool beside Andre, placing the baby monitor between them. They shared a smile over her choice of jacket—his favourite football team.

Belle pretended not to notice, smiling instead. '*Buon-giorno*,' she said. 'Pancakes?'

'*Si, grazie!*' Mary replied. 'Sebastian is finally asleep.'

'You had trouble getting him down?' Andre asked.

'Yes, he was fussing. Sometimes I wonder if he misses Dante, or just a male to hold him.'

'He's an intuitive baby,' Andre said.

'Was that your father on the phone?' Belle asked.

'Yes.' He sipped his coffee. 'The flood wasn't as bad as they thought. A cracked pipe behind the dishwasher. They've mopped and dried most of the water up. There's a small amount of damage to the walls and some of it got into the pantry; a few boxes had to be thrown out, but nothing major.'

'It could have been worse,' Mary said. 'It's good that my parents are with him.' Her eyes fell on the brochures scattered across the bench. 'What are these?' Her hands reached for them, gathering them into a pile and dragging them towards her.

'They're venues for our wedding,' Andre said.

'They're beautiful. I like this one.' She held up the Chianti venue with the large hall.

'That's my favourite,' Andre said.

'It can fit a large group—perfect for your family. And it has a church onsite. This is the kind of place you've always wanted to get married in.'

Andre leaned in close to look at it too. 'You like it?'

'I do! Didn't we look at something similar for our wedding?'

There was a sharp clearing of Andre's throat at the

same time that Belle's spine went rigid. When she glanced sideways to the bench, she saw that his cheeks had flushed the colour of beetroot. 'I don't remember,' he mumbled, shuffling the brochures into a pile and scooping them up, as though by removing them he could strike the comment from the room.

'I'm certain we did,' Mary persisted. She seemed oblivious to the discomfort she'd caused. 'There was a place near Portofino that we had our hearts set on. Remember, we drove up for the weekend to look at it. That place by the water? Then we stayed the night in Monaco.'

The baby monitor began to crackle with static, then Sebastian's cry burst through it. Andre looked equal parts mortified and relieved as Mary groaned and slid off the bench stool. 'And he is awake again.' She pushed the stool in. 'I'll be back for the pancakes later.'

She strode out of the kitchen, but it was a full minute before Andre could meet Belle's eyes.

———

BELLE CLEANED the kitchen and left Mary's pancakes on the benchtop for her to eat later. She headed upstairs to make the bed, finding Andre in there, sorting clothes for the laundry.

'I can do that,' Belle said.

'It's okay.' Andre kept his head down, eyes averted, continuing to sort.

She walked to the bed and began making it. After Mary had left the kitchen, Belle and Andre had fallen into an uneasy silence, which neither of them seemed to know how to fill, until Andre had set his dishes in the sink and left the room. He was clearly embarrassed, and she wondered what game Mary was playing, bringing up her relationship with Andre like that. The wedding plans they'd made. The night they'd spent in Monaco.

Andre's eyes were still on the laundry as he turned a polo shirt the right side out. 'Can I ask you something?'

'You can ask me anything,' she replied, straightening the sheet and tucking it in.

'Do you want to have this wedding?'

She paused and turned to face him. 'Yes, I do.'

He nodded slowly, his eyebrows drawing together. 'It doesn't feel like it sometimes.'

She sighed, her shoulders dropping. 'I'm sorry if you've misunderstood me.'

'It's hard to misunderstand you when you resist me every time I bring it up.'

Belle flinched. 'I'm not resisting you. I just have a very different idea about the day.'

'Because of the expense?'

'Because of a lot of things.'

'Because you don't want to celebrate our marriage?'

She straightened and faced him. 'No, it's not that. We're just not agreeing on what the day should look like.'

He chewed his bottom lip contemplatively, then dropped the shirt he was holding and walked to the edge of the bed, sitting on it. He gave her a despairing look. 'Why has this become so hard for us?'

She sat beside him and shrugged. 'I guess we're just not listening to each other.'

He reached for her hand and twirled her wedding and engagement rings around with his fingers. 'I want to marry you, Mrs De Luca.'

She smiled. 'We *are* married.'

He broke into a reluctant grin. 'No, I mean, a proper

wedding. The one we never got to have because we were in a rush to make things official for your visa. I want the ceremony and the guests and the food. I want a celebration.'

'I do too,' she said, 'but weddings are expensive. We could put ourselves in a lot of debt for the sake of inviting people I've never met before.' Even as she said it, she knew that wasn't the real reason. It was the idea of hundreds of people crammed into a venue like sitting ducks that made her skin crawl. But how could she tell him that? He would worry himself over it or worse, wonder why after eight months of therapy she still couldn't deal with large crowds. And he wouldn't be wrong because she asked herself the same thing constantly. *Why can't you just get over it?*

'It's the Italian way to have a big wedding,' he insisted gently.

'If you were marrying Mary.'

He frowned deeply at her. 'Why did you have to say that?'

She nudged him. 'I was joking.'

'I'm being serious, Belle. Are we having this wedding or aren't we?'

She studied his solemn expression. The wedding was important to him, whether because of his love for her or because of familial obligations—or both—it didn't matter. If it was important to him, it was important to her. She touched his cheek, determined to push through whatever anxiety she was harbouring about the size of the guest list to get on with it. 'Yes, we are. And we'll visit Chianti.'

He pulled back, blinking with surprise. 'Really? But you said—'

'We'll make it work. Whatever it takes. I love you and I want you to be happy.'

'I want you to be happy too.'

'Then call them. Today.'

'We can call a few of them. It doesn't just have to be Chianti. This is your wedding too.'

'Chianti's fine.'

He nodded and smiled, but then his face turned serious. 'That thing that Mary said, about Portofino, it wasn't right.'

Their hands were still entwined, and she squeezed his. 'I don't mean to be sensitive. Obviously, you share a past with her. These things are going to come up.'

'But what she said hurt you. I could tell.'

'I just wasn't expecting it. Mary's hardly said two words since arriving. She said more this morning than I've ever heard her say.'

'Sometimes Teresa can cast a big shadow when she's around.'

'It *did* hurt,' she admitted, glancing up at him. 'It shouldn't have, but it did. And I hate that I let silly things like that get under my skin.'

'I don't think that was her intention,' he said. 'Mary isn't like Teresa—she's not spiteful. I think the comment came out without her realising.'

It wasn't Belle's nature to be suspicious of people, but she was somewhat doubtful that Mary hadn't intended her words. How could someone be that thoughtless otherwise? 'I know you have a Mary, just like I had a Ben. I'm trying to be understanding about her being in your life—'

'But it's hard,' he finished for her. 'I know. I would feel the same if Ben was here telling me about your wedding plans.' He brought his hand to her lips and kissed it.

'There's still so many things you share with her that we don't share,' she said.

He seemed puzzled by her comment. 'Like what?'

'Like A.S. Roma and Portofino and a love of big Italian

wedding venues.' She smiled through her half-joke, but her eyes pooled with tears, and she couldn't help them brimming on her lashes and spilling over. She'd been so out of sorts lately, since before Christmas Eve, when she'd first learned that Mary and Teresa were coming, and she wasn't sure how to make everything feel normal again. Now here she was, questioning things she hadn't questioned in years, like how different she and Andre actually were. For the past year, she thought she'd slotted perfectly into his world, but maybe she'd been wrong.

She wiped the tears from her cheeks and Andre wrapped his arms around her, pulling her into him. She leaned her head against his warm body, inhaling the clean fabric of his sweater and the cologne he wore that she loved —cedarwood and bergamot.

'What about all the things *we* share?' he said. 'Like love and a house and marriage. Like cooking and travelling and wine. And you have my heart, all of it. That I will never give to anyone else.'

She chuckled tearily into his sweater. 'You'd better not.'

'Come here.' He tilted her chin up so she was facing him. 'I never want you to doubt us, ever. We're good. More than good. Okay?'

The look in his eyes was so serious, so unyielding, that she nodded. 'Okay.' She released a breath, trying to exhale all the worries that had accumulated in her chest like a dead weight. 'I'm sorry. I've been all over the place lately. My head is a bit of a mess.'

'My love, I know none of this has been easy for you.'

'Being cooped up in the house isn't helping.'

'That's true. I have an idea.' Andre moved her hair off her shoulder. 'How about we go to Florence tomorrow? For the day. You can spend time with Riley.'

She grinned. 'Really?'

'Yes. We can leave early in the morning and come back in the afternoon.'

She leaned in and kissed him, so relieved that he understood and didn't think she was being intolerable. 'What about Mary?'

He grimaced. 'We should invite her. It wouldn't be nice to leave her here while we went.'

As much as Belle wouldn't have minded that at all, he had a point. 'I suppose you're right.'

THIRTEEN

Belle woke early the next morning before the pale winter sun had breached the horizon. The sky was still grey and cold, windowpanes frosted and the world outside stirring in a half-light. Andre was already up so she yanked back the covers, showered and dress, then dashed down the stairs, finding him in the kitchen having coffee with Mary.

'All set for Florence?' he asked, drawing her in and kissing her.

'I am,' she said.

'Would you like coffee or something to eat before we go?'

She surveyed the kitchen. They'd already had breakfast, empty plates dotted with jam and breadcrumbs stacked on the benchtop ready for the dishwasher, coffee mugs rinsed and placed in the sink. She tried to ignore the fact that they hadn't woken her to join them, choosing to eat without her instead. Now time had run out and they had to get on the road. 'It's okay. I'll get something in Florence.'

Mary climbed off the bench stool. She wore a knee-length blue woollen dress with a high neck and long sleeves.

She'd paired it with black boots, her dark hair loose and wavy, her makeup carefully applied—smoky eyes and plum blush that accentuated otherwise bland cheekbones, full, sultry red lips and thick mascara.

Belle glanced down at her outfit, underwhelming in comparison. She'd thrown on simple dark jeans with a white turtleneck, brown boots and her camel coat, and had dragged her hair into a neat, high ponytail. Even with a coat of mascara over her eyelashes and a swipe of pink gloss over her lips, she felt plain and unattractive beside Mary, who had somehow blossomed overnight.

It's not a competition, she told herself, and yet, somehow, it seemed Mary was competing.

'Andre, can you help me with the baby?' Mary asked, stacking the dishes and mugs in the dishwasher and closing the door.

'Okay.' He pushed off from the bench where he was standing.

'Would you like me to do anything?' Belle asked.

'We have it under control,' she said haughtily.

Belle blanched at the dismissal as Mary strode out of the kitchen. Andre appeared not to have heard, searching for his car key and phone near the coffee machine. 'I put them here somewhere.'

'They're on the dining room table,' Belle said, still frowning.

'Ah, yes.' He leant down and kissed her. 'What would I do without you?'

She was still smarting over Mary's comment and gave him a tight smile.

But he remained oblivious. 'Will you be ready in ten?'

'I'll be ready in five.'

He touched her cheek. 'I'll see you out there.'

OUTSIDE WAS BITTERLY COLD, a brisk breeze rippling through the yard, making the pencil pines shift and sway. The previous night failed to deliver fresh snow, and the ground was slushy with ice. With little to do but watch Andre and Mary pack Sebastian's things into the car, Belle went to sit in the front passenger seat where it was warm.

The boot was open and Andre was loading the pram in, he and Mary conversing over the logistics of its positioning. There was laughter as they tried to manoeuvre it.

'Do you have the baby bag?' he asked.

'It's here,' Mary said, holding it up. 'I'll put it in the backseat with me.'

'How about extra blankets?'

'All packed.'

'I'll get Sebastian,' Andre said, finally conquering the position of the pram and jogging back to the house. He returned a few minutes later, nursing the baby in his arms. 'He was wide awake staring at the Christmas tree,' he said, gazing down at Sebastian. 'He must like the tinsel.'

'I think he's noticing more colours,' Mary explained. She leant over Andre's arm to peer at him. Her fingers brushed Andre's forearm, then rested there for a few seconds, a gesture that didn't go unnoticed by Belle as she watched them in the side mirror from the front seat.

'Let's get him in the car,' Andre said. 'It's cold out here.' He climbed in through one side and Mary through the other and together they positioned Sebastian in the infant seat and gently fed his arms through the shoulder harness. When he was safely secured, they both stared at him and sighed.

'So cute!' Andre declared, climbing out and returning to

the house to lock it. Then he jumped into the front seat, and Belle wondered if she'd ever give him the chance to look at their child like that.

A grey, mottled sky accompanied them on the two-hour drive to Florence. Belle's mood lifted once they hit the autostrada and she realised getting out of the house was exactly what she needed. Andre was also in a good mood, one hand resting on Belle's thigh most of the way, the other on the wheel. Occasionally he'd squeeze her leg and mouth *I love you*, making it difficult for her to stay upset.

Sebastian slept most of the way, Mary watching over him in the backseat. Occasionally she contributed to the conversation, but mostly she was quiet, staring out the window.

When they arrived in Florence, Andre found a parking spot near the Ponte Vecchio, and the task of unpacking Sebastian and all his necessities began. The pram, the baby bag, getting Sebastian *into* the pram, swaddling him with blankets, and putting a small beanie on his head.

'Where are we meeting Riley?' Andre asked, looping the bag strap around the pram handle.

'At Astra Caffè. It's a short walk from here,' Belle said. 'In the Piazza di San Lorenzo.'

Mary took hold of the pram handle, looking especially chic in her blue woollen dress and dark hair. As they walked, Andre grasped Belle's hand in his, and they were quickly swallowed by the maze of ancient streets and medieval candle-lit chapels. Florence's Gothic-Renaissance and Romanesque architecture was on display, like a living museum of masterpieces, and Belle thought it was arguably the most enchanting metropolis in all of Tuscany.

They crossed through Piazza della Signoria, the breeze fresh as it swirled around the square. Florence wasn't brimming with crowds like it usually was in the warmer months. A few people scurried by—faces peeking out from beneath layers of clothing—but mostly, Florence in winter-time was a quiet affair, one that belonged to the locals. It was an ideal time to visit, void of humidity, swarming tourists and buses that arrived with summer, and while most restaurants and cafés were closed for the holidays, museums and churches remained open, so too, some shops.

As they left the piazza, they entered another maze of cobbled lanes and streets, eventually reaching Piazza di San Lorenzo, hemmed by medieval buildings, cafés, and the imposing San Lorenzo Basilica. Most of the eateries were closed, but across the square, Belle saw the Astra Caffè and Riley standing out the front waiting.

They crossed the square, Mary pushing Sebastian's pram and Andre still holding Belle's hand. When they reached the café, Riley held her arms out.

'Sorry we're a bit late,' Belle said, rushing into them. She held her friend tight, feeling everything that was familiar in her embrace.

'No problem. I just got here too.' They parted and Riley hugged Andre. 'It's good to see you.' Then she cast a perplexed look at Mary. '*Ciao?*'

'*Ciao,*' Mary replied.

Riley returned her attention to Belle. 'It's packed inside, but I managed to get us a table.' She glanced at Sebastian in the pram. 'I'm not sure we'll fit the pram in there though.'

Andre studied it. 'Can you hold Sebastian in your arms?' he asked Mary. 'We can leave the pram outside.'

'I'll hold him,' Belle offered. 'I'd love to.'

Mary looked unsure. 'It will be hard to hold him the whole time. He'll need to be fed and have his nappy changed.' She stared at the café windows. 'It does look busy in there.'

'We'll help,' Andre said. 'We can take turns.'

Mary chewed her bottom lip in thought, then glanced around the piazza. 'No, it's okay. I might walk around the city until you're finished. I don't want to ruin your catch-up.'

'It's no problem,' Andre said.

'You can't walk around in the cold for two hours,' Belle added.

Mary shook her head. 'Really, we'll be fine. I'll see what shops are open. If we get too cold, we'll go back to the car and wait.'

Andre grimaced helplessly and stared at Belle. 'Maybe I should walk around with them.'

Mary touched his arm. 'You don't have to. Go inside with Belle and Riley.'

'I can't have you walking around waiting for us in the cold. It doesn't feel right.' He glanced at Belle again. 'Do you mind?'

Belle did but standing in front of the group with everyone's eyes on her left her little opportunity to say so. 'I guess it's okay.'

'It will give you girls a chance to talk properly,' Andre said, his smile uncertain as he stared at Belle, as though trying to gauge how she really felt. 'You know, without the baby waking up and needing feeding and all that.'

'Yeah.' Belle shrugged. 'Okay. Sure.'

He leaned in and kissed her, and it was deeper than she expected it to be, full of his apology. He was torn between wanting to stay with her and escorting Mary and Sebastian around Florence. He of course chose the nobler act, for he could never in all good conscience let a woman and her baby roam a city in the freezing cold alone while he sat in a warm café and drank coffee. It was one of the things she loved most about him, his thoughtfulness and empathy. She could hardly begrudge it now just because it was directed at Mary.

She kissed him back, then threaded her arms around his neck, holding him close. Riley discreetly turned away, but Mary's eyes were fixed on them. 'I love you,' she said. 'We won't be long.'

'Take your time. We'll come back in two hours.'

She watched as Mary took hold of the pram and set off with Andre across the piazza.

Riley shifted beside her. 'I feel bad. We probably could have squeezed the pram in somewhere.'

'People would have knocked it about as they moved around.'

'Yes, but...' She shrugged, as though she wanted to say more but was hesitant.

'But what?' Belle asked, staring at her.

'Well,' Riley bit her bottom lip, 'why is she here? Couldn't she have stayed at the house with her parents? You came to Florence to spend the day with your husband, and now he has to spend it with *her*.'

Belle's shoulders slumped. 'Her parents aren't at the house anymore. She stayed behind with me and Andre.'

Riley's beautifully arched eyebrows shot up.

'And he doesn't *have* to spend the day in Florence with her. He offered because he's a nice person.'

'Well, how convenient for Mary.'

Belle frowned. Riley was being protective, and she understood that, but all it did was fortify those same wretched thoughts in her head. 'Let's go inside before they give our table away.'

FOURTEEN

The café was warm when they stepped inside, the air redolent with sugar and coffee beans. It was a square room with amber-painted stone walls, tables crammed together, people in abundance. A familiar pang of anxiety slipped under Belle's skin as she scanned the area, her eyes darting around for exits and hiding places, or doorways where bottlenecks could occur. The Papilles Café flashed through her mind, fear digging its talons into her thoughts, her mouth suddenly dry.

She jumped when Riley gripped her hand and tugged her forward. 'The table's over here.'

It was the only one left and it sat flush against the large front window, with an unobstructed view of the outside. She stared through the glass at the piazza, at the people walking through it, the monuments and the grey sky, and she concentrated, trying to ground herself.

Don't disassociate, she could hear Emilio saying. She took several deep breaths—in, out, in, out. Her heart rate slowed; the weight on her chest eased.

'Are you all right?' Riley asked, watching her carefully.

Belle shook her head with an uneasy laugh. 'Nothing like a packed café to get the heart racing.'

Riley gave her an understanding smile. 'I know. I still get jittery from time to time. But I promise the pastries here will take your mind off it.'

They shrugged out of coats and scarves, draping them over the backs of their chairs, then took their seats. The table would have fit four people comfortably and probably the pram too if they'd angled it against the window, but nothing could be done about it now. Andre and Mary were already across the other side of the piazza.

Riley picked up one of the menus and flipped it open. 'I'm dying for a cappuccino,' she said.

'A milky coffee after breakfast? That's sacrilegious in Italy,' Belle teased. 'The staff might laugh at you.'

Riley snorted. 'I'd forgotten about that rule. Espresso it is if we ever want to show our faces here again.'

She rose from the table and walked to the counter to order their coffee and a plate of cannoli. She returned several minutes later, and they made small talk until their order arrived —miniature cups of espresso and a plate of cannoli filled with sweet ricotta cheese cream and ends dipped in pistachio.

'Mmm,' Belle said, as she bit into a cannolo. 'This is good.'

'So good,' Riley mumbled with a full mouth, licking the pistachio-dipped end. 'I'm glad this place stayed open over the holidays. We've been eating here most days. They have the most amazing ravioli at night.'

'*We*?'

Riley flushed at her faux pas.

'You mean your date from the *Nutcracker*?' Belle asked, wiping icing sugar from her lips and dusting her hands. 'He's still here?'

'Well, uh, sort of,' Riley stammered. 'Not really. I mean, not the date I was supposed to be with.'

Belle blinked in confusion. 'You've lost me.'

Riley dusted her hands over her plate too and sipped her espresso. She put the cup down, leaned back in her chair and pursed her lips. 'My original date stood me up.'

Belle gasped theatrically because men weren't known to stand Riley up.

Riley nodded. 'Yes, he stood me up. My Austrian from Vienna who wanted to spend Christmas with me in Florence. It was his idea to go to the *Nutcracker*.'

'So why did he stand you up? Did he make it to Florence?'

Riley crossed her arms and jutted her chin out. 'He stayed in Vienna to reconcile with his ex-wife.'

'Oh!'

'Yes,' she said soberly. 'He didn't even have the spine to call and tell me. I texted him when I was out the front of the theatre waiting. He texted me back and told me he wasn't coming.'

'Oh, Ri,' Belle said. 'I had no idea. You should have called me. I would have come and picked you up.'

Riley waved her hand. 'You had enough on your plate, kid. And I'm a big girl. I can take it. But some notice would have been nice, so I wasn't standing out there waiting like a loser.' She sighed. 'Sometimes I think that being in a relationship would be easier. You don't get stood up in Florence when you're in a relationship.'

'It was a one-off,' Belle said. 'Hardly a sign of things to come.'

'Still,' Riley said, somewhat wistfully. 'I'm getting older, and it would be nice not to have to meet new people all the time. To have that one reliable person by your side. Like you and Andre.'

The comment made Belle glance out the window. Her eyes swept the piazza, settling on Andre and Mary across the far side by a chestnut stall. They'd bought a paper cone of roasted chestnuts, and while Mary held the cone, Andre held Sebastian in one arm and with his free hand, dipped into it to grab a handful. At one point, they both laughed. Even from a distance, Belle could see how that laugh lit Mary from within.

She swallowed and turned away, staring down at her half-eaten cannolo. She might have been married, had that *one reliable person by her side*, but it didn't prevent the fear that she might have her heart ripped out if Andre ever strayed, if he shared just one inappropriate moment with Mary that there was no coming back from. It would completely devastate her.

She wanted to be understanding of her husband spending time with his ex-fiancée, to trust them both, but it was difficult watching them interact like that—Andre holding the baby, Mary beside him as though she were his wife, both sharing a bag of hot chestnuts in beautiful, wintry, romantic Florence.

Riley snapped her fingers at her, and Belle jumped. 'Hello. Earth to Belle.'

Belle threw her an apologetic look. 'I'm sorry. I drifted off. Were you saying something?'

'I was telling you that after being stood up in front of the theatre, I was mad.'

'Oh. Right. Yes, I would have been too.' Belle forced herself not to look out the window again.

'There was a guy standing next to me and he asked if I was okay. When I turned around to look at him, he smiled. Pretty adorably actually.' A softness settled in her expression. 'We started talking and I don't why I told him that my date wasn't coming, but I did. He was at the theatre alone and suggested we sit together. So he sat in the Austrian's seat.'

'Just like that?' Belle scrunched up her nose. 'Wasn't it a bit odd?'

'We singles are extremely sociable creatures. Unlike boring couples,' Riley said, eyebrow raised.

'Right.' Belle laughed. 'Fair point.' She and Andre were guilty of spending too much time together and not enough time with friends. It was something she wanted to work on next year—building friendships with other women in Italy. But since losing Avery in Paris, she was the first to admit she was afraid to make new friends, to become too close to someone and have them leave or die.

'I'll cut to the chase,' Riley continued, 'we sat together, we went for a meal afterwards, then we ended up in my hotel room. And the sex was something else!'

'And you've been in Florence with this man ever since?'

'For the past three days, yes. He's still in my hotel room now. He leaves this afternoon.'

'For where?'

'His home, somewhere in Tuscany—I can't remember the name of the town. But he's close by.'

'So he's Italian? And he doesn't have a secret girlfriend or an ex-wife that he forgot to mention?'

Riley finished the last of her cannolo and licked her fingers. 'Not that I'm aware of. He's perfect actually.'

Belle sat back and smiled. 'Wow. I've never heard those words come out of your mouth before.'

'Don't get used to it.'

'Are you going to see each other again?'

Riley considered the question as though trying to answer carefully. 'He wants to. And I think I do too.'

Belle grinned so widely for her friend that her cheeks hurt. 'That's amazing!'

'Well, I don't want to get ahead of myself. It's only early days, but he's just so... normal. And nice. And good looking.'

'All very important attributes.'

'He's invited me up to Lake Como for a couple of days.' Riley shrugged. 'Do you think I should go?'

'Of course you should go,' Belle said. 'If you like him, you need to see where it will lead.'

'I just don't want to... you know.'

'Get your heart broken?'

Riley's cheeks coloured a little.

'Like you said, it's early days,' Belle said. 'And Leo's in the past. I know you loved him, but he was young, and he wasn't willing to fight for you.'

Riley exhaled sadly. 'No, he didn't fight for us.'

'How old is this guy?'

'About our age. And I think he's a doctor or something. We haven't done a lot of talking.' She grinned impishly.

'I'm ecstatic for you,' Belle said, and she truly was. 'Do I get to meet him?'

'Let's wait until after Lake Como,' Riley suggested cautiously. 'Just in case I've dreamed up Romeo and he turns out to be a jerk.'

———————

TWO HOURS PASSED QUICKLY with just enough time left for Belle to fill Riley in on the flooded kitchen at

Valentina's and how Uncle Benito, Teresa and Giovanni had dashed back to Rome.

'Why would she stay, though?' Riley asked, referring to Mary, as they paid the bill at the counter and threaded their way through the still-packed café back outside. Belle had noticed an hour earlier that Andre and Mary had left the piazza and she scanned it, hoping to see them remerge from behind a monument or from the laneways. But the piazza was dotted with only a few people walking purposefully in the brisk wind.

'I don't know. She wanted to spend some time with people her own age.'

'With her ex-fiancée and his new wife?' Riley scoffed. 'Sounds like there's more to it than that.'

'Do you think I should be worried?' Belle dared to ask the question out loud.

Riley grimaced. 'I don't want to put thoughts in your head, kid.'

'You can't put what's already there,' she said ruefully.

'Well, any normal person would feel awkward staying. Ask yourself why she's insisting on it. What does she hope to gain? A friendship with you? I don't think so. She wants to spend time with Andre.'

Belle's stomach twisted at Riley's words. It wasn't anything she hadn't thought herself, but hearing it verbalised by someone else made it tangible. She shook her head, giving a despairing sigh.

'I shouldn't have said anything,' Riley said quickly.

'No, you should have. Because it's everything I'm already thinking.' Her eyes scanned the piazza again, wishing that Andre would appear so she could feel reassured, but all she saw were dark clouds above whipping the wind into a frenzy. 'Every second of every day I'm analysing the things she says and does, the way they interact. And I shouldn't because Andre has plenty of female friends. Why am I only doing this with Mary?'

'Because for the past five years, everyone has drilled it into you how much *they* belong together. And she clearly still wants him. I'd have my defences up too.' Riley jutted her chin out with indignation.

'I want to trust Andre,' she said.

'And you should,' Riley said firmly. 'He adores you, anyone can see that. But I wouldn't take my eyes off Mary for a second. She can't be trusted.'

Belle nodded miserably, tears threatening to spill over her lashes. She hadn't intended to talk about Andre and Mary, but she was glad she had, to know that someone else shared her suspicions. That she hadn't conjured them up in her mind.

'Did he say what time he was coming back?' Riley asked gently, glancing at her watch.

'In two hours, which was about ten minutes ago.' She wiped her eyes with the back of her hand, then pulled her phone out of her bag. 'I'll call him.' She retrieved his number on her phone and hit the call button, as the sky began to grumble and groan. It was picked up immediately by voicemail. 'He's not answering.'

'I'll wait with you then,' Riley said.

Belle shook her head. 'No, you go. Your guy is leaving Florence soon.'

'I'm not going to leave you here.'

'Nonsense,' Belle insisted. 'Andre will be here shortly. They're probably on their way now.'

Riley looked uncertain. 'Are you sure?'

'Yes. Go and enjoy your man.'

Riley shuffled in the cold, not looking entirely convinced. 'Okay, well, call me if you need me. I'll come back down.'

'I won't, but okay,' Belle said.

They hugged, Riley promising to call her after Lake Como, then she left, striding across the piazza, towards her hotel.

The sky churned as Belle tried to call Andre again, but like the previous attempt, it went to voicemail. She sighed, frustrated. Thunder rumbled in the distance as one, then two fat drops of rain landed on her head.

'Great.' It was about to pour down and she'd left the car without an umbrella. A glance back at the café window indicated that their table was now occupied by someone else, and the awning above the café was too narrow to provide decent shelter. The drops grew frequent as her eyes desperately searched the piazza again. *Where are you, Andre?*

Another ten minutes passed, and the rain came down in earnest, quickly soaking her jeans and hair. She yelped, throwing her hands above her head, trying to protect herself. She glanced around, panicked, looking for a place to shelter, but all the awnings were narrow, offering meagre refuge. All she could do was stand there and wait, eyes still searching the square for any sign of Andre and Mary. Lightning sizzled, lighting Florence up as people ran for cover, some braving the wind with umbrellas turned inside out.

Just as she contemplated returning to the car in the hope that Andre had gone straight there, she heard her name through the storm. She pushed her wet hair from her eyes and saw Andre rushing across the piazza, waving at her from beneath a large black umbrella.

'Belle!'

She ran out to him and when they reached each other, he hurriedly pulled her under the umbrella.

'God, you're soaking wet,' he said.

'Where were you?' she asked, teeth chattering. 'I've been waiting out here for half an hour.'

'I'm sorry,' he said, shrugging out of his coat and sliding it around her shoulders. 'The storm came, so I took Mary and Sebastian back to the car, then grabbed the umbrella and came straight here.'

She tried not to feel insulted that he'd ensured Mary's comfort before hers. He should have of course—Belle wouldn't have wanted Sebastian out in the storm either—but she was soaked to the bone and hurt that he'd considered her an afterthought.

'I tried calling your phone,' she said, as Andre guided them out of the piazza and towards the car.

'My battery died,' he explained, trying to control the umbrella as the wind took hold of the edges and tried to flip it inside out. 'Otherwise I would have called you.'

A violent crash of thunder erupted in the sky, and they could barely hear each other anymore as they hurried through Florence's maze of laneways, a gale driving the rain in every direction.

They eventually found their way back to the bridge, Andre's Alpha Romeo parked along the riverbank. They jogged towards it, the rain still pelting down.

Andre unlocked the car and they climbed in, Belle's thighs squelching as she sat on the front seat. She glanced at Mary, who was looking warm and comfortable in the back, watching them as they peeled off soggy coats and scarves.

'Goodness,' she said to Belle. 'Why are you soaked?'

'Because I wasn't sitting in a dry car like you,' Belle retorted.

Mary flinched. Andre glanced sharply at Belle. But she didn't apologise. She was annoyed and wet in every possible place. All she wanted to do was go home.

FIFTEEN

The drive back to the house was silent. Belle sat in her wet clothes, still smarting over the way the day had ended. Andre's eyes were fixed stonily on the road ahead and the only sound was Sebastian waking briefly and Mary coaxing him back to sleep again.

By the time they arrived home it was late afternoon. The winter sun was setting behind a sky still bruised by the storm. Andre parked the car and Belle climbed out, not offering to help Mary with unpacking, for she knew it would be declined anyway. She unlocked the front door and went upstairs to her bedroom, peeling off her boots and socks. As she was about to leave for the shower, Andre stepped into the room.

'We need to talk,' he said, closing the door behind him.

'I was about to take a shower.'

'Can it wait?'

'I'm cold. I want to get out of these clothes.'

He studied her for a moment, then nodded. 'Okay.'

She took a step towards the door, then sighed. There was no point dragging it out. She was upset with him, and they needed to get to the bottom of it. 'I'll have a shower later.'

He nodded again, then collected her robe from the edge of the bed and handed it to her. She accepted it, peeling off her wet clothes and pulling it over herself.

He sat on the edge of the bed and waited for her to finish before he spoke. 'I know you're angry because I left you waiting in the rain.'

She lifted her eyebrows in response.

'But Mary and I couldn't walk in the storm with Sebastian. I took them back to the car first. I'm sorry if you think I shouldn't have done that.'

Her shoulders dropped, her anger deflating a little. 'I'm not upset because you took them to the car first. Of course you should have made sure he was safe. I'm upset because you took so long to come and get me. Why did you leave it that late? Were you having such a good time that you forgot?'

He blanched. 'No, I wasn't having a good time. You say that like we were doing something wrong. We were just walking around. We lost track of time.'

'Mary isn't someone you should ever lose track of time with.'

He exhaled deeply, running a hand through his hair. 'It was an honest mistake, Belle. My phone was dead, I didn't realise how late it was, I did the best I could when the storm hit. I'm sorry.'

They both fell silent. The afternoon outside had receded, making the walls dark, but neither of them switched the light on.

'Is this about me leaving you in the rain or because I walked around Florence with Mary?' he asked, watching her closely.

'Both,' she said. 'Why is she even here? Surely the girl has friends in Rome she can be with. Why does she insist on spending the holidays with *us*?'

Andre lifted his palms in the air. 'I don't know. Mary's always been awkward. She doesn't have a lot of friends. Maybe she feels comfortable here.'

'She didn't look awkward today.' Not in her beautiful dress and high boots, swishing around Florence with Andre.

'Look, I understand that you don't like her—'

'It's not that I don't like her,' Belle said. 'I don't know her. But I know enough to know this situation is strange. She's your ex.'

'Who's married now with a baby. Just like we're married.'

'It was a shotgun wedding. She was pregnant.'

'What does that matter?'

'It matters a lot. Maybe Dante isn't the one she's in love with.'

'*Mio Dio*,' Andre said, dragging his hands down his face. 'She's just a friend.'

'A friend you were going marry.'

His jaw ticked. 'I can't help it if we have a past. Who doesn't these days?'

'But your past has come to stay with us.'

'Yeah well, just like your past came and found us in Paris.' He was referring to Ben all those years ago, when he'd turned up at Belle's hotel door, begging for a second chance. It was the night the city had been attacked and Ben was killed at the Papilles Café. The comment was stark, and she gasped, shocked that he would bring that up.

Andre sighed remorsefully, eyes not meeting hers. 'I'm sorry, my love. That was unkind.' He swallowed, pressing his hands together prayer-like. 'We're going around in circles, Belle. I don't want to argue with you.'

'I don't want to argue with you either.'

'Then what are we doing?'

'Honestly, I don't know. I thought I'd be okay with her being here but...'

'Then I'll drive her and Sebastian home tomorrow.'

Belle frowned. 'That will just make me look bad.'

'Then what do you want?' he asked, exasperated.

'For her to never have come.'

'It's too late for that. She's here now and if that's a problem, then she goes. Simple.'

But it wasn't simple. She wanted Mary gone more than anything, but what kind of message did that send to Andre? That she didn't trust him? That he wasn't allowed to have female friends? That Belle was so threatened by his ex that she'd send the girl and her baby packing? She knew she was being difficult and that he may not understand where she was coming from but sending Mary home would only fortify in everyone's eyes what a horrible, jealous person she'd become.

'Do you want her to stay?' she asked Andre.

He stood and walked towards her, placing his arms around her waist. She rested her head against his chest. 'I couldn't care less about Mary. I just want you to be happy.'

'I can't relax with her here,' Belle said, 'but I also don't want to be mean and send her home.'

'Tell me what to do and I'll do it.'

'Ugh.' She groaned into his shirt before pulling away. 'Don't take them home.'

He gave her a bewildered look. 'Belle, a minute ago you were—'

'I know, but I don't want to overreact.' She was torn

between wanting Mary gone and being a cool, calm, completely sane, reasonable person. What would Uncle Benito, Teresa and Giovanni think if they knew she'd kicked Mary and Sebastian out? She'd be the talk of the family.

'Sleep on it at least,' Andre said. 'I'm happy to drive them home in the morning.'

Belle nodded, relieved that he understood and was willing to do that for her. Maybe all they needed was to hit the restart button. She was the first to admit she hadn't got to know Mary properly. They'd shared brief conversations, but otherwise all they had was a strained history and Belle's deep suspicion that Mary still loved Andre.

'Thank you,' she said.

He nudged her nose with his. 'You always come first, my love.'

'Except when there's a storm, right?' she teased.

He frowned. 'That's not funny.'

'I was joking.'

But he didn't seem upset. He surprised her by dropping a kiss on her lips instead, as though the idea just occurred to him, and he was overcome with the need to do it. She thought it would be a quick, quiet peck, but his lips parted and his tongue gently sought hers. There was a subtext in that kiss—longing and apology and forgiveness too, and she responded with need and desire. They rarely fought, but all they seemed to do lately was bicker over Mary.

'Weren't you going to take a shower?' he murmured into her neck.

'What shower?' she replied.

He tugged at the belt of her robe. It unravelled in a single motion, the garment slipping from her shoulders to the floor. She was left naked before him, and she saw the moment his breath quickened at the sight of her.

He hurriedly pulled his sweater over his head, then pushed his jeans down and kicked them to the side. Despite being at odds only moments before, the heat between them rose quickly. His hands travelled to her hips, gripping them, pulling her closer, her chest against his. He forewent the bed, pulling her down onto the floor instead, as though it would pain him greatly to separate from her for even three short steps. His mouth made a journey over her body, his kisses insistent and worshipful. His arms went around her, strong and protective, and she melted into them, the only place she ever wanted to be.

Then he made love to her, there in the dark, the kind of intense, emotional, soul-binding sex that always brought them back together, no matter how far they'd drifted apart.

SIXTEEN

When morning came, Belle was the first to open her eyes. The room was still dark, and she rolled over, watching Andre sleep, his eyelashes fluttering with his dreams. His hair was unruly and in need of a haircut. She desperately wanted to run her fingers through it but didn't want to wake him.

They'd spent a long time on the floor the evening before, lying in each other's arms. He'd apologised again about Florence, and she'd conceded that maybe she'd over-reacted. She still wasn't sure what Mary hoped to gain by staying with them, but she reconciled, not for the first time, that she would have to be the bigger person and deal with it. The alternative was to send her home and Belle couldn't see how that was possible without seeming cruel. Because who could possibly understand where she was coming from?

Unable to resist, she ran a hand along Andre's chest, feeling lean muscle ripple under her fingertips. He stirred, opened his eyes, then smiled.

'Good morning,' he said, slipping his arm around her so she could nestle in.

'Good morning.'

He stretched languorously. 'What time is it?'

'Almost seven.'

He rested his chin on the top of her head. 'What's the plan for today?'

She wrapped her arms around his waist and held him close. 'I thought I might cook us lunch. Something yummy.'

He lifted his chin to glance down at her. 'Am I taking Mary and Sebastian home?'

She sighed and pulled away so she could meet his eyes. 'I don't think there's any nice way to do that, so no.'

'It doesn't matter if it's nice or not. If she makes you uncomfortable, then she should go.'

Belle chewed her lip, wanting to take Andre up on the offer but knowing the consequences that would follow. She could only imagine what Teresa would say to Uncle Benito. *She's not just infertile. She's mean too!*

'Let them stay,' she said. 'What's another week?'

'You tell me. Can you do another week?'

'I'll try,' she replied honestly. 'At least the baby's cute.'

Andre gave a reluctant chuckle. 'Yes, he is.'

'You need a haircut.' She reached up to run her hand through his hair. It was soft and long and starting to curl at the ends.

'I know,' he said, flicking it out of his eyes. 'I meant to get one before Christmas.'

'We can go to the barber in town tomorrow,' she said. 'Maybe we could have lunch while we're there. Celebrate my first year in Italy.'

Tomorrow was the one-year anniversary of the day she'd arrived back in the country. She wasn't sure if he'd remembered, and she hadn't wanted to make a fuss about it, but now that she thought of it, lunch, a little of their favourite

Barolo, and a walk around Barga sounded like a nice way to celebrate.

His eyebrows shot up with surprise. 'That's tomorrow?'

'It's not a big deal,' she hurried to say. 'I wasn't going to mention it. But if we're going in for your haircut, maybe we could do something together.'

'Of course we can!' He grimaced an apology, pulling her closer to him. 'My love, I'm so sorry. I didn't realise. Which is stupid of me because it's also the day I proposed to you. New Year's Eve.'

'You don't have to be sorry.'

'I do. How could I forget something like that?'

'We all lose track of time over the holidays.'

'That's not an excuse.' He bent down to kiss her, his thumb caressing the side of her cheek. 'Let's do it, then. We can walk to town, have a nice lunch, drink a little wine, watch the sun go down.'

'Can it just be the two of us?'

'Absolutely,' he said.

'I like this celebration already.'

'I'll make it a special day,' he said. 'One year in Italy. One year with me. And you've survived both.'

She wrapped her arms tighter around him. 'You're easy to survive, darling.'

THEY WERE LATE DOWN to breakfast, deciding on a walk through the woods first, then a shower. It was already mid-morning when they entered the kitchen. Mary was seated at the bench with Sebastian in her arms, staring morosely into a cup of coffee. She looked pretty, hair brushed until it shone and wearing a deep green blazer that made her dark eyes brighter. But she gave them a glum frown when she saw their happy faces.

'Where did you go?' she asked sullenly.

'For a walk,' Andre said. 'It's something we do most mornings together.' He ran his hands through his wet hair, winking at Belle.

Belle pushed the sleeves of her sweater up and grinned. The walk, then the spontaneous sex in the shower afterwards had put them both in a good mood. 'I'm going to bake ciabatta today,' she said. 'And who feels like pasta for lunch? I was thinking of ragu with fusilli.' Uncle Benito had taught her how to make fusilli, and it was one of her favourites to create from scratch. The curled shape of the pasta was perfect for catching chunky bits of tomato and sausage in the ragu.

'You're making me hungry,' he said, bending down to kiss her. 'I'll get the coffee.' His eyes widened suddenly, and his right hand flew to his left wrist. He groaned. 'I've lost my watch again.'

'Oh no!' She glanced at his bare wrist where his favourite watch usually sat. 'Is it upstairs?'

'I don't think so. I don't remember taking it off when we got home. But I remember putting it on before our walk.' He made an impatient clicking sound. 'It must have fallen off outside. Maybe down near the stream. I'm going to look for it.'

'You're going to retrace our steps from this morning?' she asked incredulously, collecting her apron from the hook near the pantry door. 'That will take forever. We walked for over an hour.'

'But I love that watch,' he said miserably.

'It keeps falling off,' she reminded him. 'You need a new one.'

'You could wear the one I gave you,' Mary suggested.

Andre looked at her apologetically. 'Thanks, Mary, but I really like my watch.'

'I'll come with you then.' She fixed hopeful eyes on him. 'I could put Sebastian in the carrier.'

'Another time,' he said. 'The terrain is hilly. I won't be long.'

Mary's face fell and she looked down at Sebastian, avoiding the penetrating stare Belle gave her.

Andre left out the back door and the kitchen fell silent. Belle collected flour and yeast from the pantry, as Mary sat at the bench with the baby. The quiet drew out, Belle not knowing what to say.

'Is he asleep?' she finally asked when the silence became too thick.

Mary nodded. 'Yes. I'll put him upstairs now.' She stood, repositioned Sebastian in her arms and hurried out of the kitchen.

Once she was gone, Belle exhaled in relief. She was trying to find common ground with Mary, to give her the benefit of the doubt, but it was difficult when her desire to spend time alone with Andre was becoming increasingly obvious. It took all of Belle's strength not to give her more than just a cold, hard stare.

Half an hour later, Mary returned. She shoved her hands into the pockets of her blazer and glanced around the kitchen. 'Is Andre back yet?'

'No,' Belle said. 'But we walked a lot this morning. He could be a while.'

Mary chewed her lip and nodded. She was about to leave when Belle decided to extend the olive branch. 'Would you like to help me cook?'

Mary turned back, looking surprised. 'Oh, um.' She shook her head. 'I don't want to get in your way.'

'You won't.' Although every fibre of her being preferred to be alone in the kitchen, she also wanted to get to know Mary, to know what went on inside her head and, perhaps, in some way, be proven wrong about her.

Belle pointed to the laundry door where her spare aprons hung from a hook behind it. 'Grab an apron if you like.'

Mary hesitated, then walked to the door and collected an apron from behind it, sliding it over her jacket and tying the ends behind her. 'What would you like me to do?' Her back was rigid as though she was being circled by a predator.

'You could start on the fusilli.' She assumed Mary would know how to make it and she did. She went to the bench where Belle had left the flour and a bowl of activated yeast, wiped it down, and began to make a floury well.

Belle collected vegetables from the pantry for the ragu and began chopping them. They worked in silence, Belle's knife hitting the wooden board and Mary bringing the flour and yeast together.

'It must be hard being away from Dante during the holidays,' Belle said, attempting conversation.

Mary didn't answer straight away, as she worked the newly formed dough. 'Yes, it is.'

'Do you speak to him often while he's on mission?'

Mary lifted one shoulder in a shrug. 'Sometimes. If he's working on something important, it can be difficult to reach him. Do you mind if we switch to Italian?'

Belle was momentarily taken aback, but quickly recovered. 'No, of course not.' In fact, she welcomed the chance to prove she wasn't completely hopeless at the language.

'*Grazie*,' Mary said.

'*Prego*,' Belle replied. Then, in careful Italian, 'You know, I only met Dante briefly at your wedding, but he seemed nice.'

'He is,' she replied.

'His family too.'

'They are.'

They fell silent again and Belle thought talking to Mary was harder than getting blood out of a stone.

'He misses Sebastian,' she supplied after a few minutes.

Belle nodded. 'I imagine he does.'

'And it's hard for us to get to know each other if he's never there.' A cold edge had crept into her voice.

Belle glanced up. 'Yes, that would be hard.'

'Our wedding was rushed,' she said, eyes fixed on the dough, kneading it determinedly.

'Mine and Andre's was rushed too,' Belle said. 'We had it at the town hall.'

Mary threw her a vexed look. 'Yes, but you'd known each other for years. And you're in love. Dante and I knew each other for a second.'

'I'm sure you'll get there,' Belle said. 'You just did things in a different order.'

'Like having a one-night stand?'

Belle's face warmed. 'That's not what I meant.'

'I've never done that before, just so you know,' she said defensively. 'It was my first time.'

'I'm not judging you.'

'And neither of us expected that I'd fall pregnant. We were careful, although not careful enough I suppose.'

Belle held up her hands. 'You don't owe me an explanation.' In fact, it was more explanation than Belle had anticipated. Mary suddenly had a lot to say.

Mary shaped the dough into a ball and set it in a glass bowl to rest. Her expression had grown tight, her eyes narrowed. 'Sebastian is the best thing that ever happened to me. So I *am* happy.'

'I'm glad.' Belle went to the pantry to collect olive oil, pouring a lug of it into the pot on the stove and turning it on high.

'But it was a shock to find out I was expecting. My parents were furious with me.' She gave a derisive laugh. 'I'd saved Dante's number in my phone—not that we'd ever spoken again after that one time—but my mother found it and called him, demanded that he marry me.'

Belle cringed at the thought. 'That must have been mortifying.'

'It was.' Mary draped cling wrap over the dough, then went to the sink to wash her hands. 'I'm a grown woman. I should be able to choose who I want to marry, pregnant or not.'

'I agree.'

'I never expected him to say yes,' she said. 'But he did.'

'Because he liked you.'

'No, because he's a decent man.' She dried her hands on the dish towel hanging near the sink. 'On our second date we were planning marriage and parenthood. I didn't even know his last name.'

Andre had told Belle briefly what had occurred—the one-night stand, the accidental pregnancy, the plan to marry quickly. She remembered feeling sympathetic for Mary at the time. A night of innocent fun had changed her whole life, Dante's too, and it seemed they were still reeling from it.

'Anyway, the rest is history,' Mary said, leaning against the bench to watch Belle carry the chopping board of vegetables to the pot. 'The wedding, moving in together, trying to get to know each other with a new baby.'

'I'm sure you'll both find your way,' Belle said, sliding the vegetables in.

'Maybe,' Mary said half-heartedly.

'You have to want it though,' Belle added pointedly. 'Do you want it? Or are you wanting something else?' *Someone else*.

Mary gave her a lengthy look. Finally, she pushed off the bench and headed for the kitchen door. 'You know you really need to work on your Italian, Belle. I have no idea what you're saying.'

SEVENTEEN

Andre returned forty minutes later, holding his wrist up with a grin. 'I found my watch.'

'Where was it?' Belle asked, wiping her hands on her apron. The ragu was on the stove simmering and the pasta and ciabatta doughs were rising nicely. Mary had disappeared upstairs when Sebastian cried out and was preparing to bring him down.

'It was up the mountain, just there on the grass.' He shook his head, turning his wrist over. 'Lucky the sun was out. I was able to spot it a mile away.'

'You should get that link checked again. One day you're going to lose it properly.'

'I know.' He walked to the sink and washed his hands, drying them on a towel. 'Where do you want to eat lunch?'

'I was thinking outside. It's a nice day.'

'All right. What can I help with?'

Belle glanced around the kitchen. 'Most of it's done. I just have to put the bread in the oven and cook the pasta.'

'Should we make a salad?'

'Artichoke and rocket?'

'I'll set the table, then come back in and help you.' He collected plates and cutlery and disappeared outside.

Mary wandered in several minutes later holding Sebastian. 'Did I hear Andre?'

Belle scattered flour over the clean benchtop and began stretching and kneading the ciabatta dough. 'Yes, he's outside setting the table for lunch.'

'I'll help him.' Mary marched towards the back door, letting herself out.

As she worked and shaped the dough, Belle heard conversation and laughter drift in through the kitchen windows. Andre was explaining how he'd found his watch and Mary was exclaiming her happiness over it with overexaggerated enthusiasm. Belle couldn't help rolling her eyes. Then the conversation grew quiet, serious almost, and she could no longer hear what they were saying.

Andre returned later, pushing up his sleeves. His brow was furrowed as though he had something on his mind. Belle waited but all he said was, 'The table's set. I'll start on that salad.'

———

LUNCH WAS ready and Andre and Belle carried hot ragu, artichoke salad and warm, sliced ciabatta bread to the table. Mary was out there, positioning Sebastian's rocker in the shade. The sun was high in the sky, an almost warm Tuscan winter's day.

Andre dashed back to the house to get a bottle of wine, juice for Mary, and glasses.

Mary finished settling Sebastian in the rocker and took a seat. 'This looks wonderful.'

Belle smiled at the unexpected compliment. 'Oh, thank you. You helped.'

'I only made the pasta dough,' Mary said.

'Maybe we could cook again the day after tomorrow. I'm sure you know more Italian recipes than me.'

Mary played with her cutlery setting. 'Why not tomorrow?'

'Andre and I are going into town.'

She did a double take. 'To do what?'

Belle dragged a chair out and sat down. 'He needs a haircut and I've been in Italy for a year. Well, tomorrow actually. New Year's Eve. We're having lunch to celebrate.'

Mary's eyes flashed with intrigue. 'Really? That's nice.'

There was a beat of silence, as though she was expecting an invite, but when Belle didn't offer one, she flicked her dark hair off her shoulders and pulled her sunglasses down, pursing her lips.

Andre reappeared, precariously balancing a bottle of Dolcetto, two wine glasses and a glass of juice for Mary. He set them down on the table and took a seat beside Belle, opening the bottle of wine and pouring them each a glass.

They helped themselves to food under a sky that was the kind of deep blue only winter could produce. Forested hills of chestnut trees and rows of grape vines draped across the landscape behind them, rolling north towards the Apuan Alps. It was, Belle had always thought, an impossibly beautiful part of the world.

'So you know how I called that wedding place in Chianti the other day?' Andre said, scooping pasta ragu onto his plate. 'While I was looking for my watch this morning, they called me back.'

Belle sipped her wine. 'They're calling people back over the holidays?'

'Yes. And it gets better. They're opening on New Year's Day for viewings. They've been inundated with requests since Christmas, so they're hosting a special open day. There'll be food and wine and music. This place must be good if they've had that many enquiries.'

'Oh, it will be incredible,' Mary said, shaking her head as though there could be no question of it. 'You *have* to get married there.'

'That's unusual to open on New Year's Day.' Belle hadn't heard of any place in Italy doing that before.

'They're about to start renovations next week,' Andre explained, 'so they want to get as many bookings in as they can before they close for two months.'

Belle tore a slice of ciabatta in half and dipped it into her ragu. 'Then we should go.' She had no doubt it would be beautiful—verdant hillsides, distant vineyards blazing a trail to the horizon, golden sunsets and lavender sunrises. Chianti was exquisite, as if painted by the hand of an artist. She could already envision their special day—springtime, surrounded by their family and friends, prosecco flowing as she and Andre married each other a second time. Given that it was almost their first-year wedding anniversary, it would be a vow renewal of sorts, and she began warming to the idea, if only she could get her head around the several hundred guests. But Andre was grinning happily, and she didn't have the heart to mention it, so she smiled too, resolved to get over herself and make the wedding work, however he wanted it.

The rocker began to tilt back and forth, then Sebastian's tiny cry filled the air. Around a mouthful of bread, Mary dusted her hands over her plate and turned to the rocker. 'What's the matter?' she asked him. 'I just fed and changed you.' She rose from her seat and peered inside the rocker.

'Too hot maybe?' Andre said.

'He's not hot,' Mary mused, touching her fingertips to his skin. 'Not a dirty nappy either. Just a bit unsettled from the milk probably.' She reached for him, collecting him in her arms and nursing him upright against her, his head over her shoulder, patting his back to burp him. Sebastian fussed and squirmed and wouldn't settle, even as she bounced and walked and soothed.

Andre wiped his hands on a napkin and stood. 'Let me try.' Mary transferred Sebastian to Andre's arms. Once Andre was holding him, the baby stopped crying. He cooed softly, then nuzzled his tiny head against Andre's strong arms, falling straight back to sleep.

Mary's face lit up like a Christmas tree. She clapped her hands softly, as though it were the most beautiful sight she'd ever seen. 'It's you he wants,' she said. 'You have such a way with him.'

'He's getting used to me,' Andre agreed. The way he looked down at Sebastian made Belle's heart expand and ache. He would make an incredible father. He had a depth of patience and devotion about him that she'd always loved, and it wasn't difficult to imagine the way he would be with their child, loving and nurturing. It hurt to think he may never be given that chance, that all those precious 'firsts' were being experienced with Sebastian and not his own.

Still holding the baby, Andre sat back down at the table. He nursed him in one arm and with his free hand, continued to eat, looking every bit like an experienced father.

'You will make an excellent godfather,' Mary trilled, sipping her juice. Her face was flushed, full of pride and happiness.

Belle glanced between them both. 'Godfather?'

'Yes,' Mary said. 'Didn't Andre tell you? I asked him to be Sebastian's godfather.'

'No he didn't.' She swallowed, wrong-footed. 'When did you ask?'

'Just before when we were setting the table,' Mary said.

Andre's face reddened as he met Belle's eyes. 'Sorry, I haven't had a chance to tell you yet.'

But he had. They'd been in the kitchen together for an hour while he'd helped her finish lunch. He could have brought it up then. She pushed away the sting of hurt she felt, trying to concentrate instead on being happy for him. She knew he would have been honoured to have been asked.

'That's wonderful.' She reached across the table for his hand. 'What a beautiful privilege.' She wondered briefly if she would be asked too, but neither of them mentioned it, and she felt foolish for such a thought. Teresa would never allow it anyway. 'Who will be the godmother?'

'My sister,' Mary said. 'She's two years older than me.'

'Here,' Andre said, rising from his seat with Sebastian in his arms. 'Have a hold, my love. He's settled now.'

'Really?' Belle glanced at Mary. 'Would that be okay?'

Mary waved her hand. 'Sure.'

Belle rose from her seat and stepped around the table to where Andre was standing. She held her arms out as he transferred Sebastian to her. She'd never held a baby before and she was surprised at how clumsy she felt, not sure where to put her arms, conscious of supporting his head, while her heart raced with giddiness.

Once she had Sebastian securely in her arms, his head supported, she gently rocked him, peering down into his tiny face. His eyes were closed now, his rosebud lips sucking an imaginary pacifier, and the soft, sweet smell of him penetrated all the way to her heart. She understood why Andre was captivated by him. He was utterly, perfectly divine, and she would have held him all afternoon if she could have.

But no sooner was he in her arms than his eyes opened, and he began to squirm, fists bunched together. Next followed an emphatic cry, so loud it startled the birds in the trees. She tried gently bouncing him, then walked around in small circles, shushing and soothing and rocking, but Sebastian would have none of it. He wriggled and wailed and finally, Mary stood again, looking uncomfortable.

'He's not happy,' she said. 'Maybe you should give him back to Andre.'

EIGHTEEN

Later that night, Belle and Andre made a simple Tuscan seafood stew, serving it with the sliced ciabatta from lunch. They ate it around the fire, in deep ceramic bowls, watching Sebastian in his rocker. Afterwards, the three of them stacked the dishwasher, washed and dried the bigger pots, and wiped down the benchtops. Belle stepped outside with a bag of garbage and walked it around to the side of the house, dropping it into the outdoor bin. When she returned, the kitchen was empty.

She locked the back door, hung the tea towel, turned the light off, and went in search of Mary and Andre. She found Mary sprawled out on her stomach on the floor watching Sebastian play on the jungle gym. Andre was sitting cross-legged beside her. The baby was lying on his back in a fleece onesie, his little legs and arms sticking out, his eyes wide as he stared up at the dangling animals. The gym played soft rainforest sounds, and he seemed fascinated by it.

Andre reached out to touch Sebastian's tiny fingers and Mary watched them, sighing contentedly.

Belle cleared her throat. 'There you both are.' She'd tried for unmoved, but her voice was thin and high as she took in the scene.

Andre turned around. 'Oh Belle.' He patted the spot beside him. 'Come and watch the baby. He's doing the cutest things.'

Belle walked to where Andre sat and lowered herself beside him, crossing her legs.

He placed his hand on her knee. 'Look how fascinated he is with the toucan.'

Her irritation momentarily diminished as she watched Sebastian play. He really was the most adorable boy. His mouth was shaped in a perfect O, lips rosy and puckered, as he stared at the soft bird dangling down, his eyes two captivated saucers. His little arms reached for it, flailing, not long enough yet to catch it, but he seemed intent on trying.

Mary was still on her stomach, staring at him. Her chin rested on her hands, a pensive expression on her face. 'He's my entire world,' she said, almost to herself.

'Babies are a blessing,' Andre agreed.

'When are you planning to have them?' she asked.

Andre smiled at Belle. 'Soon.'

'You'd make a wonderful father, Andre,' she said. 'You're a natural.'

Andre grinned. 'Thanks.' He reached for Belle's hand and squeezed it reassuringly. 'It's taking time but we're hopeful.'

Mary rolled onto her side and sat up. 'Are you having problems conceiving?'

Her feigned ignorance irked Belle. She knew perfectly well they were having challenges. She'd stood beside her mother in the kitchen only days before while Teresa called Belle infertile.

Andre shrugged. 'Not problems exactly.'

'Have you been to the doctor?' she asked.

'It hasn't even been a year,' Belle said, even though she was the first to acknowledge that they'd waited long enough, and she was desperate to see the doctor again. But she would never admit that to Mary. 'We were told not to worry about tests until then.'

'Well, I got the test done, remember?' Andre said, like she'd forgotten.

How could she forget? It had been a day of mixed emotions—joy at discovering Andre's test results were clear coupled with the fear that she was the problem, none of which she wanted to discuss with his ex.

'And what were the results?' Mary asked eagerly.

'Everything was fine.'

Mary looked at Belle. 'So the issue is with you?'

Belle blanched.

'It doesn't mean that at all,' Andre said firmly. 'It's just not happening as quickly as we'd like it to. That's not unusual when someone has dealt with trauma.'

Mary, unapologetic, nodded slowly. 'Like Paris, you mean?'

'Yes, like Paris.'

Mary chewed her lip, watching them closely. 'That was a terrible thing. It was a while ago though.'

'I didn't know there was a time limit on healing,' Belle snapped.

Andre cast her a startled look.

'That's not what I meant,' Mary said. 'If it was a while ago, then maybe you'll feel better soon, and you can have a baby.'

Belle sniffed indignantly, turning away to stare into the fire, feeling herself simmer like the flames. Paris and her fertility issues were painful enough. Was it too much to ask that she deal with them in private? Did they have to talk about them with Mary, who seemed to gloat at their misfortune.

'I'm sure it will happen one day, when you least expect it,' she said, stretching out her legs.

'Yes, it will.' Andre gave Belle an encouraging smile. 'And if not, we have options to consider.'

'Like adoption?' Mary asked.

'Well, that, and IVF too. Surrogacy. Maybe intrauterine insemination.'

'Oh.' Mary's face screwed up. 'That sounds complicated. I suppose you'd love a little boy though.'

Andre leant back on his hands and stretched his long legs out too. 'I'd love either, as long as they're healthy.'

'You could teach them football,' she said.

'I will definitely teach them that.' He was grinning now.

'You can teach Sebastian too. As his godfather, you can step in when Dante's away.'

Andre nodded, giving Belle an uncertain look.

Belle climbed to her feet. She was tired and irritable and didn't want to discuss her fertility challenges or how Andre could step in for Dante when he wasn't around. 'I'm going upstairs.'

Andre reached for her hand, gently pulling her back towards him. 'To bed? It's still early. I thought we could have some wine.'

She pried her grasp from his. 'Not tonight. I'll see you up there later.' She'd had enough of Mary's goading and decided it was best to slip away before she said something she might regret. *Be the bigger person.*

Up in the bedroom, she sat on the edge of the bed facing the window. The curtains were open, and she could see outside to a sky that was dark and clear. Minimal light pollution in her neighbourhood, in Northern Italy generally, allowed millions of stars to be visible, the whole sky splashed with them.

The conversation surrounding her fertility challenges had left her feeling hollow. She brought her knees up to her chin and wrapped her arms around them, her thoughts drifting to Avery, Ben and her father, who were no longer alive to witness the beauty of star-soaked nights like this one. And because of that or because she hadn't felt like herself lately, their absence seemed heavier, more profound than it had in a while. Time and her work with Emilio had diminished her grief so that she'd been able to remember happier moments spent with them and not always the anguish of losing them. But that night, their loss was inexplicable.

'I still miss you,' she whispered to the sky outside. 'All of you.' The breeze whispered back, rattling the windowpane slightly, and for a moment, she felt very alone.

Footsteps sounded on the staircase, then down the hall, pausing at the bedroom door. She turned and saw Andre leaning against the frame, holding two wine glasses and a bottle of Barbaresco.

'I thought I'd bring the wine to you,' he said, holding up the glasses.

From her spot on the bed, she swivelled around to face him, crossing her legs in front of her. 'Maybe just one then.'

He walked into the room and climbed onto the bed, sitting opposite her. He handed her a glass, set his down on the quilt cover, then opened the bottle. Pouring wine into their glasses carefully, he wore a look of bewilderment, as though he could sense something was off but didn't know what it was.

'You left downstairs in a hurry,' he said, leaning over to place the bottle on the nightstand.

She sipped her wine, then glanced down at it and shrugged. 'Just feeling the ghosts tonight.'

He sipped his wine too, then gave her an apprehensive look. 'I wanted to talk to you about Mary asking me to be Sebastian's godfather.'

Belle managed a smile. 'I'm happy you were asked.'

'Really? Because I haven't said yes. I mean, I'd like to do it, but I told her I'd need to speak to you first.'

She reached out her hand and touched his arm. 'You should accept. Sebastian would be lucky to have you in his life.'

He nodded slowly, chewing his bottom lip. 'Are you upset because you found out from Mary first?'

Belle shrugged. 'It was a bit of a surprise. I would have liked to have heard it from you.'

'I wasn't keeping it from you. She asked me while we were outside setting the table for lunch. I didn't get a chance to tell you.'

'We had an hour in the kitchen together.'

'Yes, but we were cooking and talking about other things, and Mary was walking in and out. I wanted to speak to you alone, properly. I was going to do it tonight, actually. As in now, over wine. But Mary beat me to it.' He gave her a chagrined look. 'I can tell it's upsetting you and I'm sorry.'

'That's not what's upsetting me.' She sucked in air, realising she was uncomfortably close to tears. She tried to blink them back because she didn't want to unravel in front of him. In a voice that trembled slightly, she said, 'Did we need to discuss our fertility issues with her?'

Andre grimaced apologetically. 'It just came up.'

'She was enjoying it.'

'She was curious and asking questions.'

'No, she was taking pleasure in our situation.'

'I didn't get that impression.'

'You always defend her.'

Andre flinched as though he'd been slapped. 'No I don't.'

'Every time the two of you are together, I become the outsider. Like the third wheel.'

He looked appalled. 'I make you feel like that?'

'Not you,' she said. 'But Mary does. Or maybe the way you two seem to just fit together without trying.'

They fell silent, her statement settling between them. Andre played with the stem of his glass and Belle stared out the window again. The air in the room was taut with everything unsaid, everything Belle wasn't sure she *should* say. She'd left the living room earlier to avoid saying something she'd regret, to keep her words and thoughts to herself because they would only cause an argument. And there she was, launching straight into self-destruct mode.

Andre gave her an earnest look. 'We're just good friends, Belle. We've known each other for years, since we were kids. I know her sister and brother too. They're like family.'

'But you were engaged to her once. She loved you. She still does.' And Belle was struggling to compete with all that unshakeable history. Her five years with Andre paled against Mary's forever.

'She doesn't love me,' he said with strained patience. 'Well, I don't know, maybe as a friend, but she has a husband. She loves him.'

'I'm not so sure,' Belle said.

He sighed. 'Does it matter what Mary thinks? Do you honestly believe I'd let anything happen between us?'

Belle hesitated for a second too long.

'Oh. Wow.' He looked deeply hurt. 'Belle.'

'Sorry, what do you expect me to think?'

'Not that!' he cried. His whole body slumped like he'd been kicked in the stomach.

Guilt plucked at Belle's insides. God, what was she doing? She'd just accused Andre of being untrustworthy, maybe even unfaithful. She hadn't even had to utter the words; her silence had inflicted the wound.

'Look that all came out wrong,' she said eventually.

'I'm not Ben.'

'I didn't say you were.'

'You basically did.'

Belle avoided his eyes, desperate not to see the hurt there. All the words she needed to say, to make it right, seemed to evaporate. What was left was the carnage of her implication, that she may have just broken her husband's heart with her insinuation. Of course she trusted him, with everything. It was Mary she didn't trust.

'I'm sorry.' She reached for his hand, a sob lodging in her throat. 'I'm not myself tonight and I'm saying all the wrong things.'

He swallowed thickly, his voice full of emotion. 'I know it's been hard having Mary here. Believe me, I understand. She's my ex and yes, we have history that sometimes shows. But I'd never...' He let out a disbelieving breath. 'I'd never be unfaithful to you. You know that, don't you?'

She nodded. 'I shouldn't have implied otherwise. It came from nowhere.'

'If it's how you feel...'

'It's not,' she said. 'The conversation downstairs just got me in a mood.'

He stared at her, then reached for her hand across the

bed. 'You're right. The ghosts are everywhere tonight.' He rubbed his thumb across her fingers.

Her lips trembled. She was dangerously close to tears again, her heart squeezing painfully in her chest. She wanted to turn back time and erase the last few minutes from both their minds. She was still feeling prickly about Mary and unsure how to make things right with Andre. And she was angry with herself for taking her frustration out on him instead of the woman downstairs, who deserved it most.

'Are we okay?' he asked.

She brought his hand to her cheek, nestling against it. 'I want us to be.'

He smiled and the sight of it lifted the tension a little. 'Then we will be.'

Belle took a large gulp of wine from her glass, letting the burn soothe her throat. She was still wracked with guilt, and she hoped Andre could put her misplaced accusation down to a bad night. A tough week.

'Lunch tomorrow will be nice,' he said, bringing his wine glass to his lips too.

'I'm looking forward to it,' she agreed. 'We need this.'

And the way his hand squeezed hers told her that yes, they did, desperately so.

NINETEEN

Belle woke later that night to find their room dark. Movement outside the bedroom had roused her and when she rolled onto her side, she saw a strip of light shining along the space between the door and the floor. The hallway light was on. There was a soft murmur of voices, then Sebastian's hungry cry.

She reached sleepily for her phone and scooped it up, turning the screen towards her. It was two am. Belle dropped the phone back on the nightstand, then her other hand went instinctively to the place where Andre slept beside her. 'Sebastian's awake,' she said groggily. But there was no reply; Andre wasn't in the bed with her.

Belle forced herself onto her elbows and glanced at the door again, wondering what was happening. She pushed the covers away and padded across to the door, opening it. There was no one in the hall, but she heard voices drifting from Mary's room, accompanied by Sebastian's persistent wail.

Belle slipped out into the hall and walked quietly to Mary's door. It was partially open and through the slim gap, in soft lamplight, she saw Andre slowly pacing the room, holding Sebastian, as Mary sat on the edge of the bed, looking up at them, half-asleep.

Belle didn't want to acknowledge what that sight did to her chest, the way it tightened, making her heart thump unpleasantly, even though Andre was only helping Mary settle Sebastian.

Dante should be doing this, she thought. *Not my husband.*

Andre glanced at Mary and asked her in quiet Italian, 'Do you want to try to feed him again?' She shook her head miserably and he sighed. 'I'll make up a bottle. Go back to bed and get some sleep.'

Belle stepped away from the door and tread softly back to her bedroom. She climbed into bed and pulled the covers over her. A few minutes later, Andre walked in. He went to his robe, draped across the blanket box, and tugged it on.

'What's happening?' Belle asked, watching him from the pillow.

He yawned, pushing his feet into slippers. 'Mary's breasts hurt.'

Belle balked. '*Andre!*'

He looked startled. 'What?'

'Can you please not talk about Mary's breasts?'

'Well, they are. She can't feed the baby. It's too painful and she said she's feeling unwell.'

Belle reached out her hand to turn the lamp on. 'Does she have mastitis?' She'd read about it in one of the many pregnancy books Grace had bought her over the past year.

'I don't know. What's that?'

'Inflammation in the breasts. It can be common in breastfeeding mothers.'

'I have no idea. Will she be okay?' he asked.

'I'm sure she will be. I think it's best to try to feed through the pain.'

Andre shook his head. 'She won't. It hurts her too much.'

Belle pushed herself up onto one elbow. 'Can I do anything?'

He ran a hand through his hair and down his face, scrubbing the stubble on his jaw. 'I'll make Sebastian a bottle and get him back to sleep. That'll give Mary time to recover.'

'Would you like me to come downstairs with you?'

He walked to the bed and bent low, dropping a kiss on her lips. 'No, you should sleep too. We have our celebration tomorrow.' He frowned. 'Well, today.'

Sebastian's cry pierced the silent house and Andre straightened, giving her one last tired smile before he turned the lamp off and left the room.

THE NEXT MORNING, Belle woke to pale sunlight soaking the edges of the curtains. She yawned and stretched, then sat up, checking the time on her phone. Eight am. She glanced at the spot beside her to find that Andre wasn't there. And as she reached out and touched the sheets, she realised they were cold and that he'd not been beside her for some hours.

It had taken her a long time to fall back to sleep after he'd left the room the night before. She'd heard shuffling and low voices, and Sebastian fussing downstairs as Andre tried to feed him. The hallway light had remained on for hours, until Andre had finally turned it off and crawled into bed beside her, falling into a deep, exhausted sleep. By then, dawn was lighting the room, turning the walls grey, and the sun was creeping over the horizon as Belle tossed and turned.

She rubbed her tired eyes and ran a hand through her matted hair, trying to force enthusiasm into her muscles. It was New Year's Eve and she and Andre had their day planned in town for her anniversary. The thought of this made her climb out of bed with newfound motivation.

It was quiet out in the hall—Mary's room was empty. She trotted down the stairs and into the living room. The fire was crackling, and Sebastian was in the rocker sleeping soundly, his lips making an occasional puckering sound. Belle smiled as she tiptoed past him.

In the kitchen, she found Andre studying his phone and Mary sitting at the bench, hunched over.

'Hey,' Belle said. 'What's happening?'

Andre glanced up. 'Mary's developed a fever. I'm going to take her up to the doctor in town.'

'Oh no.' Belle went to Mary's side and placed her hand on her back. 'Are you in pain? What can I do?'

Mary met her gaze. Her skin was pasty and her eyes glassy, her body trembling. 'I thought I was coming down with the flu, but I think I have mastitis.'

Belle nodded and gently rubbed her back. 'Would warm compresses on your chest help?'

'I need antibiotics,' Mary said.

'I wasn't able to get an appointment,' Andre said, pushing his phone into his back pocket, 'but they said we could come straight up, and they'll fit her in. Hopefully, it won't be too busy. Being New Year's Eve, everyone might be away.'

'Should I come too?' Belle asked. 'I could help with Sebastian.'

'That's okay,' Andre said. 'We won't be long. Then we can go into town for our lunch.'

'I could stay here with him. It'll be one less thing for you to worry about in the waiting room.'

Mary shook her head. Belle caught the wary look in her eyes. 'We'll take him with us. Andre can help me look after him.'

Determined not to be hurt by the dismissal, Belle nodded. 'Would you like me to help you get dressed?'

Mary shook her head again and slid off the bench stool. 'No, thank you.' She looked at Andre. 'Give me thirty minutes and I'll be ready to go.'

She shuffled out of the kitchen. Andre watched her leave, then sighed heavily, turning to the coffee machine. He filled the portafilter with coffee grounds and tamped it.

'Our parents will kill me if I don't look after her,' he murmured, his voice full of apology.

'No, it's fine,' Belle assured him. 'You *should* take her to the doctor. She's not well.'

His back was to her, but she saw the exhaustion in his broad shoulders.

'If today isn't good for lunch...' she said.

He spun around to face her, his expression serious. 'No, we're doing it today. This celebration is special to you.'

'To *us*,' she corrected him.

He closed his eyes, then opened them again with a remorseful smile. 'That's what I meant. It's special to us. Sorry. Two hours sleep and I'm not saying the right things.'

She walked to him and threaded her arms around his waist. 'The joys of babies, huh?'

He let out a huff. 'It would be easier if Dante was here. I'm a little out of my depth.'

'What can I do? I feel a bit useless.'

He dropped a kiss on her nose. 'You can hold me up while I fall asleep on your shoulder.'

She laughed, then pressed her lips to his and he returned the kiss deeply, his hands cupping her face. Her stomach flipflopped the way it always did when he kissed her like that, slowly and with intent.

Later outside, with a pale sun in a blue sky, Belle placed the baby bag in the car as Mary curled up in the front passenger seat, and Andre secured Sebastian in the infant seat in the back.

'My phone is charged,' he said, holding it up to her after he'd climbed out from the backseat. 'No flat battery this time.'

'Text me later,' she said.

He gave her a quick kiss and a hug, then trotted around to the driver's seat. His Alfa Romeo kicked up gravel as it rolled down the driveway, around the bend, and out of sight.

TWENTY

There were a few hours to kill before they left for lunch, so Belle took advantage of the quiet and did chores. While clothes were washing in the machine, she made toast and a coffee and ate outside in the sun.

A mild winter's day had turned the sky vivid and the mountains in the distance shimmered blue. The snow had moved on, but she remembered from the previous year how winter in Tuscany could be unpredictable, and she had no doubt that the snow would return in January.

Closer to ten-thirty, as she was hanging the washing on the line, her phone tinged. She retrieved it from the pocket of her sweatpants and glanced at it. It was from Andre.

Still waiting to see a doctor. There are eight patients in front of us.

Belle grimaced. There was nothing worse than waiting to see a doctor when you were feeling as unwell as she knew Mary was. *I guess not everyone went away!* she typed back. *How's Mary?*

A few seconds later, his reply came. *Not great. And*

Sebastian is unsettled. We should have left him at home with you.

She *had* offered, but something in Mary's words had told her that she wasn't trusted to look after Sebastian yet. It was hardly surprising, she supposed, given she'd held him the day before and he'd cried.

Text me later and let me know how you're going, she tapped into her phone. She sent the text, then slipped it back into her pocket, humming a tune as she finished hanging the washing. The weather was showing off, gloriously bright and not too cold. And she wasn't worried about time—they still had three hours before they had to leave for lunch.

———

AN HOUR LATER, Andre texted her again.

We still haven't seen a doctor. Mary's temp is high. Reception said to come back later. Too busy. Thinking of trying the hospital.

On some level, Belle wasn't surprised. Andre had been optimistic in thinking everyone in Barga would vacate for the holidays. People preferred to stay home too, and those seeking medical help likely wanted to do so before the New Year holiday.

The hospital was a ten-minute drive from the doctor's surgery and although time was ticking on and their lunch was soon, Belle knew Mary had to see a doctor.

Hospital is a good idea, she wrote back.

A minute later, he replied. *I'm sorry, my love. I didn't want this for your anniversary.*

She felt his despair all the way to her heart, wanting to

make it better. *It's okay. It can't be helped. Should I meet you at the restaurant?*

There was no reply and she figured he was occupied getting Mary and Sebastian back into the car for the drive to the hospital. She busied herself tidying up and unloading the dishwasher, then went upstairs and showered.

Stepping out a few minutes later, she dried herself, then chose a paisley floral dress that she'd bought in Milan months earlier. It was long-sleeved and belted and fell effortlessly to her ankles, and she wore it with boots and a brown felt hat. It was Andre's favourite of all her outfits, and he often said that the copper tones in the print made her eyes bluer.

She wore that dress for him today, and for her, because she always felt beautiful in it. She smiled with a renewed sense of excitement for their day together, in the mood now to let her hair down and celebrate, to put the last few days behind them.

Belle finished her hair and makeup, pulled on her boots and hat, then collected her handbag and skipped down the stairs. It was almost one and she checked her phone for an update from Andre.

There was nothing, so she typed out a text. *How's it going?*

His reply was immediate. *At the hospital. Mary's being triaged. Hopefully not too much longer.*

Is it busy there? she asked.

Packed.

Belle ignored a flicker of concern as she glanced again at the time. Few restaurants operated over the holidays in Italy and while she knew their favourite one—Caffè Capretz— was open that day in town, she also knew they would probably close by early evening before New Year's Eve celebrations commenced.

You've got time, she told herself.

Belle turned the TV on and watched part of a football match, then flicked over and caught the end of *Fatal Attraction*, dubbed in Italian. When it was over, she stood and studied the top of the fireplace mantel. It was dusty, so she wiped it down. Then she straightened the cushions on the sofa, sat down, stood again, checked there was enough firewood, straightened the cushions once more and touched up her lipstick.

Another hour passed and she was becoming hungry and restless. *How's it going now?* she asked Andre, at the risk of nagging.

We're in. Just waiting for the doctor.

Belle sighed with relief. *Do you know how much longer you'll be? It's almost two.* And they were late.

Thirty more minutes?

She could live with that. There was still time to eat and go for a walk before the sun went down. *I'll head into town and wait for you at the restaurant*, she texted back.

His reply was swift. *Are you sure?*

Yes. Otherwise, they'll give our table away. Drop Mary and Sebastian at home, then come meet me. I'll order the wine!

He replied with two smiley faces.

With some semblance of a plan, Belle turned the television off, grabbed her handbag, ensured the dying fire was properly extinguished, and locked up the house. She walked down the driveway, glad to have worn her long-sleeved dress, as the breeze picked up, making the shadows cool.

It was a fifteen-minute walk into the village of Barga, mostly downhill and pretty. The town was surrounded by forest, the same woodland that stretched to the back of the farmhouse and further up towards the peaks of the Apuan Alps. And it was perched high on a hilltop, far from the main tourist route. Belle loved it even more for its anonymity, untouched by coaches, tour groups and even backpackers, a welcome respite from the packed streets of Rome.

She entered the village, making her way to their favourite restaurant in Piazza Salvo Salvi. Following the dense network of narrow lanes, accompanied by flights of steep, old stairs, she climbed and spiralled her way around buildings, expansive views of the alps and valleys indulging her along the way. Barga was a place to lose yourself, she'd always thought, unveiling its charm little by little, cobblestone by cobblestone.

It took her hardly any time to reach the piazza and their favourite little bistro, Caffè Capretz, in the heart of Barga's old town, under the sixteenth-century merchant's loggia near the town hall. She walked quickly through the loggia and reached the front door, greeted immediately by the maître d. He had a wide smile and oversized belly, reminding her always of Uncle Benito. He extended his hands to her.

'*Ciao, signora.* Lovely to see you again,' he said, kissing both her cheeks.

She hugged him. Everyone knew everyone in Barga. If you ate a handful of times at a restaurant, you were considered a friend. '*Ciao*, Gerardo. Sorry, we're late. Is our table still free?'

'Of course!' he said, his gaze drifting past her. 'No Andre today?'

'He's on his way. He had something to do this morning.'

'He mentioned it was a special occasion,' Gerardo said, winking. 'One year in Italy, no?'

Belle smiled. 'Sì.'

He clapped his hands together, beaming. 'Then we make it a celebration. I have a table on the terrace waiting for you. Come.'

He collected two menus from the stand at the front, then Belle followed him through the bistro, threading their way around tables and between chairs, towards the staircase. The café was packed, and she felt the first stirrings of anxiety settle under her skin, which she tried to ignore. *Not today.*

Outside on the terrace, a cool breeze blew, but the view more than compensated—cluttered rooftops jostling for space, the sweeping Serchio River Valley and Apuan mountain range in deepest green, and the imposing grey cathedral perched high on its throne above the town. All the tables, except hers, were occupied, and the conversation was lively.

Gerardo held out a chair for Belle to sit on and laid down the menus in front of her.

'Thank you again for holding the table,' she said, switching to Italian and taking the seat.

'No problem,' he replied genially. 'What can I get you to drink?'

'We'll start with a bottle of Barolo,' she said.

Gerardo nodded his approval before flashing her a smile and disappearing down the stairs.

Belle took her hat off and smoothed down her hair, placing it on the table next to her. She glanced around the terrace. Although she'd been there hundreds of times, her mind still sought places to hide if the bistro was attacked. Especially up on the terrace where access was by a narrow staircase only. In the past, she'd even found herself looking over the wall to see how far the next roof was in case she and Andre had to jump.

Crazy thoughts.

That was months ago though and with Emilio's help, she'd stopped searching for the nearest roof to jump to even if she still kept one eye on the exits.

She turned to face the view now, watching people move around down below, trying to refocus her thoughts. While Barga was undeniably a small Italian town, it was also well known for its strong Scottish roots, with many families in the early twentieth century emigrating to Scotland, then returning some years later. It wasn't unusual to hear Scottish accents or bagpipes in the streets, and she knew it was why Callum had grown so fond of that tiny pocket of Tuscany.

Her thoughts drifted to her mother, with Callum in New York, and she wondered what their impromptu time together would bring. A holiday romance? A lasting love?

It had been difficult for Grace to move on after Edward's death, for she'd carried the guilt of her affair with Callum for many years, but Belle knew firsthand how exhausting it could be to nurture the ghosts of your past too close to your chest. She didn't want that for her mother or Callum. Although she'd been resistant to them spending time in New York with each other, she had no right to feel anything but happiness for them. She loved Edward, she always would, but Grace and Callum had earned their time together too, and her blessing.

She was jolted from her reverie when a waiter appeared at her table, carrying a bottle of Barolo, a jug of water, and glasses.

'Here you go,' he said, setting it all down on the table, arranging it.

'Thank you,' she said.

He poured Barolo into the wine glasses, then topped up their table glasses with water. 'Are you ready to order?' he asked.

'Um.' Belle wondered if she should order both meals but decided against it. 'Can we have another ten minutes? I'm just waiting for my husband to arrive.'

'Of course. I'll bring some bread.' The waiter smiled, then turned and left, checking on the other tables as he headed back down the stairs.

Belle pulled her phone out of her handbag and glanced at the time. It was close to three in the afternoon. 'What time do you close today?' she asked the same waiter when he returned with a basket of bread.

'Five o'clock,' he said.

Belle thanked him and typed a text to Andre. *I'm here, upstairs on the terrace. Bistro closes at five. Will you be here soon?*

A few minutes later, his reply came. *Yes. We're home. Mary is trying to feed Sebastian, but it's painful.*

She had a sudden vision of Andre beside Mary, while she held Sebastian, her breast out, Andre whispering reassurances as she tried to feed the baby. Maybe his arm around her, consoling, comforting, encouraging.

The two of them alone in the house.

Belle shook the thought from her head, instantly berating herself. She'd almost caused irreparable harm to her marriage the night before with thoughts like that. There was nothing sexual about Mary trying to breastfeed through a painful bout of mastitis while her baby cried. Of course Andre should be there to help her—Dante certainly wasn't. But it didn't stop Belle from feeling just a little, once again, like she was on the outside looking in.

Okay, she replied to his text, swallowing back that old niggling insecurity. *I'll see you soon.*

The waiter returned several minutes later and asked again if she'd like to order.

'Another ten minutes,' she said, grimacing.

But he was kind about it. 'Sure.'

He retreated and Belle reached for a square of bread. It was focaccia, soft and still steaming from the oven, glazed with garlic, olive oil and rosemary. Her stomach was rumbling, and she ate it in a few bites, delicious with the wine, wishing that Andre would hurry up so she could enjoy it with him.

The breeze whipped up stronger, turning cold with the slipping sun, and Belle wrapped her arms around herself. When she'd set out earlier that afternoon, the day had been mild, and she hadn't thought to take a coat with her. But as the sun went down now, taking the warmth with it, she regretted leaving the house without it.

The couple at the table next to her finished their meal and left, then the next table along did the same. The terrace was slowly emptying as the sun dipped lower, casting Barga in the shadow of the mountains.

She fidgeted with the stem of her wine glass, checking the time again on her phone. The minutes kept ticking over. At three-thirty, she texted Andre again. *Are you still coming?*

It was a full ten minutes before he texted back. *Mary went to bed. I'm giving Sebastian a bottle.*

She tried not to sigh, even though her jaw tensed.

Another text came immediately. *I'm sorry. I'm doing everything I can.*

There was frustration in his words too, and her shoulders dropped at the helplessness of the situation. She didn't respond, just drained her wine glass, and topped it up again.

At four o'clock, Gerard came up the stairs, an uncomfortable look on his face. 'No Andre yet?'

She'd almost finished the bottle of wine and the bread too. The terrace was empty now, save for her. She shrugged. 'He was helping a friend today. It's taking a bit longer than we thought.'

Gerard nodded. She almost couldn't stand the kind, pitying look he gave her. 'It's just that the kitchen will stop taking orders soon. Would you like to order something?'

'Oh!' Belle flushed. 'I'm so sorry. Yes, it's New Year's Eve. You want to get out of here, I'm sure.' She snatched up the menu, but she was overcome suddenly with such humiliation that her eyes began to prick with tears. She'd been sitting there for two hours, and it was clear she was being stood up, like some first date gone wrong, except the person standing her up was her husband, on her anniversary. She was mortified. 'Can I have five more minutes?' she asked, unable to concentrate, worried she'd dissolve in a puddle of tears.

'Please,' Gerard said, pressing his hands together as if in prayer. 'Take your time.'

He stepped away and disappeared back down the stairs. Belle stared at the menu, but the words blurred, and she couldn't focus. She picked up her phone again and found a text had arrived from Andre while she'd been talking to Gerard.

Belle, I don't think I'm going to get there in time. Sebastian's unsettled. Mary's in bed. I don't know what to do.

She'd known this was coming. The longer she'd sat there, with the hours falling away, she'd known deep down that he would cancel on her.

Mechanically, with fingers that felt like wood, she replied. *Just forget it.*

As she finished the last of the wine, more than a little drunk now, she stared out at the view, the mountains wrapped in late afternoon shadows. The day had been a disaster. The holidays too. And her place in Andre's life... she wasn't even sure about anymore.

TWENTY-ONE

She left Caffè Capretz with the pitying looks of Gerard and the other waiters following her out the door. She apologised profusely to them, even though she wasn't sure what she was apologising for. All she knew was that she was deeply embarrassed.

Outside, she fixed her hat in place, then strolled around the town, in and out of petit piazzas and up and down ancient, cobbled stairs, lingering, not wanting to go home yet. Andre must have sensed her dispiritedness in their last exchange and called her several times as she walked, but she was a little drunk and sad, so she ignored the calls, not in the mood to hear his excuses. Not wanting to feel the pang of guilt later once they argued over it and she walked away feeling like she'd overreacted, again.

The wine and lack of food had gone to her head and a headache began to crawl up the back of her neck, settling on her temples and forehead. She bought a bottle of water, gulping it down, as the sun gave up and slid behind the alps. A few taverns were still open for the New Year celebrations, especially the Scottish ones, and soon celebrations would commence up at the cathedral, with a party and fireworks, followed by the bells tolling at midnight. But Belle's sense of revelry had deserted her, and she felt neither excitement nor a desire to partake in it.

The afternoon grew darker, and she conceded that it was too cold to walk around the town anymore without her coat. She left Barga behind, exiting the way she'd come, and followed the winding streets back to the house.

Andre's car was in the driveway when she arrived. It was dark, the night setting in. Her head was pounding from the Barolo and the return walk uphill, and probably her disappointment too.

When she stepped into the living room, Andre was bent over the rocker, checking on Sebastian, who was sleeping soundly. He glanced up, then stood, hands held out in apology or a question, she couldn't tell.

'Where have you been?' he asked. 'I've been calling you.'

She took off her hat. 'I left the bistro, then walked around for a bit.' She met his eyes and saw it there— remorse, self-reproach. He looked as defeated as she felt.

'I'm so sorry,' he said, still standing by the rocker. He didn't approach her. Maybe he wasn't sure what reception he'd receive. 'It got crazy here. Mary was unwell. She took her antibiotics and went to bed, but I couldn't leave Sebastian by himself crying. It was a bad afternoon.'

'It's okay,' she said, not really sure that it was, but what was the point in saying so? She wanted to explain how low she'd felt sitting there for hours waiting for him, how humiliated she'd been as the wait staff stared at her with commiserative expressions, but that would make her heartless considering Mary was sick. So she buried her feelings away because they hardly seemed justified in the face of mastitis.

'I'll make it up to you. I promise,' he said. 'We'll go to Chianti tomorrow to look at the wedding venue, then the day after that, we'll celebrate your anniversary. I'll take you into town or wherever you want to go. Pisa maybe. Or Siena.'

She nodded, then walked woodenly towards the stairs. 'I have a headache. I'm going to lie down.'

He held out a hand to her. 'Belle, wait...'

She paused. 'Yes.'

'I really do feel awful.'

She gave him a sad smile because she could tell that he did. 'I know. It wasn't your fault.'

'Did you get to eat, at least?'

She gave a tired laugh. 'I drank all the Barolo.'

'Ouch,' he said. 'No wonder you have a headache.' He pushed his hands into his jeans' pockets, still looking repentant. 'Can I bring you up some food? Or maybe when you come down later, we can eat together. I'll make us something nice for New Year's Eve. We still have time to celebrate.' He was hopeful, one shoulder raised in a half-shrug.

'Yes, maybe later. My head's about to split open.' She climbed the first two steps, then stopped and glanced down at him, her hand on the banister. 'Is Mary feeling better?'

He nodded. 'I think so.'

'That's good.' She walked up the stairs to their bedroom and closed the door. Once inside, she kicked off her boots and stripped out of her dress, pulling on a sweater and track pants. Her head really was about to split open. She drew the curtains closed and climbed into bed, longing for sleep, to distance herself from the thumping in her head, the tightness in her shoulders and neck, the heaviness in her heart. But all she could do was stare up at the ceiling instead.

The day was in stark contrast to the New Year's Eve

before, when she'd stepped off the plane in Rome and Andre had greeted her at the airport. There had been tears and kisses of joy, exquisite longing and a promise of forever. He'd whisked her straight to the farmhouse, lit the fire and had got down on one knee to propose, as though unwilling to risk losing her again. It had been the happiest day of her life.

Twelve months later and the day couldn't have been more different. An epic failure, in fact.

'Happy anniversary to me,' she whispered to the ceiling, as a tear broke free and scurried down her cheek.

THE ROOM WAS STILL DARK when a hand gently shook her awake. She opened her eyes to find the doorway lit by the hallway light, casting Andre's silhouette into shadow.

'Belle,' he said softly.

'Hmm,' she murmured. As she came to, so did the pounding in her head. She pressed her hand to her forehead to stave it off. 'What time is it?'

'Almost midnight. You've been asleep all evening.'

She struggled to sit up, but her migraine forced her back down. 'My head.'

His expression tensed with concern. 'You still have a headache?'

'It could be a migraine.'

'Would you like pain relief?'

She nodded. 'And water.'

He kissed the top of her head, then disappeared out of the room. She blinked after him, the hallway light too bright, hurting her eyes. Her stomach churned and she thought she might throw up.

He was back a few minutes later with a glass of water and two paracetamol tablets. 'Here, this will help.'

'Thanks.' she said, forcing herself into a sitting position. The pain radiated to her neck and shoulders, her arms and her back, as though it were trying to colonise her entire body.

She rarely got headaches like these, this one arriving out of nowhere and with a vengeance. She was certain the stress of the past week had caused it, the disappointment of the day, the bottle of Barolo she'd nursed while she'd waited for Andre. She'd hoped for something stronger to curb its assault on her, but paracetamol would have to do.

She popped the pills into her mouth and gulped them back with water. Andre smiled helplessly at her. 'Do you think you can make it downstairs?'

All she wanted to do was go back to sleep, but it was New Year's Eve and she wanted to salvage some of the day with her husband, even if it took every effort to do so. She nodded. 'I'll come down.' He pulled the covers back and helped her swing her legs to the floor. She stood, the relentless pain in her head making the room tilt.

'I opened a bottle of prosecco,' he said, as they left the room behind.

She almost gagged at the mention of it but nodded again. 'I'll have a small glass.'

'Good. Mary's awake too. The antibiotics seem to be working.'

They walked down the stairs, Belle's head thumping with every step. She went straight to the sofa and sat, pulling a blanket that was lying there across her legs, as Andre retreated to the kitchen.

Mary was sitting beside Sebastian in the rocker, rocking it gently with her hand. The fire was crackling in the hearth, the room warm, and a small pile of party blowers were laid out on the coffee table next to a bottle of prosecco.

Mary glanced up at Belle and gave her a small smile.

'Are you feeling better?' Belle asked.

'A little,' she said. 'Thanks to Andre. He was incredible today.'

Belle's eyebrows lifted, but she didn't say anything. There was no apology for ruining her anniversary, or remorse for occupying Andre all day. Just the smug tone, it seemed, of someone who'd got what she wanted.

Mary sighed and returned her gaze back to Sebastian.

They fell silent, then Belle said, 'Have you spoken to Dante? Does he know you were unwell?'

Mary's back stiffened. 'No, not yet.'

'So you haven't called to wish him a happy new year either? I'm sure he'd like to hear from you.'

Mary's eyes met hers briefly, then darted away. 'I'll call him tomorrow.'

Andre returned with three champagne flutes, holding one up to Mary that was filled with juice. 'Is this okay for you?' he asked.

She nodded, looking relieved that he was back. 'Juice is fine.'

He placed the flutes down on the table and scooped up the bottle of prosecco. He popped the cork and filled their glasses, handing one to Belle, then he dropped down beside her. He clinked his glass gently against hers with a smile. 'Are you hungry? I could make a cheese platter.'

'No, I'm okay.' It would be enough to keep the alcohol down. The lack of food and earlier dalliance with the Barolo and now the splitting migraine had left her nauseated.

Andre glanced at the clock. 'One minute until midnight.'

Mary stood and grabbed a party blower from the coffee table, then handed one to Andre and Belle.

Andre also stood, helping Belle to her feet. They placed their champagne flutes on a side table, then he wrapped his arms around her, in anticipation of the countdown. Mary returned to Sebastian's side, a distant, pensive look on her face.

'Ten, nine, eight...' Andre said, dropping a kiss onto Belle's nose.

'Seven, six, five, four...' they all chimed in unison.

Andre stared into Belle's eyes and for a moment, Mary, Sebastian and the last eight days fell away, and it was just the two of them, saying goodbye to her first year in Italy and welcoming in a second one.

'... three, two, one. Happy New Year!' they all sang, blowing the party blowers.

Andre picked Belle up and swung her around, setting her back on her feet again. '*Buon Anno*, my love,' he whispered, touching his forehead to hers. 'And happy one year anniversary.'

'*Buon Anno*,' she whispered back.

His lips met hers and they kissed, the first of the new year, the way she hoped every new year would begin. In Andre's arms.

Mary cleared her throat and they separated. Andre's arms dropped from Belle's waist, and he stepped around the coffee table towards her, arms outstretched. '*Buon Anno*, Mary,' he said.

She fell into his embrace, her hands wrapped firmly around his torso, as he kissed each of her cheeks. '*Buon*

Anno, Andre,' she replied. Her cheeks turned scarlet when she noticed Belle watching, and she promptly stepped away, back to the rocker. She bent low and collected Sebastian out of it, then she held him out to Andre. Sebastian was awake, eyes wide, a grin spreading across his face when he saw Andre.

'Ah, my little guy,' he said, taking Sebastian from Mary. '*Buon Anno*, Sebastian. Your first New Year.' He bounced him gently around and Sebastian gurgled with delight, unable to tear his eyes away from Andre.

'Do you think I could have a hold?' Belle asked Mary after a while. 'Just for a few minutes.'

Mary's mouth pulled into a grim line. 'If too many strangers hold him before bed, he will fuss all night.'

'Oh.' It sounded like Teresa talking.

'Just one hold won't hurt,' Andre said, preparing to hand Sebastian over.

'No, it's okay,' Belle said. 'I don't want to unsettle him.' She took the hint and stepped away, returning to the sofa. Andre transferred Sebastian back to Mary, then walked to Belle, sitting beside her.

'Are you tired?' he asked, placing his hand on the back of her neck and massaging the pain.

She nodded. Her head was pounding and the light in the room was starting to hurt her eyes. And she had a niggling sensation that she was now locked in mortal combat with Mary for Andre's attention. It twisted in her belly, made her blood pulse in her ears. Made her dislike Mary even more.

After a few minutes, she stood, folded the blanket she'd used earlier and placed it neatly at one end of the sofa. 'I'm going to bed.'

Andre glanced up at her, reaching for her hand and

entwining his fingers through hers. 'Okay, my love. I'll put the fire out and come up.'

She said goodnight to them both and walked to the stairs, eager to get back to bed and lie her thumping head down. She was also desperate to get away from Mary. She may have been unwell, but she'd ruined Belle's first anniversary in Italy, a day that she'd never get back. It was gone, as fleeting as it was disastrous. And Belle wasn't sure the reason was entirely down to mastitis. She had an overwhelming feeling that Mary had exploited Andre's kindness, keeping him home longer, drawing out the time.

Now more than ever, Belle was looking forward to spending the day with him in Chianti. Just the two of them. Alone. Planning their wedding.

And Mary wasn't invited.

TWENTY-TWO

Belle woke the next morning to Andre gently nudging her. Early morning sunlight pressed against her eyelids, the migraine from the night before resurging across her head, down her neck and along her shoulders. It radiated to her stomach, making her nauseated.

When she opened her eyes, he was sitting on the edge of the bed beside her, looking down with a concerned expression. 'What time is it?' she asked, her hands reaching for her forehead, applying pressure.

'It's almost nine,' he said. 'You slept late. I didn't want to wake you, but we need to get on the road soon.'

She studied him through her migraine fog. He was already dressed for Chianti in a white long-sleeve polo and jeans, his jacket draped across the edge of the bed. She tried to sit up, but the pain forced her back down again. 'Ugh,' she groaned. 'It hurts.'

'You still have it?' he asked.

She closed her eyes and nodded. She'd hoped to be better, but she wasn't. And she didn't know how she would manage a two-hour drive to Chianti and back, a full day of walking and talking, expressing enthusiasm at wedding venues when all she wanted to do was lie down in a dark, quiet room with a cold compress to her head. But she desperately wanted to go because the day before had been terrible for them, and they needed this.

'Are you going to be able to do this today?' Andre asked, seeming to read her thoughts.

She nodded, but even that hurt to do. 'I want to.'

'Do you want more paracetamol?'

'I can try, but it didn't do anything last night. I'll need something stronger.'

'All the chemists are closed today. It's a holiday.'

'Then I probably need to sleep it off.'

He nodded slowly, registering the implication. 'Sleep it off. That means...'

'What if we went another day?' she asked, grimacing, even as she said the words.

He frowned. 'Belle.'

'I want to go, more than anything,' she insisted, 'but I'm not sure I can even get in the shower at the moment. And I want the day to be special. I don't want to feel unwell.'

'If we don't go today, we'll have to wait until February,' he said. 'They're closing for renovations.'

'February's only a month away.'

'But we'll be back at work, rostered on the weekends. We'll never get there.'

'Then maybe we should take the plunge and book it. Who cares if we don't see it first?'

'I do,' he said. 'Because I don't want you to tell me in two months' time that you've decided you hate it. Then we'll be back to square one.'

She flinched at his words. 'I wouldn't do that.'

'You might.'

Belle's heart sank. Something was happening to them; she could feel it. That unmistakable chink in their armour again. 'I know you're disappointed. After yesterday, I am too.'

He stared down at the quilt cover for a long time and she saw many things pass over his expression—uncertainty, sadness, frustration. It was all the things she'd felt the day before waiting for him at the bistro. No. She was determined not to have *this* day turn out like that. 'You know what? You're right. We should get it done. I'll get up.' She flicked the covers back and swung her legs to the floor, but the room spun, and her head thumped in protest.

Andre's eyes assessed her. 'Belle, if you're not up to it...'

'It's fine. This is important.'

He put his hand on her shoulder, gently pushing her back down. 'It is, but not at the expense of making you feel worse.'

'A minute ago you were angry at me for not coming,' she snapped.

'I wasn't angry, I just...' He sighed with weary resignation. 'I can see you're not well. It's okay, I understand.'

'Do you really, though?' she asked.

He touched a hand to her head, pressing lightly, making the thump momentarily cease. 'I do. I'm just sad for us.'

She reached for his hand, bringing it to her lips and holding it there. 'I don't want you to be sad for us.' Sad meant they weren't in a good place, and although she felt it too, she was terrified of acknowledging it.

'You know what I mean,' he said. 'We'll go another time. Just rest.' He bent to kiss her, to rest his hand lovingly on her aching head again and pull the covers up around her chin.

'I'm sorry,' she said as he rose from the bed and walked to the door.

He paused and turned to look back at her. 'You have nothing to be sorry for.'

Then he smiled softly and left the room, closing the door behind him.

BELLE SLEPT most of the day. When she woke later, the colours in the room had changed, and she realised it was afternoon. She stretched and placed a hand on her forehead. The wretched migraine that had left her debilitated for nearly twenty-four hours had dulled to a slight ache. She sighed with relief. It wasn't the best start to the New Year, but at least she was feeling better.

Belle rolled onto her side, looking for her phone on the nightstand, noticing instead a plate of cornetti and a glass of juice beside her. Two paracetamol pills lay next to the juice. *Andre*. She smiled. It was what she loved most about him, his attentiveness, the way he always cared for her, and she promised herself she'd make the wedding venue a priority as soon as it reopened after the renovations. To make *their marriage* a priority.

She sat up and reached for the plate, taking a bite out of the pastry. Her stomach yowled in response. The last thing she'd eaten was a small basket of bread at Caffè Capritz the day before and her appetite was awake. She licked her fingers as she finished half of it, sipped the juice, swallowed the paracetamol—better to be safe than sorry—then flicked back the covers.

The room was freezing, and she tucked her feet into slippers, wrapping her arms around herself. The fire downstairs mustn't have been lit—she couldn't smell woodsmoke either—and she wondered why. She slipped out into the hallway, noticing Mary's bedroom door open but the room empty. The house was quiet and still, like Belle was the only occupant.

Downstairs, she discovered the living room and kitchen empty too, and decided Andre and Mary must have gone for a walk with Sebastian until she passed by the front windows again and noticed Andre's car missing from the driveway.

They went for a drive? She chewed the inside of her cheek, staring at the empty spot where his Alpha Romeo was usually parked. The last of the afternoon sun streaked through the pencil pines, dappling the gravel. The day had obviously been glorious, one of those winter sparklers. Why should they stay home just because she'd been stuck in bed with a migraine? But even as she told herself that, the empty spot on the driveway stared back at her with mute provocation.

Back upstairs in her room, she reached for her phone on the nightstand and dialled Andre's number. It didn't ring, picked up instead by voicemail, so she left a message.

'Hi, just wondering where you guys are. I'm up and feeling better. Call me back.'

Her voice sounded strained and unnaturally high even to her ears, as her mind began leaping all over the place. *Where did they go? How long have they been gone?*

She distracted herself by making the bed and starting the fire. The kitchen was clean and the house tidy; there wasn't much else to do. It was just silent, and her thoughts kept circling back to Andre and Mary's whereabouts, so she called her mother and Callum in New York to wish them a Happy New Year, then Riley, but none of them answered.

At six-thirty, well after the sun had gone down, head-lights shone through the front windows, the familiar sound of Andre's car rolling up the driveway. Belle was sitting on the sofa, watching the fire, picking at a loose thread on the sofa's arm.

The front door opened and Andre and Mary walked in, talking animatedly. Mary carried Sebastian and Andre had the baby bag slung over his shoulder. He caught sight of Belle on the sofa and smiled. 'Ah, you're up. How are you feeling?' He dropped the bag near the doorway and slipped off his jacket.

'Better,' she said. She glanced at Mary, all flushed cheeks and bright eyes. 'Where did you go?'

'Chianti,' Andre said.

Belle froze, as though someone had thrown an icy bucket of water over her. '*Chianti?*'

'It was amazing, Belle,' Mary sang. 'The wedding rooms were exquisite.'

'Chianti?' Belle repeated. This time Mary didn't mistake the tightness in her voice. The smile disappeared from her face, and she glanced uncomfortably at Andre.

'Yes, we went to Chianti,' Andre said cautiously, as though realising he may have made a grave error. 'We decided to go since we had nothing else to do.'

'You went without me?' Belle shot the accusation at them, rising from the sofa. She was astounded and deeply hurt. While she'd been unwell upstairs in bed, her husband had taken his ex-fiancée to see wedding rooms, to drive through beautiful Chianti together, on a day that should have been theirs. He couldn't even wait for her to get better.

Andre swallowed hard, Adam's apple shifting. 'I didn't think you'd mind.'

'Well, I do mind,' she said. 'We should have done that together.'

'But you were sick.'

'We were supposed to go when it reopened,' she shot back, her voice rising.

'I said I would take *you* when it reopened. I didn't say I would wait until then.'

'Are you kidding?' She was trembling now with a rage that had been building since Christmas Eve and was now on the verge of exploding.

'Belle, Andre was excited to go.' Mary's voice was patronising. 'I only went to give him a second opinion.'

'Don't *you* talk to me!' Belle said, pointing her finger at her. Mary gasped. 'You and your mother have caused nothing but trouble since you arrived. I wish you both never came.'

'Belle,' Andre cautioned.

'I'll get Sebastian's bath ready,' Mary murmured, collecting the baby bag from the floor and scurrying up the stairs.

'That was unnecessary,' he said, once she was gone. 'Mary isn't to blame. If you're going to be angry at anyone, be angry at me.'

'Oh, I'm angry at you too,' she said. 'How could you go without me? This is something you and I should have done together. Not you and Mary.'

He threw his hands up in the air. 'I didn't think you'd care.'

'Of course I care.'

'Frankly, I've been nagging you for the past six months to look at places with me and you keep making excuses. At least Mary *wanted* to go.'

Belle inhaled sharply liked she'd been slapped in the

face. Her heart dropped into her stomach as they stood facing each other, an incomprehensible confession laid out in front of them.

Andre was the first to concede. He drew a shaky breath, running a hand over his jaw. 'I'm sorry, I shouldn't have said that.'

'No, please, continue to speak to your mind.' Belle's voice wobbled. She was torn apart inside, her heart ripped to shreds. Something unfathomable and unstoppable was happening to them and she didn't know how to wrap her hands around it, slow it down.

'You know that's not what I meant,' he said.

'I wanted to go with you today,' she said. 'But I was unwell. It's interesting that when Mary's unwell, you cast me aside to be with her, but when I'm sick, you spend the day with her instead.'

Andre's face screwed up, as though searching for an explanation, but then his shoulders fell with realisation. He shook his head and looked down at his hands.

She looked down too, and it was then that she noticed it. The watch Mary had given him, wrapped around his wrist, large and gaudy, but there. 'You're wearing her watch.'

He looked confused for a second, then glanced at his wrist, turning it over. 'Yeah, I... I didn't want to lose my favourite one in Chianti.'

'But why would you wear that? You know how I felt about her giving it to you.'

Andre's jaw tightened. 'It's just a watch, Belle.'

'What are you playing at?' she asked.

His brow knitted together. 'I'm not playing at anything.'

'Are you falling in love with her again?'

'*What?*'

Hot tears pushed at her eyelids, her heart hammering in

her chest. The fact that she even had to ask made her sick to her stomach.

'What kind of a question is that?' he said, his voice high again.

'It's a question I need you to answer because I don't know what to think anymore.'

'Well I'm not going to answer it,' he said, crossing his arms over his chest.

'Because you are?'

'No, because it's insulting! Are we doing this now? Accusing each other of falling for other people?'

'But how could you not?' Belle cried. 'She's everything I'll never be. A mother, Italian, your childhood friend.'

'That's ridiculous and you know it.'

'Well, what am I supposed to do? Not ask? Just sit back and let it happen?'

'Nothing is happening!' he exploded.

A silence fraught with pain filled the room. Andre was breathing heavily, and Belle's entire body trembled.

'How would you feel if I spent time with my ex,' she said, forcing calm into her voice. 'Taking him to look at wedding venues and walking around Florence with him, letting him look after our baby and nursing me back to health? If that was Ben, what would you think?'

Andre quietly scoffed.

'No, honestly, tell me,' she insisted. 'I want to know.'

He looked at her for a long time and she saw it in his eyes. Fear, realisation, shame. There was a quiver of vulnerability in his voice when he spoke. 'I'd hate it.'

'But my ex is dead, so you don't need to worry about that, right?'

The comment clearly stung, and he flinched. 'Belle...'

A sob escaped her lips and she took one step back, then

two, turning towards the stairs. Andre was silent, standing in the same spot by the front door, his head hung in remorse or embarrassment, maybe defeat—she didn't know. All she knew was that somehow, her marriage had become irrevocably broken. She'd lost trust in Andre, and he'd lost faith in her, and they were crumbling before her eyes.

She climbed the stairs on legs that felt wooden, feeling as though she wasn't in her body, and walked into their bedroom. Her eyes stung with hot tears, but she refused to let them fall. She changed into jeans and a sweater, pulled on shoes, and reached for her handbag and coat.

When she went back down the stairs to the living room, Andre was gone. She heard the coffee machine whirring in the kitchen, a chink of a teaspoon against an espresso cup, then the back door open and close. He was going outside to cool off and she needed to also. Never had they fought so ferociously before. One thing was for certain, she wanted to get away from the house. From Mary. From their closeness. For an hour or two... or ten, she didn't know. She just needed to leave.

She went to the desk by the window and collected a pen and paper from the drawer, scribbling a note to Andre. *I'm going to Florence to see Riley. I don't know when I'll be back.*

Or if she would come back.

With a last look at the living room, with its warm fire and Christmas tree still twinkling in the corner, she let herself out the front door and walked up the driveway, away from the house she'd called home for the past year.

TWENTY-THREE

It was a cold, clear night, the streets dark and hilly. Belle wasn't sure how she was going to get to Florence exactly— she hadn't thought that far ahead—motivated only by adrenalin and a need to leave the house. Trains ran from Barga to Lucca, then Lucca to Florence, but it was New Year's Day and almost seven o'clock at night. She wasn't sure what services would be available.

Belle pulled her jacket tighter around her, her head bent against a breeze that stung her cheeks, walking determinedly before she could ask herself what she was doing.

Twenty minutes later, she reached the train station, an ivory-coloured building nestled a few kilometres out of town. Pale-coloured villas were scattered around the terminal on a street that curved gently before fading into the stillness of the countryside. There was a small carpark with two cars in it, and the station was deserted, save for a bored-looking attendant sitting behind the ticket window. There were no buses or taxis queued outside, no souls roaming or waiting for trains, just flickering streetlights, the dark expanse of sky overhead dotted with stars, and a waning crescent moon.

The quietude had a lonely presence to it and before she could talk herself out of being there, Belle walked to the ticket counter and pulled her purse out of her bag. 'When is the next train to Lucca?' she asked in Italian.

The attendant, an older male, with a grey moustache and droopy eyelids, glanced up from his crossword. 'Eight-fifteen is the next and last one. You have one hour to wait.'

'Can I purchase a ticket please?'

'One-way or return?' he said, tapping his keyboard.

One-way or return... 'One-way.'

He tapped the keyboard again, then printed her ticket and slid it under the window to her. She paid with her credit card, then collected the ticket.

'Part of the route is serviced by bus,' he called out as she stepped away from the window.

She sighed. *Great.*

THE TRAIN DEPARTED at eight-fifteen sharp. There were only a handful of passengers in her carriage, and she dropped down into her seat, closing her eyes against the harsh interior lights as the train pulled away from Barga. Andre must have discovered her note for he tried calling her several times. She let each one go to voicemail, then turned her phone on silent. She had no words left for him, for them.

The thought had occurred to her that leaving the house might provide Andre and Mary with the opportunity to be alone, a thought that left her feeling ill, even as she tried to pivot away from it by staring out the window at dark hillsides rolling by. She wouldn't be there to prevent anything happening, but she also reasoned that if her marriage had come to that, if they couldn't be trusted alone, then what kind of marriage was it anyway?

Or was she simply being an irrational, jealous person? She'd never been like this before, not with Ben. But she'd never had a reason to, she supposed, until he'd cheated. Jealousy was fuelled by insecurity, and insecurity was fuelled by past hurts. Did that mean her and her insecurities were partly to blame? Were she and Andre so out of touch with each other that someone like Mary could diffuse their marriage in as little as a week?

She didn't know what to think anymore and she spent the entire trip to Lucca, with the bus change in between, wishing, despite everything, that Andre was with her.

The train pulled into the Lucca station at ten past nine that evening. The terminal was busier there than the tiny one in Barga, with people in endless replication. She bought a coffee and a small bowl of penne napolitana and eventually found a spot to sit and eat. The train to Florence wasn't due to depart for another hour, so she had time, her stomach hollow from lack of food and her head dull and in need of caffeine.

After she ate, she rummaged in her handbag for her phone and pulled up Riley's number. In all her distress, she'd forgotten to let her know she was coming. She wanted nothing more than to see her best friend's face, to listen to her perspective or the one where she automatically sided with Belle—that was good too. She needed to know someone was in her corner, that she wasn't going crazy, that any sane, rational person would have reacted the same way to Mary and Andre's day in Chianti. To all of it. The entire holidays.

But it was then, as she was about to hit the call button, that she realised with a jolt that Riley wasn't in Florence! She'd forgotten. Riley was at Lake Como with the man she'd met at the *Nutcracker*.

'Ugh!' She groaned audibly.

The couple at the next table shot her a look. Belle muttered several curse words under her breath, trying to think of what to do. She was alone. Utterly, depressingly alone, at a train station in the middle of Tuscany, with nowhere to go. Should she go on to Florence or turn back to Barga with her tail between her legs? Should she stay in Lucca and find a hotel for the night, gather her thoughts somehow?

She flicked through her phone and found herself searching for the only other person she knew who lived in Tuscany—Emilio. She would make an appointment to see him in the morning, if he was available, even if he charged her an exorbitant fee for interrupting him during the holidays. She needed to climb out of her head, disentangle herself from her thoughts, and Emilio had always been good at helping her do that.

She dialled his number, second-guessing the idea as soon as she did, but knowing it was too late to end the call, for he would see her name on his screen.

'Belle?' he answered with surprise. 'How are you? Happy New Year.'

Tears pushed against her eyelids, emotion clogging her throat so thickly that her voice wobbled. 'Hi, Emilio. I'm so sorry for calling you on New Year's Day.'

'That's okay.' His voice was full of understanding. 'Is everything all right?'

She swallowed hard, trying not to burst into a flood of tears. 'Not really. I just... I wanted to know if...' She could barely get the words out. 'Can I see you tomorrow? I'm just feeling a little lost right now.'

There was a short pause, a clearing of the throat. 'I'm not in Pistoia, Belle. I'm away for the holidays.'

'Oh.' She shook her head, cheeks flaming with embarrassment. 'Right. I'm so sorry. Of course. That's fine.'

'Are you okay? Are you in danger?'

'No.' She shook her head again. 'Nothing like that. I just... I don't know.'

'Are you with Andre? Can I call someone for you?'

'I'm not with Andre,' she said, trying to steady her voice. 'We had a fight and I walked out. I'm not sure what I'm doing or where I'm going.'

There was a shuffle in the background, then a woman's voice that sounded oddly like... Riley's? The voice halted abruptly, then there was more shuffling, as though Emilio was on the move suddenly, leaving whatever room he'd been in.

Belle's body went from flushed to ice cold as her brain hurried to understand. Surely not. But there could be no mistaking it. She knew her friend's voice anywhere, could pick it in a room of a thousand voices. 'Where are you?' she asked.

'Excuse me?' Emilio asked.

'Where are you? Right now? On holiday.'

There was a pause. 'Belle...'

'Are you at Lake Como?'

His silence confirmed it and she knew the woman's voice she'd heard *was* Riley's. That somehow, in some other strange twist of fate, the universe had thrown her psychologist and her best friend together. 'Oh, God!' she said, her hand flying to her mouth. 'Really?'

'Belle,' Emilio said again, 'this isn't appropriate... I mean, we should probably talk about this face to face.'

'You're with Riley? *My* Riley?'

Emilio hesitated. 'Yes. Your Riley.'

'But when? How?'

'We met in Florence... and well, we only realised recently that you and her... uh.' He was stammering too. 'We were going to tell you, not like this, obviously. We need to navigate this properly, since she's your friend and I'm your therapist, and this is normally not a good idea.'

'No,' she said, stunned into disbelief. 'It's not.' Her heart was racing a million miles an hour. Riley and Emilio? Together? She was overcome with that familiar and unpleasant sensation of being on the outside looking in again. Now her friend was keeping things from her? 'I have to go,' she said suddenly, her hand shaking as it held the phone.

'Belle, wait—'

'Happy New Year,' she blurted, then hung up.

Belle stood quickly, gathering up her trash and tossing it in the bin as though she could escape what she'd just learned. Hearing Riley's voice had shocked her—she hadn't been expecting it—but there was something else there too. Betrayal. She'd been lied to by the two people she'd thought she could count on—her best friend and her psychologist. What would this mean for her therapy with Emilio? Would they have to end her sessions? And how could Riley not have told her the truth?

She walked towards the ticket queue on trembling legs, numb, dispirited, her sense of everything retreating into itself. She joined the queue, and inched forward, eventually reaching the counter.

'Destination?' the attendant said from behind the window.

And before Belle's brain could catch up with her mouth, she was uttering the words. 'A one-way ticket to Rome, please.'

TWENTY-FOUR

The train pulled into Roma Termini at three-thirty the next morning. Belle disembarked, bleary-eyed and exhausted, having had little sleep under the garish interior lights of the carriage.

By the time she reached Rome, she had twelve missed calls from Andre, six from Riley, and two from Emilio. It wasn't her intention to make them worry, but she couldn't find the right words to unpack the complexities of her relationships. Friendships were tricky, marriage trickier, and all it left her with was a deep, tangled sense of sadness that she couldn't articulate.

She climbed up the escalators to the street level, the roads and sidewalks slick with rain, even though it wasn't falling anymore. There were only a few people out. It was cold, the restaurants and bars were closed, and she breathed in the familiar smell of ancient Italy and modern-day pollution. She wasn't sure what had drawn her to Rome, only that she craved a time when things were easier, and the year she'd spent in Rome with Andre, Avery and Riley had been one of the best of her life. This time round, she was questioning everything, like Andre's love for her and Mary's motives—the girl had been undermining her since she'd arrived—even her own future in Italy. Had she ever belonged, or had she always been an outcast?

She blinked suddenly and realised that she'd walked some distance away from the station, her legs subconsciously carrying her in the direction of Piazza Navona. Working at Valentina's during the week gave her no cause to enter the piazza or Corsia Agonale, the lane where Avery used to live, for she and Andre could simply skirt around it on their way to and from the trattoria. But there she was, having arrived at Piazza Navona's southern entrance, staring at her grief head-on. Her heart began to ache indescribably, for a past lost and a future not quite found.

She crossed the piazza, fountains trickling, the air suffused with garlic and basil from the few pizzerias that had opened that evening but were now closed. Bats beat their wings overhead and she was reminded with a sharp pang of all the times she and Andre had followed these same steps, pausing at the fountains to cast wishes into them, the conversations they'd had until the sun rose.

Then she turned into Corsia Agonale, her brain telling her not to put herself through the torment, but her heart begging her to. And there it was, the small building where she'd lived for a year with Avery before Paris, looking exactly the way it had back then, as though time in that lane had stood still. Her breath caught; her hands trembled. She felt neither the cold nor the late hour, just the past rushing upon her like wild horses, making her heartsick.

Belle dropped her handbag to the ground and sat on the top step, pulling her knees up to her chest. It was the same steps she'd sat on countless times before, the concrete engrained with a thousand conversations. What Belle wouldn't give for the front door to open and for Avery to be standing there, full of mischief and life, with those golden plaits and freckles on her nose. Belle would race up the stairs and hold her and never let her go, and Avery would roll her eyes playfully and hug her back. Just to have one more second with her, one minute, one hour, one day. Belle would tell her how much she loved her and how sorry she was about Paris, because being in Belle's life had ended hers.

Tears slid down Belle's cheeks again as the weight of unbearable sadness closed in, causing her heart to fracture into a thousand pieces. She was exhausted, thirsty and cold. She hadn't eaten in hours and desperately needed sleep. She needed to lie down, close her eyes, and stave off the ache in her soul that lingered.

'I want to go home,' she whispered to the night, but she wasn't sure where that was anymore—not Sydney, Tuscany or Rome, not her old life or her new life. She was homesick for all of it, but she suspected that most of all, she was homesick for Andre.

Belle rearranged her handbag on the step, laid down, and rested her head on it. She curled herself into a ball and closed her eyes. She might not have been able to go up to the apartment, walk into her old bedroom and sleep on her old bed, but those steps were as familiar to her as any of it. The street, the building, the balcony above, everything about it was a part of her. And she missed it terribly.

Sleep came before she had a chance to acknowledge how hard or cold the concrete was.

BELLE OPENED her eyes to a kind face peering into hers. She started, sitting up, realising that the face staring at her was Uncle Benito's.

'You scared me,' she said, her heart racing in her chest. She glanced around. A slip of moon was barely visible as it inched towards the tops of the buildings, the sky slowly colouring with dawn. She realised she must have slept for a few hours.

'Belle,' Uncle Benito said, his eyes full of bewilderment. 'What are you doing out here?'

She closed her eyes, then opened them again, her body stiff and sore as though it had been put together wrong. She wondered how many people had passed her during the night and thought she was homeless or drunk.

Uncle Benito sat beside her on the step. 'Did you sleep out here?' he asked kindly.

'Not all night.' She glanced at him, confused. 'How did you find me?'

'Andre called. He's been frantic, looking for you.'

'I told him I was going to see Riley. Why would he be frantic?'

'He called Riley. She said you weren't with her.'

Belle shook her head, still confused. 'But how did Andre know I'd be here, in this exact spot?'

Uncle Benito smiled. 'He knows you better than you think.' He glanced back at Avery's apartment with sorrow. 'He knows how much you miss her, my niece.'

Belle couldn't reply. The bitter pain of loss coated her throat, making it impossible to swallow. She dragged her hands over her gritty eyes, then through her dishevelled hair, more to distract herself from the tears that were building than anything else.

Uncle Benito turned back to her, watching her closely. 'Andre told me you and he fought.'

Belle raised her eyebrows. 'That's an understatement.'

'Why didn't you come to my apartment? Why did you sleep here on the steps?'

She shrugged. 'I don't know. Because nowhere feels like home right now.' A stubborn tear slipped from her lashes and dripped onto her cheek.

She swiped it away, but not before Uncle Benito saw it and nodded sadly. 'You're homesick?'

She swallowed a sob. 'I guess.'

'The last year has been hard for you.' It wasn't a question.

'I hadn't thought so. But maybe I was wrong. Maybe I don't belong here.'

He sighed heavily. 'It's my fault.'

She glanced at him. 'Why do you say that?'

'Because I should have welcomed you more.' He looked ashamed. 'You know I love you like a daughter, but I haven't always made it easy for you.'

She nudged him. 'It's okay. I know I wasn't your first choice for Andre.'

He didn't laugh at her half-joke. Instead, he blinked sorrowfully. 'That's true. You weren't. I feared what a long-distance relationship would do to him. I thought it would break his heart. Mary was a safer option.' He drew in deep breath, shaking his head. 'But anyone can see what you mean to him. You're his entire world; you have been from the start. I didn't trust in that. I tried for a long time to make him love someone else. I was a fool!'

Belle watched him, surprised by his candour.

'When you arrived here a year ago, and he told me he was going to propose, I was happy for you both, truly. And I loved you as I should have always loved you. Like a daughter. Like family. But I still should have tried harder, done more for you.' His eyes grew shiny, and he cleared his throat. 'It's not right that you only had Andre when you got here. You should have had me too. As your father-in-law.'

'I don't blame you for any of this,' she said. 'The fight Andre and I had was about Mary, not you.'

'Still, if you'd felt secure, you wouldn't have had a reason to doubt him.'

Maybe, but maybe not. Andre had taken Mary to Chianti when he shouldn't have, had allowed her to come between them, had continually defended her actions. That's what had broken them in the end. But perhaps their fight hadn't been just about Mary. Perhaps it had been a culmination of lots of things—her PTSD and homesickness, feeling like a foreigner, and the baby they struggled to have. Maybe that was enough to put their marriage under strain and Mary had simply been the card that had toppled it.

'You love him, don't you?' Uncle Benito asked.

Belle didn't hesitate. 'More than anything. But I'm not sure he feels the same way.' Saying the words out loud made her soul feel hollow. 'I don't think we'll ever have what he and Mary have.' A natural connection born from their childhood years together.

'Andre and Mary have known each other a long time, yes,' Uncle Benito conceded carefully, 'and she was devastated when he ended their engagement. We all were, her parents and me. But as much as it used to upset me, I see it now. Andre doesn't love Mary; he never did, not like he loves you. And I'm good with that. But it angers Teresa because she's holding onto the past.'

Belle gave a soft snort. Teresa was a whole other subject.

'I know she was tough on you over Christmas and that was my fault too. I should never have invited them knowing how she felt about you. It wasn't fair to put you through that.' He glanced at her with broken-hearted conviction. 'No one should treat my daughter that way.'

Belle leaned her head against his shoulder, and he reached across and patted her hair in a fatherly way. 'It's your house, Papà. You can invite anyone you like.'

'Ah,' he wiggled his finger at her, 'but it's also *your* house. Yours and Andre's. And I should have asked you first. I'm sorry.'

Although they'd been sitting on the step for only half an hour, she felt as if they'd climbed a mountain of revelations. Still, as daylight crept over the horizon, casting the spires and campaniles in a peach sunrise, she was more confused than ever. There were many things about her fight with Andre that were unresolved, questions about him and Mary that she wanted to ask but didn't want to know the answers to, like if he'd resurrected old feelings for her. Deep down, Andre was the only one who could say.

'What would you like to do?' Uncle Benito asked as though sensing her thoughts.

She shrugged and shook her head. 'I want to go back to Sydney.'

He looked surprised and saddened. 'Really?'

'Yes.' She sighed. 'But only because it's easier than dealing with everything.' Andre, Mary, Teresa, Riley, Emilio.

He nodded with understanding. 'Will you let me take you home first? To Tuscany?'

Home. Tuscany. His words settled on her like an unexpected blanket. She met his eyes and saw in them what she needed desperately—a father. Someone to hold her hand

and guide her, to give her advice and to love her. And she needed Andre. No matter what they'd been through, she needed him, and she suspected that he needed her too.

She nodded, a solemn tear trickling down her cheek that she didn't wipe away. 'Okay, let's go home.'

TWENTY-FIVE

Belle napped for the first part of the journey back to Barga, Uncle Benito waking her near Montallese for food and coffee. Afterwards, she remained awake, and they talked about Valentina's and the pipe bursting in the kitchen, skirting any mention of Andre and Mary, which Belle was thankful for. She was too emotionally drained to contemplate her crumbling marriage or what would be waiting for her when she got home. If Andre was angry, if he wanted her to leave, if she even wanted to stay.

The sun was high in the sky when they arrived, cold buttery sunshine drenching the hills in the distance, a light breeze shifting the pencil pines that bookended the house. Andre's car was out the front as they rolled up the driveway. Uncle Benito parked beside it and shut the engine off.

They climbed out of the car and walked to the front door, Belle letting them in with her key. The living room was warm, a low fire crackling behind the grate. Andre was sitting on the sofa and he glanced up when they entered, rising to his feet.

Uncle Benito shrugged out of his coat, hung it on the

coat rack, and walked to his son. They embraced, exchanging a murmur of words before Uncle Benito clapped his hands together. 'Who wants espresso?' He must have sensed that he needed to make himself scarce, for he strode purposefully to the kitchen and out of sight.

Belle met Andre's eyes and saw her hurt and confusion mirrored in them. 'Where's Mary?' she asked.

'She took Sebastian for a walk.'

'And you didn't go with them?' She cringed. Her remark sounded like a cheap shot, but she'd only meant it as conversational, something to ease the awkwardness.

Andre's expression tightened. 'No, I didn't want to go.'

Belle nodded, sighed, glanced around, anywhere but his eyes. Her hands were clasped in front of her, fingers locked together. There was a stretch of deep silence that neither of them filled. She didn't know what to say or where to start, and she suspected he didn't either.

'Why did you leave last night?' he finally asked.

'Because I needed to,' she said. 'I was hurt.'

'You wrote on the note that you were going to Riley's, but I called her, and she was at Lake Como.'

'I didn't remember that until I got to Lucca. I decided to go to Rome instead.' She wasn't sure if Riley had told Andre about Emilio, although she suspected she had. It was just another thing she would have to work through, but there were too many other things jostling for space in her brain at the moment.

'You should have called me,' he said. 'I would have come and picked you up. You didn't have to go to Avery's old place.'

'I wasn't ready to see you. I wanted to go somewhere familiar. Somewhere that felt like home.'

'*This* is your home,' he said, stepping forward, eyes imploring hers like a searchlight. 'Here, with me.'

'Is it?' She met his gaze directly.

He flinched, shoulders dropping. She walked to the sofa and took a seat. He lowered himself beside her and they sat there, close, legs not quite touching. Mere millimetres and yet they spoke volumes, like oceans were separating them once again.

'What's happening to us?' he asked, his voice thick with emotion.

She glanced at him, the love of her life, and had no answer. Somehow, a single thread had been pulled and they'd unravelled. 'I'm not sure,' she replied honestly. 'All I know is that Mary's tried to come between us, and you've let her.'

'How can I *let* that happen if I can't see it?'

'So you think it's all in my head? I've imagined the things she's been doing?'

He closed his eyes. When he opened them again, there was an odd sense of hopelessness etched in them. 'I'm not saying that you've imagined them. But you think Mary is here for one reason—because she's still in love with me. She hasn't said or done anything to give me that impression.'

'So going with you to look at wedding rooms while I'm not there is a normal thing to do?'

'She offered to come with me. I didn't think anything of it.'

'You don't look at wedding venues with another woman's husband, especially when that man is your ex.'

'How am I supposed to know that?'

'It's common sense,' she said. 'What about Florence?'

'The pram wouldn't fit in the café,' he said.

'We offered to help her with Sebastian. She refused

because she knew you'd never let her walk around Florence on her own.' The memory of Mary standing in the piazza eating hot chestnuts with Andre still made her blood hot. 'The watch she gave you, then. This is not all in my head.'

Both their gazes fell to his wrist. He'd taken Mary's watch off and had replaced it with his own again.

Belle looked away and took a deep breath. She was overwhelmingly exhausted. 'Why did you take her to Chianti yesterday?'

He gave her a pained expression. 'I didn't think you wanted to go.'

'I had a migraine, Andre.'

'I know.' He grimaced. 'But you've been resisting the wedding all year. I got it in my head that you weren't interested. And Mary was excited to go...' He trailed off and sighed heavily. 'I shouldn't have taken her, that was wrong, but it wasn't because I wanted to spend the day with her. I took her because I wanted to see the place where I'd marry you again. And I wanted company on the drive. That's all.'

'You should have waited for me,' she said. 'I would have waited for you.'

His eyes were full of self-recrimination. 'I know. I'm sorry. It was stupid.' He rubbed his forehead as though staving off a headache. 'And I shouldn't have worn the watch she gave me. I wasn't thinking.'

Everything about his apology was sincere, but she couldn't let him take the blame entirely. She hadn't been a saint either. 'I'm sorry as well.'

He looked confused. 'For what?'

'For making you think I didn't want to celebrate our wedding. I *have* been resisting, but not because I don't want to marry you again.'

'Then why?'

She gave him a sheepish look. 'Because I'm scared.'

He turned his whole body to face her. 'Scared of what?'

'Of all of it. Of people and a wedding that would become bigger than me. I'm scared of not being able to cope, of losing control, of becoming swallowed by it.'

'Our wedding isn't Paris, my love,' he said gently.

'I know. But I...' Her lower lip trembled, and tears flooded her eyes, dripping onto her cheeks.

'Oh, Belle...' He looked crestfallen, wrapping his arm around her and drawing her into him. 'Why didn't you tell me?'

'Because I didn't want to acknowledge it myself,' she said. 'Because then all my hard work this past year would have been for nothing.'

'It's not for nothing,' he said, resting his chin on her head. 'You've made good progress; even I can see that. But if the idea of a big wedding was frightening you, you should have told me.'

She nodded and dabbed her cheeks and nose with her sleeve. 'Mary was excited about Chianti,' she said. 'I knew at that point I couldn't tell you the truth. I would have just been a disappointment to you.'

'You would never be that. God, Belle, don't you know me by now?'

He was right. She should have trusted him. It had never just been about the expense of a huge wedding or that she'd never met half of the guests. It had been about Paris, plain and simple. She should have trusted him enough to tell him the truth.

'You're right. I should have mentioned it sooner,' she said. 'All I did was make it worse. Sometimes I think you ended up with all my broken parts.'

He gave her a small smile. 'I love your broken parts.'

She elbowed him.

'Let's make a promise to each other,' he said, 'to always be honest. To talk more, even about things that are crazy and stupid and that scare us. Because I can't lose you, Belle. You're my whole world.'

The love in his voice made her eyes well and she buried her face into the clean cotton of his shirt, trying not to drench it in tears. She was emotionally and physically drained—bone-weary, her heart bled dry. Maybe she'd become *too* good at compartmentalising things—Ben, Avery, Paris, her father, her complicated grief. She'd stored the past in neat little boxes for so long, placing them high up on the shelves of her subconscious, but she was learning that it took the slightest tremor to bring them toppling down around her. That was PTSD. She would never be free of it, would just need to get better at managing it. She supposed it was something to keep working on with Emilio, until she remembered that he was dating Riley now and that she'd probably need to find a new psychologist.

'So where to from here?' he asked, solemnity in his expression.

She inhaled shakily, needing an answer to a question that still plagued her. 'I want to ask you something, and I need an honest answer.'

'Okay,' he said.

'Do you still feel something for Mary?' she asked. 'Even just a little? Did spending time with Sebastian make you think about her in ways that you shouldn't have? I won't be angry. I just need to know.'

He shook his head. 'Belle, no.'

'I know how badly you want children. And clearly, Mary can have babies. So I would understand if being with her and Sebastian confused you a bit... attracted you to her again.' She faltered on those last words. It killed her to say them, but she was determined to see it from his perspective. She was faulty goods after all and if he had known that before he proposed, would he still have?

Andre reached for her hands and held them tight in his, forcing her to look at him. 'No,' he said, firmer this time. 'Not once. Not ever. Mary is my friend. God, she's like my sister.'

'You were engaged once. She's hardly like your sister.'

He pursed his lips. 'You know what I mean. Mary loves Dante. The father of her baby.'

Belle wasn't convinced that Mary did love Dante, but she *was* convinced that Andre's feelings for her were platonic. Her soul calmed and her heart settled a little, not quite so bruised with hurt. It helped to hear the ferocity in his words, the way his eyes met hers directly and didn't waver. There was no guilt in his expression, and she would know if he was lying, like she knew every emotion that made his dimples hollow and his eyes crinkle, the shadows that crossed his face when he was uncertain. And right now, there was nothing uncertain about his relationship with Mary.

'I'll take her and Sebastian home tomorrow,' Andre said.

Belle nodded, disappointed that it had come to this. 'I think that would be best.'

He reached out and traced his fingertips gently down her cheek, his countenance full of regret. 'I really am sorry I missed your anniversary the other day.'

She gave him a half-shrug. 'It doesn't matter. It was stupid anyway.'

He pulled back. 'It wasn't stupid. It was a special day and I ruined it.'

'It wasn't your fault. And I was just embarrassed sitting there on my own.'

'I know you were. You had every right to be.'

'As long as you don't miss our first wedding anniversary,' she said, waving her finger at him. 'That's the important one.'

He laughed. 'That one I definitely won't miss.' He gave her an abashed look. 'Were you going to leave me?'

She met his eyes, knowing she might well break his heart with her response. 'I was thinking about it.'

He dropped his gaze, his Adam's apple shifting with emotion. 'And now?'

She glanced down at her wedding and engagement rings and thought of all the years they'd waited to be together, how much she loved Andre, and how much she loved living in Italy. She wouldn't let anyone make her doubt her marriage or her life here again. 'You lucked out,' she said. 'I'm staying if you'll have me.'

His face split into a wide grin and he leaned across the sofa, pulling him to her. His lips were on hers, then on the top of her head, burying himself in her hair, kissing her all over. He held her so tight that she almost couldn't breathe. But she didn't move. Not an inch. Because there may have been little left to say, but there was a lifetime of words in that embrace.

TWENTY-SIX

Belle was in the kitchen an hour later, cradling a cup of coffee, watching light outside the window recede over the trees like silk. Earlier she'd showered and dressed in clean clothes, then Uncle Benito had made her a bowl of hot pasta that she'd been ordered to sit down and eat. She was glad she had. Her hollow insides were now warm and full; she felt human again.

Andre was out on the driveway with his father, the hood lifted on the Fiat, checking an oil leak. Their voices drifted occasionally through the open front door into the kitchen. Mary was somewhere with Sebastian. She'd returned from her walk and had avoided Belle, slinking like a cat upstairs and out of sight. It was for the best. Belle had nothing to say to her, that was civil anyway.

She returned her attention to the afternoon outside but was interrupted when Mary entered the kitchen. The girl halted, as though startled to find Belle standing there.

'I thought you were outside,' Mary said tentatively. Her eyes darted away like she wanted to flee. 'Sebastian's asleep. I was going to make a coffee.'

Belle ignored her and gazed back out the window. She heard Mary move to the coffee machine, fill the portafilter with coffee grounds and tamp it. A cup was removed from the cupboard, the milk jug taken from the fridge. Uncomfortable silence.

'Andre wanted to take you home,' Belle said.

The activity by the coffee machine stilled.

'After Florence. He said he'd take you home because having you here was causing problems. And I told him no. I wanted to give you the benefit of the doubt in case I'd been wrong about you. Turns out, I wasn't wrong. Was I?' She turned to face Mary, fixing a piercing stare on her.

Mary blanched. 'Andre wanted to take me home?'

'Yes. And I let you stay. Stupid me.'

Mary swallowed, glanced down at the milk jug in her hand, then lifted her chin, eyes defiant. 'Don't blame me because you and Andre are fighting.'

Belle scoffed loudly. 'Are you kidding? The only reason we've fought is because of you. Ever since you and your mother arrived, all we've done is fight.'

Mary's eyebrows lifted but she didn't reply.

'Why are you really here?' Belle asked, placing her coffee cup on the bench, then leaning back against it, crossing her arms.

'Because I wanted company over the holidays.'

'You should have left with your parents when the pipe burst at Valentina's.'

Mary's mouth fell open at Belle's directness. 'You're acting like I've done something wrong.'

'Are you going to tell me I've imagined the whole thing?' Belle retorted. 'The watch you gave Andre for Christmas, enticing him to walk around Florence with you, the trip to Chianti to see *our* wedding venue.'

'You weren't able to go so I went with him.'

'Don't pretend like you were doing me a favour. You went because you wanted to spend the day with Andre, alone.'

Mary appeared speechless again. She stared at Belle, then looked away, down into the milk jug.

'Well?' Belle asked.

Mary shrugged. 'It's been hard without Dante here.'

'That's not an answer. You don't come into someone's home and make a play for their husband because you miss yours.'

'That's not what I was doing,' Mary said vehemently.

'Oh, come on. You never stopped wanting Andre. But he's moved on. And you need to as well. For God's sake you're married.'

Tears filled Mary's eyes and she chewed her bottom lip, then turned back to the coffee machine. But she didn't make her coffee. She stared down at her hands, bravado deflated, hair hanging limply in her face. Compassion rippled through Belle, softening her anger, but she tried to ignore it because she didn't want to feel sorry for Mary.

'We fought before I came here.'

Belle stared at the back of her, confused. 'What?'

'Dante and me. We fought.' Mary turned around to face her. 'Right before he left to go away with the navy, and I came here with my parents. I said I wanted to leave him.' She sniffed, wiping her nose with her sleeve.

Belle shook her head. 'I'm sorry, but I really don't care.'

'We've been fighting a lot.'

'Like I said—'

'He's away so often,' Mary continued. 'I'm trying, I really am, but it's hard to make a marriage work with a husband who's a stranger.'

'That doesn't mean you come into someone else's home and try to break up theirs.'

'I wasn't doing that.' She gave a panicked, defeated sort of sigh. 'Well, maybe... I don't know.' She fell back against the bench, dropping her face into her hands. Then a muffled sound erupted from behind them. 'I actually don't know what I'm doing.'

Belle watched her, slightly dumbfounded.

'I'm not an awful person,' Mary pleaded, dropping her hands and staring at Belle.

'I don't think you're an awful person. I just don't trust you.'

'I haven't given you a reason to.' She sniffed again, her eyes pooling with tears. 'I didn't come here meaning to cause problems. But when I arrived, I was upset with Dante and I just...' She exhaled a long, unsteady breath. 'I just remembered how Andre and I used to be. How easy our relationship was.'

'So you came here hoping to revive it?' Belle asked, feeling a rush of indignation again.

'I don't know,' Mary said with a hopeless shrug. 'Being here with him has confused me, made me wish I could turn back time. And my mother, she's never liked Dante. She was in my ear, telling me that Andre might still have feelings for me. And I let it make me feel good again.' She placed her hands over her face and groaned into them. 'God, I'm so embarrassed admitting this to you.'

'You should be,' Belle said. 'And you shouldn't blame your mother for all of it. You did inexcusable things too. I invited you into my home.'

Mary wiped her eyes, looking deeply ashamed.

'And you came here with one intention. To ruin my marriage. What would Dante think if he knew?'

Her eyes widened. 'He'd be horrified.'

'He would be.' They might not have had a perfect start to their marriage, but she was his wife. Any man would be heartbroken by the emotional cheating.

'I'm so sorry Belle,' Mary said, fresh tears welling. 'I don't even know what to say.'

'I can't have you or your mother here again.'

She cried softly, small sobs making her shoulders quake. 'I understand.'

'And you should go back to Rome. The sooner the better.'

Mary's shoulders slumped.

'But I need to know something first.'

She glanced up. 'What's that?'

'Did Andre ever give you a reason to hope?'

She inclined her head. 'What do you mean?'

'Did he encourage you, tell you that he...?' She couldn't finish the sentence.

Mary shook her head emphatically. 'No, Belle. It was all me. You don't need to worry about that. Andre loves you. Anyone can see it.' She looked down at her hands, twisted together, and sighed. 'You might not believe me, but I didn't want to take him from you. I just...' she shrugged miserably, 'I just missed what we used to have. I guess, for a few days, I wanted to feel close to him again.'

Belle wasn't sure she believed that, not entirely, but she was too exhausted to argue about it anymore. She was deeply relieved that Andre had been faithful, that he hadn't encouraged Mary. That she could trust him unreservedly, and she did. He'd made some naïve choices, but they were forgivable. An emotional, not to mention physical, affair was not.

Mary gave Belle a small conciliatory smile and turned

back to the coffee machine. 'Would you like another coffee?' It was a peace offering.

Belle glanced down at her cup on the bench next to her, still half-full, lukewarm. 'No thank you.'

Mary nodded. 'I'll make this, then go upstairs and pack.'

Footsteps sounded in the dining room, then Andre appeared in the kitchen. He wiped oily hands on an old rag. 'There you both are.' He glanced at each of them warily. 'Is everything okay?'

Mary stole a glance at Belle. 'I guess.'

He flicked the rag over his shoulder. 'Mary, you have a visitor.'

She blinked. 'I do? Is it my parents?'

'No, Dante.'

Mary stilled, went pale. 'Dante?'

'He drove in just then.'

'Oh.' She placed the sugar jar down by the coffee machine and swallowed. 'I had no idea he was coming.'

'Well, he's here.'

Yes.' She cleared her throat. 'I suppose I should go out to him.'

Andre frowned. 'Of course you should.'

Mary nodded, tucked a wayward strand of hair behind her ear, and strode out of the kitchen.

Andre raised an eyebrow at Belle. 'What's up with her?'

'We got a few things off our chest,' Belle said, tipping her cold coffee down the sink and rinsing the mug. 'I'll tell you later. What's Dante doing here?'

'I have no idea. I guess he got early leave from the navy.' He held his arm out for her and she walked across the kitchen and stepped into it. He drew her close to him and kissed the top of her head. 'My love,' he murmured.

'I'm tired.'

'Me too.'

They walked together to the living room, finding Uncle Benito climbing the stairs in a huff. He paused and threw the front drive a grimace. 'Don't go out there. They're having a big argument.'

He disappeared upstairs and Belle walked to the window, parting the curtain discreetly to peer out. Dante was standing by the Fiat in his naval uniform, a duffel bag on the ground beside him. Mary was telling him in Italian that she was struggling with their marriage. He frowned, hands on his hips, shaking his head. When Mary began to cry, Dante's posture softened.

'Why don't we give them some space?' Belle said to Andre, letting the curtain drop just as Dante's arms went around Mary.

TWENTY-SEVEN

Although they'd both had little sleep the night before, Belle and Andre decided to walk, taking their usual route down to the stream, where roe deer grazed on wild grass, then they headed up to the hills. The cold afternoon air was cleansing, the sun sinking behind the landscape, dragging the light with it, plunging the sky and forest into a riot of colour.

'What were you and Mary talking about earlier?' Andre asked as they journeyed up the hillside.

'Lots of things,' Belle replied.

'I think she and Dante are having problems.'

'They are,' she said. 'And I called her out on her behaviour. She didn't deny it.'

His brow creased. 'What do you mean?'

'She told me she's been uncertain about her marriage, and she thought she'd like to be with you again. That you might like to be with her.'

He stopped walking and faced her, a surprised look on his face. 'She *said* that?'

'Yes.'

He blinked, then frowned.

'You can ask her if you want.'

Andre shook his head. 'No, I believe you. I just...' He seemed lost for words. 'I'm shocked.' Then realisation crossed his face, and he held up his hands in defence. 'I swear, I never gave her a reason to think that. I never encouraged her.'

Belle reached for both of his hands, pulling them down. 'I know. She was confused. She'd had a fight with Dante and Teresa was in her ear, telling her things.'

'Teresa,' he muttered. 'Still, that's no excuse. Mary's a grown woman. A *married* woman. She should know better.' He ran a hand through his hair. 'I thought it was just nice to have my friend back without the pressure of her wanting more. I never thought...' He trailed off, an expression of intense concentration on his face. Belle could almost hear his thoughts ticking over, replaying the moments he'd spent with Mary in his head and seeing them in a new light.

'I did try to tell you,' she said gently, without accusation.

He closed his eyes and breathed deeply before opening them again. 'You did. And I didn't want to hear it. I kept defending her. Pathetic.'

'You try to see the good in people. I won't ever hold that against you.'

'You can. I should have listened.' He shook his head, still looking bewildered. 'She didn't say she was unhappy with Dante. In fact, I thought she seemed very happy.'

'Happy to be spending time with you.'

'She never made a move. I promise. Otherwise, I would have said something to her. I would have told you.'

'I guess she was more subtle around you than me.'

He winced apologetically. 'I'll speak to Dante tonight. They can go home tomorrow.'

'I think they should.'

With the sun finally setting, they headed back down the hill towards home. In the distance, the lights of the farmhouse lit up the property, guiding their way. When they reached the back door, they kicked off their shoes, greeted by the scent of fresh bread and something tomatoey cooking on the stove.

'You're back,' Uncle Benito called out from the kitchen. 'Just in time. Dinner's ready.'

They sat down at the table to eat, Mary beside Dante, Sebastian awake in his father's arms, wide-eyed and mesmerised by his face. Dante's gaze dropped often to his son, his long, large fingers touching the child's milky cheek, stroking his tiny head. Mary was quiet throughout the meal, watching them intently while she picked at her cacciatore, an almost bewildered expression on her face.

After dinner, they helped Uncle Benito clean up then, while everyone retreated to the living room to drink more wine, Belle slipped into her coat and out the back door to sit on the step. The moon was large and glowing in the sky, stars in their billions painted across a black canvas. She sank further into her coat, letting the snap of cold sting her cheeks and clear her head. She breathed it deeply into her lungs.

It was the moment she needed to collect her thoughts and be alone. A lot had taken place in such a short time that she'd barely had a moment to register it. Things had been said and done, maybe to be forgiven but not forgotten. What she didn't want to do was dwell. She'd spent years dwelling on past hurts—Paris, the loss of her friends and father—and she knew she couldn't cling to this hurt with Mary if any of them had a hope of moving past it.

Her solitude was interrupted when the back door opened and Mary stepped out, staring down at her with a cup of coffee in her hands. 'May I sit with you?' she asked.

Belle shuffled over on the step, allowing room for Mary to drop down beside her. They both stared in silence up at the sky.

'It's pretty out here,' Mary said.

Belle nodded. 'It is.'

Mary sipped her coffee, then wrapped her hands around the cup. 'I told Dante everything.'

Belle glanced at her. 'Everything?'

'Yes, this afternoon. About my behaviour, what I did, how I disrespected you... and him.' Her expression contorted in shame. 'He was devastated.'

Belle raised her eyebrows, turning to stare out at the night again.

'I thought he was going to take Sebastian and leave me. I've never seen him so upset before.'

'Can you blame him?'

'Of course not.'

'No one wants to learn that their wife has been thinking about another man.'

Mary swallowed, looking down into her coffee. 'I'm the worst kind of person.'

'At least you told him. Most people wouldn't have.'

'I don't want to lose him.' She bore her gaze into Belle, almost imploring her to believe the words. 'Despite what you think of me, I need you to know that.'

'And will you lose him after what you told him?'

Mary sniffed, then shrugged. 'Once he got over the shock of it, he said he understood. We've had our challenges, but we both want our marriage to work, even if what I did was inexcusable.'

'He sounds like a good man.'

'He's more than I deserve. I'm going to make things right.'

Belle met her eyes with conviction. 'Then make them right.'

LATER UP IN THEIR ROOM, Belle was changing into her pyjamas while Andre was folding clean laundry. The house was quiet; everyone had retreated to their beds. It had been the longest day, hard for Belle to believe that less than twenty-four hours earlier she'd been at the Lucca station calling Emilio and learning about Riley, then boarding a train to Rome.

'I spoke to Dante tonight,' Andre said, putting a pile of his underwear away in a drawer. 'He said Mary told him everything. They're going to leave for Rome first thing in the morning.'

Belle pulled her pyjama top over her head. She didn't reply and Andre narrowed his eyes at her. 'What?' she said.

He frowned. 'Don't say it.'

'Say what?'

'That you want them to stay.'

'I didn't say anything.'

'You didn't have to. I can see it all over your face.'

She smiled. 'How can you?'

'Because I know you better than anyone. And the answer is no. They're *not* staying.'

Belle grimaced. 'It's just that I was thinking—'

'God, Belle.' Andre threw his hands up in the air. 'You did this last time. I offered to take them home and you said no. And look what happened. Why would you want them to stay?'

'Because Dante's here now and don't you think they need this? To make things right. Time for the three of them to be together without Teresa interfering?' As the words tumbled out, she knew how crazy they sounded, especially after everything that had happened. But since speaking to Mary outside on the step, she'd been thinking a lot about her and Dante. She knew if they went back to Rome, they wouldn't stand a chance with Teresa's meddling.

'That's not my problem,' Andre said. 'And it's not yours either.'

'No, you're right, it's not,' she agreed, 'but I want them to have a chance, to be happy.'

'So you've forgiven her?'

Belle's nose twitched. 'Not forgiven, but I can understand why she did it.'

Andre put his hands on his hips and dropped his head, exhaling with exasperation.

'Have you forgiven her?' Belle asked, stepping towards him.

He glanced down at her, eyes heavy with exhaustion. 'I don't know. I feel betrayed and stupid. Because of her, I let you down. Because I'm an *idiot*, I let you down.'

She pulled him towards her and wrapped her arms around his waist. 'We were both stupid. But I think for us all to move on, they should stay.'

He sighed deeply. 'I don't want this blowing up in our faces again, Belle.'

'It won't. I feel certain that everything will be better now that Dante's here. He's trying to move past it. We should try too.'

'Most people would just want them gone. You're too nice.'

She shrugged coquettishly as Andre's hands cupped her

face and he kissed her gently. Then he pulled away and stared into her eyes so intently, her heart galloped.

'My love for you terrifies me sometimes,' he whispered.

'Mine does too,' she whispered back. That almost painful love that was at times simple and sublime, and at others, an ocean of complicated need. She loved this man with her entire being, the closeness they shared unlocking the deepest parts of her soul in a way she struggled at times to comprehend.

She pushed herself to him, every inch of her skin wanting his touch suddenly, her lips wanting his mouth. His hands found the hem of her pyjama top, drawing it up slowly over her shoulders and head, discarding it on the floor. She repaid the favour, helping him out of his sweater, so they were shivering against each other. His fingers glided down her neck and along her collarbone, his slow caress, reverent and solemn, as gentle as time, making the nerves in her body rustle to life.

His fingers moved to her pyjama pants, pushing them down slowly. As she climbed out of them, he abandoned his jeans, then in one smooth motion, he picked her up, her legs wrapped around his hips, and he carried her to the bed. He lowered her gently down, his body moving over the top of hers, lips finding the hollow in her neck.

'I can't lose you again,' he said, his voice full of uncertainty and desperation.

'You won't,' she said, every emotion, every desire, racing to the surface.

'It killed me not knowing where you were last night.'

'It killed me thinking you wanted someone else.'

He closed his eyes, then opened again, anguish stamped all over his features. 'I could never...'

He didn't finish the words and she didn't need him to.

They'd always shared a complex love, deep and daunting and bigger than both of them, but if there was one thing she was learning, it was that Andre's love for her wasn't all that complicated. It was raw and fierce and protective, but it was also pure. The purest, most devoted kind of love she'd ever known.

He removed her underwear, then his, and made love to her in that same pure and flawless way, taking them both to the edge and back again. Later, as they lay with the sheets carelessly draped across them, staring at each other, warmth filling all the holes the past week had left in them, Andre smiled.

'My beautiful Belle,' he murmured. 'I've loved you for so long.'

She smiled too. 'Grow old with me?'

He delivered his answer on a careful and adoring kiss. *Of course I will.*

They laid like that for a time, the room dark. Belle was unbearably tired, her muscles growing heavy and lethargic, eyelids closing.

'Have you spoken to Riley?' Andre asked.

She was coaxed awake by the question and shook her head. 'Not yet.'

Riley had left several messages for Belle to call her back, but she hadn't returned them. She hadn't a clue how to approach the situation with Emilio, if sessions with him were possible now that he was seeing her best friend. She didn't want to be the reason they couldn't be together and yet, a small part of her still needed him. There was so much she wanted to tell him about the holidays and Mary and Andre, and the thought of not being able to do that after Epiphany, of having to start fresh with someone new, was enough to put her off the idea. She was tempted not to bother with therapy again, to leave it behind, despite knowing she still needed it.

'You should call her,' Andre said. 'I'm sure she feels terrible.'

Belle rolled back onto her side to face him. 'I know she does. And I will. I've just been dealing with one thing at a time.'

'Tomorrow then,' he said, not letting her off the hook.

She gave him a reluctant smile. 'Yes, tomorrow.'

TWENTY-EIGHT

Before Belle had a chance to make her first coffee of the morning or to consider calling Riley, there was a knock on her bedroom door. She was making the bed; her brown hair still damp from the shower she'd had after her walk with Andre.

She turned to find her best friend standing in the doorway, looking hesitant. 'Hey,' Riley said.

Belle dropped the pillow she'd been holding onto the bed and gave her a small smile. 'Hey.'

'Can I come in?'

'Sure.'

Riley stepped into the room. She looked around, as though she wasn't sure what to do. Her fingers were locked together, her expression tight. She wore jeans and a navy and white striped sweater, her long dark hair pulled back into a messy high bun. She wore no makeup but was still effortlessly beautiful in a way that only Riley could be, with her high cheekbones and deep green gaze.

'You're here early,' Belle said, more to sever the awkwardness than anything more. It was nine o'clock. Lake

Como was five hours north, which meant Riley would have left before dawn that morning.

'Actually, we left Lake Como yesterday. I stayed in Pistoia last night. At Emilio's.' She averted her gaze as she said this, chewing the inside of her cheek.

'Ah,' Belle said, taking a seat on the edge of the bed. 'I hope you didn't cut your trip short on my account.'

Riley took a step forward and shrugged. 'Well, you did worry us when you called from the station. But we were planning to come back anyway. Emilio wanted to go into the office. And I spoke to Andre. He said you were okay.'

'So Emilio's not here?' Belle asked. She'd wondered if he was downstairs, socialising with the very people she spoke about in her sessions—Mary, Andre, Uncle Benito—and she realised all over again how precarious their situation had become.

'No, he's not. We thought it best if I came alone.'

Riley walked to the bed and lowered herself down beside Belle. 'I'm sorry that you found out the way you did,' she said, clasping her hands in her lap. 'I should have said something sooner. I think Emilio and I were both in shock once we put two and two together.'

'How did you work it out?' Belle asked.

Riley smiled ruefully. 'He figured it out before I did. I'd told him all about you, obviously, and there aren't too many Belles in Barga. Finally, he told me that he'd been working with you for the past year. I'd had no idea. I'm sure you'd told me your psychologist's name in the past, but I hadn't taken much notice. I was always more interested in how you were doing than the names of people.'

She could imagine Riley and Emilio having that conversation—Riley freaking out and Emilio calmly, patiently, trying to assess the situation. It was a perplexing thought imagining them together, both from different parts of her life, like two ends of a straight line forming a circle when they really shouldn't. Because Emilio was part of her life, but still separate. That's what made therapy work.

'Your sessions are important to him,' Riley said. 'We didn't tell you straight away because he was working out what to do about it. It blurs the boundaries of your therapist-client bond.'

'It does,' Belle agreed. 'It's become a dual relationship. Through you, he and I have a connection outside of therapy.'

'Yes, that's what he called it too. A dual relationship. It's considered unethical.'

Belle shrugged. 'I guess the client would be worried that their private sessions would become other people's knowledge. Did he tell you the things we talked about?'

'Of course not,' Riley said adamantly. 'And I would never have let him. Belle, he's professional. And he's devastated by this. We both are.'

'It doesn't matter anyway,' Belle conceded. 'It's not like you don't know everything about me.'

'Still,' Riley insisted, 'he never once spoke about your sessions. That's between you and him.' She sighed deeply. 'Anyway, we're going to end things.'

Belle inhaled sharply. 'End things? Isn't that a bit premature?'

'There's no other way to fix this. Emilio and I have discussed it. The last thing we want to do is jeopardise your therapy.'

'I'll find a new therapist. They're a dime a dozen in Tuscany,' Belle said, as light-heartedly as she could. The truth was, it would be difficult to start over with someone new, but she would try, for Riley.

'You know it's not going to be easy starting over,' Riley said. 'We would never ask you to do that. I'm the one who came in late, so I'm the one who should bow out.'

'That's ridiculous.' Belle shook her head. 'We'll find a way.'

'It's not a big deal,' Riley insisted. 'Emilio and I have known each other less than two weeks. A fling, really, in the scheme of things.' She smiled, but it was touched with sadness. 'I'm not a relationship kind of girl, you know that. It's not worth risking your therapy over.'

A stretch of silence followed, the weight of everything unspoken settling between them. Riley might not be the relationship kind, but when she fell for someone, when that one person penetrated her armour, her whole heart became invested. And quickly.

'Do you like him?' Belle asked eventually.

Riley shrugged, but that small, insignificant action said so much more, a doorway into her soul.

Belle reached for her hand and squeezed it. 'Then I promise we'll find a way.'

TWENTY-NINE

Four days later, on a blustery winter's day, Epiphany arrived, chasing the mild weather of the new year away.

Belle and Andre were in the kitchen. He was making coffee and she was stirring caramelised apples on the stove. She'd learned over her time in Italy that Epiphany was a day of sweets, and she honoured the custom, rising early to make biscuits, sugared pastries and small spiced cakes with cinnamon and blood orange. She'd prepared dinner too—fresh gnocchi rolled and ready for the napolitana sauce, ravioli stuffed with duck, a ball of pasta resting for the seafood spaghetti, and several antipasto platters loaded with Tuscan cheeses and salamis. It was Three Kings Day, and therefore, on Epiphany, everyone ate like a king.

'Here's your coffee,' Andre said, setting an espresso down beside her on the benchtop.

'Thank you, my love,' she said, taking a sip. It was hot and silky, in Andre's trademark way, and she thought, not for the first time, that he was the best barista in the world.

'Where do you want the seafood?' he asked, taking bags of fresh baby clams, mussels and shrimp out of the fridge.

'Can you clean them, then we can set them up in bowls along here?' She pointed to an empty spot on the bench.

Laughter peeled throughout the house, reaching Belle from the living room—Riley's throaty chuckle, Mary's delicate titter, Uncle Benito's well-rounded belly laugh. They were pulling the Christmas tree down—it was bad luck to leave it up beyond Epiphany—but Uncle Benito had already plied them all with several glasses of mulled wine, even Mary, who'd expressed her milk earlier so that Dante could bottle feed, and Belle suspected the simple act of pulling down the tree had turned into something else entirely.

Riley had arrived alone that morning. When Belle had enquired about Emilio, she'd mentioned vaguely that he was visiting his family in Bologna, but didn't elaborate further, and Belle didn't ask. She wasn't sure if they were still together or what their future held. It was no longer her place to know, even if under normal circumstances she would have compelled Riley to tell her everything. And because she wanted the best for her friend, she was already debating whether to attend her first session with Emilio after Epiphany.

'I don't want you leaving therapy,' Andre had said to her the night before. 'You're making good progress.'

'I know. And I don't want to leave,' she admitted, 'but maybe I could find another psychologist.'

'We both know if you leave Emilio, you won't see anyone else. It was hard enough getting you to him in the first place.'

He was right, of course. She probably wouldn't start again with someone new. She would just tough it out, try to use everything Emilio had taught her and progress on her own. 'If they want to be together, how can I be the one who prevents that?'

'Their relationship came after. That's not your fault.'

'Tell that to two people who really like each other.'

Tipsy laughter burst in from the living room again and Belle stared at the caramelised apples on the stove. 'Let's leave this for now,' she said, turning the heat off and pouring the apples into a bowl. 'I want to watch them pull down the tree.' She loved cooking, but sometimes it meant missing out on the fun.

Andre washed his hands, dried them, then slipped his arm around her waist as they left the kitchen and walked to the living room.

It was only one in the afternoon, but Riley's face was already pink from the wine and Uncle Benito was in exceptionally high spirits. Even Mary looked shiny-cheeked, sipping from her glass and giggling, while Dante sat beside her, giving Sebastian a bottle. Despite being absent for some of Sebastian's life, he appeared at ease, the baby nestled comfortably in the crook of his arm, gulping milk from the bottle, eyes fixed on his father with intense concentration. Dante's smile could have lit up space, his dark eyes bright, his tall, lean body beautifully at odds with the tininess of his son.

'Who can reach the angel?' Uncle Benito said, pointing to the top of the tree. 'I'm too short.' There were decorations everywhere, yet to be boxed up, tinsel strung across the sofa and through Mary's hair.

Riley stepped forward. 'It's a tall person's job. Stand aside.' She scooped the angel from the top of the tree with ease and handed it to Uncle Benito.

'My love,' he said, his eyes shining as he kissed the angel. 'My Valentina.'

Belle glanced at Andre, who was watching his father, a tender, nostalgic smile on his face.

'Who's hungry?' Belle asked. 'I could bring out the platters.'

'I'm always hungry,' Riley said.

'Yes, bring the antipasti.' Uncle Benito tucked the angel carefully away in her box until next Christmas. 'And the focaccia with the oil and vinegar.'

'I'll help you,' Mary said, climbing to her feet.

With an unexpected blast of cold wintry air, the front door swung open, causing them all to turn around. Standing there in the foyer, by the coat rack, was Teresa and Giovanni. The draught from outside fanned the flames, stirring up the fire, and Giovanni quickly closed the door again. He unravelled his scarf, slipped out of his coat, and clapped his hands together.

'Buone feste!' he cried. Happy holidays! He made a beeline for Uncle Benito who was waiting for him with a delighted smile and a glass of mulled wine.

Teresa took a little longer to thaw, digesting the scene in the living room first—the decorations scattered about, Andre's arm around Belle, Mary looking giddy with red tinsel through her hair, Dante feeding Sebastian. She glared at Giovanni as he gave Riley a playful hug and a few too many kisses on her cheeks.

'Buone feste,' she murmured, slipping out of her coat, her lips drawn tightly together like an old string purse.

'Ah, Teresa, come and have a drink,' Uncle Benito said merrily. He swayed a little before righting himself.

'Not before I see my grandson,' she said in Italian, striding towards Dante, still feeding Sebastian on the sofa. 'My beautiful boy!' she said loudly, startling Sebastian. 'Come to Nonna.'

'He's feeding,' Mary said. 'Leave him with Dante.'

'Nonsense. I will feed him,' she replied coolly, as though it was preposterous that Dante should even be there.

Belle had forgotten how ubiquitous Teresa could be, blasting into the room like a gale. It had only been a few minutes, but Belle was already tired of her. As she glanced at Mary, she realised she was too—the frown and tense set of her jaw, the way her shoulders went rigid when Teresa leant in and tried to take the bottle off Dante.

'No,' she said firmly. 'Dante will finish feeding him.'

Teresa wheeled on her with a look of surprise. 'Don't be silly. I haven't seen him in ten days. And for goodness' sake, speak in Italian.'

'Dante hasn't seen him in four weeks,' Mary insisted in English.

'Whose fault is that?'

'I think he's finished anyway,' Dante said, leaning forward and placing the bottle on the coffee table. He pulled Sebastian to him and began gently patting his back.

Teresa's beady eyes studied Dante like an ant under a microscope. 'You're doing it wrong.'

'God, Mamma!' Mary cried. 'Why are you always mean to him?'

Teresa gasped, then responded in a spray of rapid Italian that Belle only just managed to catch, something about Dante being a part-time father, away all the time, and now he couldn't burp the boy right.

'Will you stop? Just *stop*!' Mary yelled.

Teresa jumped. The room fell silent.

Sebastian burped.

'You're mean to everyone,' Mary said with exasperation. 'To Dante. To Belle. Even to Papà. And you always inter-fere. Why can't you just be kind?'

Giovanni belched loudly. 'She's right, Teresa. Don't be angry. It's Epiphany.'

'I'm not angry,' Teresa yelled back.

Uncle Benito placed a hand solemnly on her shoulder. 'Teresa, you are my dearest friend, but you are not being a nice person now.'

Teresa inhaled sharply.

'If you come to this home, to Belle and Andre's home,' he said, 'you will treat them with respect, okay? You will treat everyone with respect, or you don't come back.'

The woman's mouth fell open. 'Benito.'

'And we speak Italian *and* English in this house,' Andre added.

Riley raised her glass. 'Amen to that.'

Teresa glanced around the room, at the seven pairs of eyes staring back at her, and the unexpected intervention that had taken place. A retort seemed imminent on her lips, but as though thinking better of it, she blinked and lifted her chin. 'Fine,' she murmured, pushing her sleeves up. 'I can see when I'm not wanted. I'll be in the kitchen getting the food ready.'

Belle took Andre's hand. 'There's no need. We have the kitchen under control.'

Teresa glowered at her, but her face fell when Mary took Sebastian in her arms and reached for Dante's hand too. 'We'll come with you, Belle.'

Andre led them out of the living room, leaving the older parents and an awkward silence behind. There was a low murmur from Giovanni, a clinking of glasses, then the sound of decorations being placed in boxes, but Teresa was quiet for the first time since she'd arrived on Christmas Eve.

In the kitchen, Mary returned Sebastian to Dante and

placed both palms down on the island bench, taking several deep breaths. She looked at everyone and grimaced. 'I'm sorry about that.'

'What happened in there wasn't your fault,' Belle said.

'I just wish she was nicer to people.'

'Why *is* she so angry?' Riley asked, holding her empty wine glass up and looking around the kitchen for a bottle of wine to refill it with.

'I think that has to do with me,' Dante said with a boyish smile.

'And me,' Belle said, raising her hand.

'And me,' Andre added.

'Jesus,' Riley muttered.

This made everyone laugh. Andre found the bottle of wine Riley was searching for and Belle collected more wine glasses from the cupboard. He uncorked the bottle and topped up everyone's glasses.

There was no laughter coming from the living room, just low talking, the tinkle of decorations being stored away, and the crunch of branches and pine needles as Uncle Benito and Giovanni hauled the tree out the front to be repurposed for outdoor firewood.

'She's gone quiet,' Mary said with a pained expression. 'I feel bad. I shouldn't have yelled at her like that.'

'Maybe you're the one she needed to hear it from, to understand how she's upset people,' Dante said.

'You did the right thing,' Andre added.

'I would still like her to apologise to everyone.' Mary met Belle's eyes as she said this.

Belle wasn't sure she'd ever receive an apology from Teresa—the woman was too stubborn for that. But as she contemplated whether this bothered her or not, her gaze met Mary's again, over the heads of the others, gathered around the island bench, sipping wine and talking football. A gentle smile passed between them, then a nod. Eyes soft with understanding.

And, for the first time ever, there was respect.

THIRTY

Two days after Epiphany, Belle had her first scheduled appointment of the new year with Emilio. Andre offered to drive her to Pistoia that morning, to wait for her while she had her session, but the sun was out and he had things to do around the house, so she decided to drive herself.

She looked forward to the open road and the solitude while she tried to figure out what her approach would be. Andre was adamant he didn't want her to give up therapy. Belle was adamant that Riley deserved happiness. Riley was adamant she should walk away.

A new psychologist was likely the answer, but Belle wasn't sure she had the energy to start again with someone new and it was what worried Andre the most.

Pistoia was busy that day and she circled the town for fifteen minutes looking for a parking spot. She'd forgotten that it was Wednesday, when Pistoia's main square, Piazza del Duomo and all its surrounding streets, transformed into a bustling marketplace, a lively sea of colourful awnings and eager shoppers.

She eventually spied a spot a few blocks from Emilio's

office, parked the Alfa Romeo and walked the rest of the way under a gentle sun. When she reached the office, she climbed the stairs to the top floor and found Greta inside, behind her desk, tapping on her keyboard.

'*Buongiorno, come sta?*' the older woman said, a navy-blue scarf looped elegantly around her slick grey bob.

'*Salve. Bene grazie, lei?*' Belle asked, shrugging out of her jacket.

'I am good,' Greta said. 'Did you have a nice Christmas and Epiphany?'

There wasn't an easy answer to that and, at the risk of spending an hour going into detail, she simply smiled and nodded. 'It was nice. I hope yours was too.'

'It was lovely. Emilio won't be long.'

Belle thanked her and took a seat on the sofa, reaching for a new issue of *Vogue Italia* on the coffee table. She thumbed through it, only a few pages in when Emilio's door opened, and he stepped into the waiting room. 'Belle,' he said, smiling.

'Emilio.' For some reason her cheeks reddened, and she couldn't quite meet his eyes. She was embarrassed, she realised, for the awkward call she'd made to him on New Year's Day, and because he was dating her best friend, and because everything that had once seemed clinical about their relationship now seemed oddly personal.

'How are you?' he asked, gently waving her through the doorway with his hand.

She stole a glance at him and saw that he shared the same overly deferential, slightly uncertain look she was wearing. 'I'm good, thank you.'

She took her usual seat on the sofa as he reached for her file on his desk, sitting opposite her. He adjusted his glasses, his Adam's apple working in his throat, and she knew he'd found himself in uncharted territory too.

'Right, shall we get started? I'd like to discuss how the holidays went.'

'No.' The words were out before she could fully comprehend what she was saying. All she knew was that she couldn't sit through a whole session like nothing had happened. 'I'm sorry. We need to talk... about Riley.'

Emilio shifted on his seat, a closed hand to his mouth, clearing his throat. 'Okay, I *was* going to get to that.'

'We should get to it now,' Belle said. 'I'm not going to be able to concentrate otherwise. I need everyone to be frank with me and to know where we all stand. Because Riley and I haven't been the same since I found out about you both, and I hate that. I hate the secrecy and the tiptoeing around and the not knowing what comes next.'

Emilio considered her for a long time, then he nodded. 'I agree. Let's clear it up now.'

She exhaled shakily. 'Yes. Good.'

He hesitated and she could see this was difficult for him too. 'I want you to know that I'm deeply sorry for what happened over New Year's,' he said. 'It wasn't my intention for you to find out about me and Riley over the phone. I had no idea she was your friend when we met. It became to clear me after a few days and I should have addressed it there and then but,' he spoke quickly, wincing apologetically, 'nothing like this has ever happened to me before.'

'I understand,' she said. 'And you don't have to apologise. It wasn't anyone's fault.'

'Actually, it *was* my fault. You needed support that night and instead you received a terrible shock. I'm only too aware of what that can do to someone's recovery.' He looked ashamed. 'It was unprofessional of me and a complete breach of your trust not to have been honest with you from the start. I should have handled it better.'

'I'm not upset,' she said quickly. 'I'm just not sure where we go from here. Can you date my friend while treating me? What are the rules?'

He leant forward on his chair. 'Well, some rules cover more complex situations, like engaging in a sexual relationship with your patient. That's illegal, in fact. Other rules are more like guidelines—dating a client's friend, for example, is not illegal, but it's not advised either.' His brow furrowed slightly, as though he was searching for the right words. 'Ethics and trust form a critical part of our relationship. You confide in me and, in return, I give you objective guidance. That balance can be jeopardised if I become part of your social circle, for example, if I start dating your best friend. It throws out that balance, that trust.'

'I tell Riley everything, so it wouldn't matter,' Belle said.

'Still,' he said, 'if you and I become friends outside this room, there's a risk my clinical judgement could become impaired.'

'I know it wouldn't though. I trust you,' Belle said.

He smiled. 'That's kind of you to say.'

Belle uncrossed her ankles and leant forward too. 'Do you like her? Because she really likes you.'

Emilio coughed with surprise. 'I can't get into that with you, Belle.'

'Sorry,' she said, cringing. 'But she does. And I think you want to be with her as well. I won't be the reason you two can't be together.'

'Your recovery is the priority here,' he said, in his doctorly way. 'I don't want you to become distracted by this.'

'I already am.'

He stared at her, inscrutable. Then he sighed, glancing down at her file, running his palm over the cover. Eventually, he looked up, meeting her eyes. 'Fine. Let's have an honest discussion then because I owe you that at least.'

She nodded. 'Please.'

'I'd like to keep seeing Riley,' he said.

Belle chortled a little at his candidness. 'That's great!'

'Yes.' He smiled. 'And I'd like to continue being your therapist too.'

'Is that possible? Can we do both?'

'We can,' he said slowly, carefully. 'But for it to work, we need to put strict boundaries in place.'

'Okay,' Belle said.

'In our sessions together, please don't ask me about my relationship with Riley, and I won't let her ask me about your therapy.'

A sensible rule.

'When we're in session together and you want to talk about her, I'll guide you objectively, so you don't need to worry about telling me things. If I feel I can't remain objective, then I'll let you know.'

'Right.'

'And I won't attend your social gatherings—birthdays, Easter, Christmas, dinners out. We shouldn't muddy the waters.'

'Understood. No social gatherings or dinners of any kind.'

'Thank you,' he said formally.

But she couldn't help herself. 'So we just pretend you don't exist?'

He shrugged, chuckling. 'Think of me as her imaginary boyfriend.'

She wasn't sure if this was hilarious or depressing. She

didn't want Riley to have an 'imaginary boyfriend', the kind they weren't allowed to see or speak about for fear of blurring the lines, but she saw how hard Emilio was trying, how important these boundaries were if they had a hope of maintaining their sessions together, and so she would make it work.

'Look, you've made incredible progress over the last year,' he said.

'I'm not so sure about that,' she replied. 'I rang you on New Year's Day from the train station, remember? That wasn't so incredible.'

He gave her a stern look. 'Belle, post-traumatic stress disorder will be with you for life. One year or three years or a lifetime of therapy isn't going to make it magically switch off. I know you know this.'

'But I *was* doing better until the holidays.'

'And you will continue to have good and bad days. Things will trigger you, make you relapse. There's no silver bullet. It's how you manage those bad days that will determine how we move forward. You're not ready to leave therapy yet, but I know you won't need me forever. I don't want to put a timeline on it, but if you continue to improve, continue to take the tools that I teach you and apply them to your life, then we could think about reducing your sessions to once a month, then maybe once a quarter, if you felt comfortable.'

'Then we can actually call you Riley's boyfriend?'

His shoulders quivered with amusement. 'Let's cross that bridge when we come to it.' He pushed his glasses up his nose and opened her file. 'Right, can you concentrate now?'

'I can,' she confirmed.

'Then let's talk about the holidays.'

THIRTY-ONE

In the end, it was the wedding Belle hadn't realised she'd wanted.

A late spring affair, on the eve of their one-year anniversary, just before the stifling heat of a Tuscan summer set in, at their house in a garden full of new blooms—sun-kissed red poppies, cheerful climbing pea vines and exotic hydrangeas. Potted lemon and orange trees ornamented the flagstone paths, and the intoxicating scent of basil and sage brought the promise of food.

Perfumed mountain air drifted down from the alps, catching the fragrance of the birches and beeches on the way, the chestnut trees and warm, cut grass delivering a bouquet for the senses, that quintessential smell that made Belle feel as though she were at home and on holiday at the same time. Not like the rushed wedding a year ago at Rome's busy Town Hall, on an uneventful Monday, which she'd quietly adored, but which couldn't compare to a day like this.

She inhaled the sweet scent of their back garden and smiled at Andre, standing at the wedding arch with her, her hands tucked in his. He gave them a light squeeze, followed by a reassuring wink. For all her reluctance to have a second wedding, she was glad they had. It wasn't Chianti or a private beach, and it wasn't in a church, but her husband was before her, handsome in a charcoal suit, his dimples impossibly perfect, his grin wide, and that was all she needed. They'd just finished their vows, conveyed in Italian because she'd been determined for the ceremony to be conducted in his native language and the priest was preparing them for the exchanging of the rings.

'Are you okay?' Andre whispered to her.

She felt an overwhelming urge to giggle. There were nerves and one hundred sets of eyes trained on her, and children who couldn't be tamed by their parents, already bored and wanting to run up and down the slope of the backyard.

But every part of it was divine.

She grinned. 'I'm great.'

He beamed at her, deep brown eyes drinking her in, as though he couldn't possibly drag them away. She wanted to kiss him, so she did, stepping forward and meeting his lips, even though they weren't up to that part yet.

The priest gasped, stricken. Andre responded, a lingering kiss that attracted the cheers and whistles of some of his cousins.

'Easy there,' Callum chastised from the front row. 'That's my daughter.'

Everyone laughed.

She glanced at the front row where her mother and Callum sat, Riley beside them, a proud smile on her face. The chair on her other side was empty. Belle had been hopeful Emilio would come, had even hand-delivered the invitation to him during their last session together, an act that had attracted a slight frown, even if he'd looked secretly touched by the gesture. He had of course declined. She'd even suggested that she was ready to leave therapy, which would remove the complexity of him dating her best friend and no one being allowed to talk about it. Then he could come to her wedding.

But he'd advised against that idea, keen to work with her for a little longer, and she realised that he was, if nothing else, a consummate professional and committed to her recovery. And so, at one session a month, and still a little way to go, she remained just as committed.

Belle and Andre exchanged their rings, white gold bands to add to their sets, then with a triumphant, '*Puoi baciare la sposa!*' from the priest, he shut his bible and Andre kissed her.

———————

WAITERS WITH TRAYS of prosecco roamed along white-clothed tables, topped with lanterns and centrepieces of roses and peonies. The party was held under a large marquee, the ceiling strung with fairy lights. Music mingled with conversation, laughter ringing out, children dancing with bare feet and sweaty hair.

The sun was still high outside, warming the grass and the wine, but those standing out there didn't seem to mind the late heat. A humid breeze lifted the tablecloths and the walls of the marquee, toying with the train of Belle's gown.

Belle glanced around at the party. Dinner was finished and everyone had abandoned their tables for others, like musical chairs. She saw her mother and Callum walking towards her from across the marquee, their eyes soft, smiles relaxed. Grace looked a decade younger in an elegant jade dress, intricate beadwork covering the bodice, a matching hat donned with an organza bow. Callum was beside her, gallant in a black suit.

'Sweetheart.' Grace wrapped her arms around Belle, then stood back to survey her. 'What a lovely day.'

'It's been great.' She was still brimming with relief over how well it had turned out, how she'd found herself enjoying the crowd rather than recoiling from it. Andre's idea to hold the wedding at the house, a place she'd always loved and felt safe, had been one she'd instantly warmed to. She wondered why they hadn't thought of it sooner.

'You've been hard to catch,' Callum said, leaning in and kissing her cheek. 'I've wanted to steal ye away for a dance, but ye'r very popular.'

She'd already danced with all of Andre's little cousins and his cheeky Uncle Joe, and she thought her feet might fall off. 'I promise to dance with you later.'

'I'll hold ye to that,' he said, grinning. 'Can I get either of ye a drink?'

'I'm fine,' Belle said, and Grace declined also.

He left them, heading to the bar across the other side of the marquee.

Belle smiled after him, then smoothed down her gown, a flowing white tulle skirt with a lace bodice and a plunging neckline. It was romantic and elegant and slightly bohemian, not too formal. She'd felt like a princess trying it on for the first time several weeks ago and she felt like one now, even if her heels occasionally sank into the grass.

She glanced at her mother who was still watching Callum make his way across to the bar.

'Will you both stay in Italy a while?' she asked. After New York, Grace had returned to Sydney and Callum to

Kirkcudbright, but she was almost certain their correspondence hadn't ended there.

'We'll stay until you leave for your vacation next week,' she said, her eyes still on Callum, as he chatted to the bartender. 'Then he's invited me to join him in Scotland.' She said the words diffidently as her gaze slid to Belle's. Her neck and cheeks flushed a deep magenta. 'And he's asked if I'd like to stay with him for a few months.'

Belle's mouth fell open a little. 'That's... wow.'

'Yes.' Grace gave an awkward cough. 'It was a nice invitation. And since I'm already in Europe, it makes sense to visit Scotland. I do adore it there; I haven't been back in years. And I'll be close to you. You can come visit, or we can come back here.'

Belle raised her eyebrows. 'They're all great reasons, Mum. But what's the real one?'

Grace fidgeted, then a slow smile lit up her face. 'We're just taking it one day at a time.' She swallowed and glanced at Belle. 'I don't want it to be strange for you, honey.'

'I thought it might be, but it's actually not. I'm happy for you,' Belle said.

'Really?' Grace asked. 'What if I moved to Scotland permanently or Callum moved to Sydney?'

Belle was left momentarily speechless. 'Oh! I didn't realise you were at that stage already.'

'We're not,' Grace clarified. 'Not yet. But... life is short. We've spent so much time apart and we're not looking to waste any more years.' She shrugged with that reticent smile again. 'It was just a thought.'

Belle reached for her hand. 'It's a great thought. And I *am* okay with it.'

'He'll never replace Edward,' Grace insisted. 'I know how much you miss your dad.'

Belle felt the back of her eyes sting with unexpected tears. She missed her father terribly, the gruffness in his voice which always belied something softer, and those last precious months when they'd made amends before he died. It had been a difficult time for her, in the aftermath of Paris, but he'd stepped up and supported her, had called her often, just to talk and see how she was. They'd had their ups and downs over the years, but she would wish him back in a heartbeat if she could, because he'd died before she could tell him how much he meant to her. And that was, perhaps, one of her greatest regrets in life.

'Your dad would be so proud if he could see you now,' Grace continued, her voice thick with emotion. 'Happy and beautiful. Gosh, he'd love Andre too.'

The tears moved to the front of Belle's eyes, brimming on her lashes. She fanned them, giving a watery laugh. 'Don't make me cry, Mum.'

Grace fanned her eyes too. 'Goodness, yes. Sorry! Enough with the waterworks. I think we need that drink after all.'

'Prosecco?'

Grace touched her arm, smiled, then tottered in the direction of a wandering waiter, balancing a tray of flutes.

Belle turned and saw Riley enter the marquee. She waved her over. 'Hey!'

'There you are.' Riley strode towards her.

Belle held her arms out and her friend stepped into them.

'You're hard to catch, kid,' Riley said, hugging her fiercely.

'I know. Sorry. Lots of people to say hello to.' She'd stopped by so many tables and spoken to so many guests, most of whom she was meeting for the first time, that her head was spinning.

'The food was something else.' Riley pulled away to look at her. 'I couldn't stop feeding my face.'

Belle was ecstatic to hear it. She and Andre had painstakingly designed the seven courses themselves, right down to the last pinch of salt, and she'd hoped the caterers wouldn't become overwhelmed with their requests. But they'd been kind and accommodating, excelling in fact, and every course had far outweighed her expectation.

She hadn't seen Emilio at dinner, and she glanced around, wondering if he might have made a late entrance. 'I was hoping Emilio would come, even for an hour.'

Riley's expression grew sad. 'Me too. But he's a professional. We know that.'

'It's actually the thing I admire most about him.'

Riley sighed ruefully. 'Still, I hate not being able to talk to you about my relationship. It still feels weird.'

It was ironic how therapy healed Belle while at the same time, creating a barrier between her and Riley. They both understood why and respected it, but some conversations were now off the table, as though everything they'd ever spoken freely about before—men, sex, love—had to be carefully navigated.

'Well, if nothing else, I've loved having you close,' Belle said. 'We might not be able to talk about some things but being with Emilio means you've stayed in Tuscany for the last three months. And we couldn't have made this wedding happen without you.'

Riley waved her hand. 'It was nothing.'

'No, it was everything. You're my best friend. I can't do life without you.' The tears threatened her eyes again and she blinked them back, not before Riley noticed them.

'Don't get me started,' she cried. 'I've been an emotional wreck all afternoon watching you get married again.'

Belle laughed, tears dripping down her cheeks. God, where was that prosecco?

'Now, I'm going to allow you five more minutes of socialising, then we're hitting the dancefloor.' Riley smacked a loud kiss against her cheek.

Belle laughed again. 'Okay.'

Riley left her side and made a beeline for her seat, intercepted on the way by one of Andre's slightly hopeful, flirtatious friends. The band launched into a cover of Ed Sheeran's 'Photograph' and an almost tangible conviviality rippled around the party. It was like pure joy—the crescendo of Italian, the colour of the flowers, the waiters and children and happy, beautifully dressed adults mingling inside the marquee and the garden outside. The music, the champagne, the warm setting sun. She took a moment to inhale it all, immensely glad that she'd persisted with the wedding. That she hadn't let fear prevent her from celebrating the day.

Her periphery caught a small group heading her way and she realised it was Mary, Dante, and Teresa.

'Belle,' Mary said, quickening her pace and reaching her, kissing each of her cheeks. 'You look beautiful. Congratulations.'

'Thank you. I'm glad you could all make it.' Her eyes met Teresa's, who was holding Sebastian. The older woman nodded, then buried her face in Sebastian's hair.

Mary's midnight blue dress was long and fitted, clinging to her new bump. Belle glanced at it and smiled, trying to ignore the painful emptiness that flared inside her own stomach, for the pregnancy she and Andre had yet to have. 'How far along are you now?'

Mary placed a hand on her growing child. 'Twenty weeks. We're having another boy.'

Belle gasped. 'That's incredible! I'm so happy for you all.' She waved at Mary's husband, standing beside her, tall and distinguished in a matching dark blue suit. 'Hi, Dante.'

He bent down and kissed each of her cheeks, hugging her. 'Thank you for inviting us. We're happy to be here.' He gave her a meaningful look, and she smiled, knowing what he meant. The Christmas holidays had been a calamity, Mary and Teresa's behaviour reprehensible, but they'd all tried their best to move on from it. On some level, it had wiped clean a slate that had always been muddy, forcing everything to the surface for them all to face. Mary, particularly, seemed happier, as though through her actions, she was able to purge herself of the past, even if it had almost cost two marriages.

Momentarily distracted, Belle almost missed Teresa giving her a rare smile. 'Yes,' the woman said in English, 'it was a lovely wedding. We are happy to be invited.'

'*Grazie*, Teresa.' It was the closest they would ever come to being friends, but Teresa's sentiment seemed genuine, and that was enough for Belle.

Mary, Dante and Teresa drifted back to their table and Grace finally returned with a glass of prosecco for Belle.

'Sorry, I got stuck talking to Benito's brother. He's quite flirtatious,' Grace said, cheeks flushed.

Callum returned too, jacket and tie discarded, collar open, looking relaxed and mischievous. 'I'm stealing yer mother,' he called to Belle, reaching for Grace's hand and dragging her away.

Belle laughed, watching them walk back to their table, his hand on the small of her back, as a surge of warmth overwhelmed her. Her mother deserved happiness, that first love, schoolgirl crush kind of happiness that she'd known once with Callum and seemed to have found again. And it wasn't a betrayal of her father's memory, she realised. They both loved him and always would. It was about not getting lost in the past.

Satisfied that she'd spoken to most people in the marquee, she decided on fresh air and stepped outside with her glass of prosecco, into the warm breeze. The sun had dropped now, drawing the last of the light with it, leaving behind a deepening twilight.

Her gaze found Andre and Benito, standing nearby, sipping beer and talking. She picked up the train of her dress and made her way across to them.

Andre noticed her approach and placed his beer on the garden wall, holding his hand out to her. 'My love.' He looked carefree and devastatingly handsome in his suit, and she was already thinking about when the guests would leave, and they could be alone in bed.

'*Sei bellissima*,' Uncle Benito said, cupping her face in his thick hands and kissing her loudly on each cheek, as though he were trying to gobble her up. 'You make me so proud. Both of you.' His face was rosy, and she suspected that he'd already had more than a few red wines. 'My heart is full. I love you so much.' He mopped his eyes as they began to leak profusely.

'Oh, Papà.' She put her arms around him, squeezing him. 'We love you too.'

He looked at them with a serious expression. 'I don't ever want you to worry about the *bambini*, eh? I know it makes you sad.' He shook his head as though trying to impress the words upon them. 'But it doesn't matter to me. Your happiness is the most important thing.'

Belle knew his words were intended to soothe but her heart clenched anyway. She didn't want him to be okay with it, to accept what her soul could not yet accept. That she and Andre, both only children, may never carry on their family lines. That they might not hold their babies in their arms. That they would need to be content with the children of others. And that the problem was *her*. Every day she grappled with it, knowing she was the one depriving everyone of that gift.

She'd become a master at hiding the pain, so once again she smiled it away, as she'd done before with Mary, and let Uncle Benito hug her, before he wobbled away, searching for another glass of wine and Giovanni.

Andre stared at her closely. Although he was an expert at seeing through her brave façade, he refrained from commenting and she was relieved. 'Are you enjoying your day?' he asked instead.

'Yes. I'm mostly enjoying your family. They're wonderful.' His uncles had been full of compliments and his aunts warm with hugs; his male cousins playful with dirty jokes and his female cousins curious. His nonnos and nonnas, still alive and robust, could hardly understand a word she said, whether it was in English or her heavily accented Italian, and she had nodded and hand gestured her way through conversations with them. They were all a noisy, boisterous, cheeky lot, and she'd loved threading her way to each of them.

Andre wrapped his arms around her waist and pulled her close, dropping his lips to hers and kissing her. Someone wolf-whistled at them. 'How does it feel being Mrs De Luca all over again?'

'I could be Mrs De Luca a hundred times over,' she said, moving aside a stray lock that had fallen into his eyes, watching his dimples deepen. The same dimples that had first drawn her to him.

He smiled, then his face grew serious. 'I want you to know—I *need* you to know—that no matter what happens, we'll be okay. You and me. That's all we need.'

She sensed what he was referring to, and despite the longing for a child that lived so deeply in her heart, she believed him. They *would* be okay. They had survived tragedy and trauma, long distance, doubt and grief, and it hadn't torn them apart. It had only made them stronger and now more than ever, she needed to trust in that. To trust in him.

Her blue eyes locked on his brown and she was, as always, drawn into his calm and optimistic view of the world, and as certainly as the sun would rise, she felt it too. 'Yes, my love. We're going to be fine.'

ACKNOWLEDGMENTS

I'm lucky to have an amazing family who supports me. I always thank them first because, without their love and patience, my books wouldn't make it to publication. I doubt I'd even get words down. To Brett, Eve and Connor, my four seasons and all the days in between, I love you dearly.

Enormous thanks to my editors, Lynne Stringer and Marcia Batton. We have worked together for a long time now and I wouldn't have it any other way. As usual, your keen eyes and expertise have made this a far better book than I could have hoped to achieve on my own.

I'd like to thank my closest friends, Liz Butler, Natasha Spiteri, Joanne Libreri, Bianca Nash and Erika Slaby. My world is brighter with you guys in it. And to Nikki Divis, who always finds the time to come to my events.

Love and thanks to my parents and in-laws, Carmen Montebello, Joe and Michelle Montebello, Rhonda and Joanie Flynn-Scott, and Roger and Paula Campbell. It's nice to talk books with you. I love the recommendations, the new authors we discover together, and the support you always have for my work.

To Kris Dallas, thank you for another stunning cover, and to my early and ARC readers, Emmie, Rosemarie, Brenda and Shelly, thank you for your support and friendship.

To Craig and Phil, we may live in different states, but we still manage the lunches, dinners, cocktails and conversations. Thank you for being beautiful souls. To Helen Sibbritt, deepest thanks for your love, dedication and unwavering support. I'm honoured to know you. And to author extraordinaire and my dearest pal, Tanya Nellestein, you've always got my back and I'll always have yours.

Finally, to my readers, thank you for staying the course with Belle and Andre. You always lift me with your unfailing warmth and generosity, like a loving net of constant support. Thank you for always catching me.

ALSO BY MICHELLE MONTEBELLO

www.michellemontebello.com.au

Seasons of Belle Series

The Summer of Everything

To Autumn, With Love

The Colour of Winter

The Spring Farewell

Historical Romance

The Quarantine Station

The Lost Letters of Playfair Street

Contemporary Romance

The Forever Place

Beautiful, Fragile

The Spring Farewell

MICHELLE MONTEBELLO

ABOUT THE AUTHOR

Michelle Montebello is a writer from Sydney, Australia where she lives with her family. She is the internationally bestselling author of *The Quarantine Station*, *The Forever Place*, and *The Lost Letters of Playfair Street*.

Her books have won several awards. *The Lost Letters of Playfair Street* won the ARRA 2020 Favourite Historical Award. *The Quarantine Station* was a finalist in the 2021 International Book Awards for Best Historical Fiction and *The Forever Place* was shortlisted for the 2022 RWA RuBY and 2022 ARRA awards.

Michelle has been shortlisted three times for ARRA Australian Author of the Year.

When Michelle is not writing, she has a keen passion for reading, tennis and travel.

If you would like to subscribe to her newsletter, visit www.michellemontebello.com.au.